THE KILLING STAR

THE KILLING STAR

CHARLES PELLEGRINO
AND
GEORGE ZEBROWSKI

An AvoNova Book

William Morrow and Company, Inc.
New York

THE KILLING STAR is an original publication of Avon Books. This work has never before appeared in book form. This work is a novel. Any similarity to actual persons or events is purely coincidental.

AVON BOOKS
A division of
The Hearst Corporation
1350 Avenue of the Americas
New York, New York 10019

Copyright © 1995 by Charles Pellegrino and George Zebrowski
Published by arrangement with the authors
Library of Congress Catalog Card Number: 94–31367
ISBN: 0–688–13989–2

Library of Congress Cataloging in Publication Data:

Pellegrino, Charles R.
   The killing star / Charles Pellegrino and George Zebrowski.
      p. cm.
1. Twenty-first century—Fiction. I. Zebrowski, George, 1945– . II. Title.
PS3566.E418K55 1995   94–31367
813'.54—dc20   CIP

First Morrow/AvoNova Printing: April 1995

AVONOVA TRADEMARK REG. U.S. PAT. OFF. AND IN OTHER COUNTRIES, MARCA RE-
GISTRADA, HECHO EN U.S.A.

Printed in the U.S.A.

QP   10   9   8   7   6   5   4   3   2   1

To Walter Lord and Arthur C. Clarke,
our literary fathers.

I

PUNCTUATED EQUILIBRIUM

*And there fell upon men
a great hail out of heaven....*
—Revelation

1

Spring, A.D. 2076

FOR THOSE FEW WHO LIVED TO LOOK BACK, THE MOST fearsome deaths were the quickest. Those who did not survive the first human contact with the Intruders were alive in one moment, the billions of them—happy or unhappy, seeking new loves, leaving old loves behind, or choosing to be alone, building toward small dreams, large dreams, or having no dreams at all—and then, over an entire hemisphere of Earth, their consciousness dissolved, as if they had been the dream of something alien suddenly awakening.

The first ship came from the direction of Sagittarius. It came with fire in its belly and venom in its mind. It was an old ship, without a crew. Only machines, small and crablike, stirred within its ceramic rigging. It came with antihydrogen tanks nearly empty; but this did not matter. It was never meant to decelerate into any solar orbit or to voyage home. At 92 percent of light speed, the ship slipped through the heliopause, one light-day from the Sun, with an easy stealth, trailing only dead silence across the entire electromagnetic spectrum, until it was too late for it to be noticed. Long before reaching heliopause, it had calved four times, sending large pieces of itself toward Mars, Earth, the Moon, and Mercury. These components zeroed in on the signatures of an electronic civilization, whose radio and photonic emissions outshone even the Sun on certain frequencies, as clear and easy to follow as the sweep of a lighthouse beam.

From the ship's swift perspective, all the heavens were compressed into a mighty dome, with the stars astern pulled into its forward view. It moved with a velocity that aged it at only one third the rate of the rest of the universe. All the energy put into achieving that velocity had transformed the Intruder into a kinetic storage device of nightmarish design. If it struck a world, every gram of the vessel's substance would be received by that world as the target in a linear accelerator receives a spray of relativistic buckshot. Someone, somewhere, had built and was putting to use a relativistic bomb—a giant, roving atom smasher aimed at worlds.

Cold, cheerless, and determined, the ship knew itself and its purpose. It calved again—this time into two halves. One half kept what was left of the antihydrogen fuel and began to brake just enough to insure its arrival at Uranus's small moon, Miranda, only a few hours behind the leading half, where it would strike the opposite hemisphere, guaranteeing a complete kill.

As the leading half dipped into the plane of the solar system, it encountered increasing numbers of dust particles in its shields. They ionized harmlessly ahead of the ship, blushing faint radio waves that would be detectable, if anyone on Miranda happened to be listening. The gamma-ray shine of the decelerating half was also detectable, but it made no difference. One of the iron rules of relativistic bombardment was that if you could see something approaching at 92 percent of light speed, it was never where you saw it when you saw it, but was practically upon you.

Six minutes out from Miranda, the leading half blossomed into a cluster of ten thousand relativistic bomblets—bursting forth as an expanding shroud which, by the time it reached this world 472 kilometers in diameter, would custom-fit its dimensions.

Ahead, just below the surface of Miranda's ice fields, tanks of supercooled chemicals—millions of them—would soon be detecting anomalous emissions in the sky. The ship had no way of knowing whether or not the operators of the solar system's largest astronomical observatory would have time to realize that the blue-shifting gamma-ray sources were interstellar lances, or that they and their liquid telescope array were targets. The ship's mind was certain that even if someone at the target did comprehend what was about to happen, he was already powerless to prevent it. Armed with this knowledge, and with indifference, the Intruder hurried on.

2

Miranda Station

THE VISITING SCIENTISTS' QUARTERS WERE ALL FULL, making it necessary to put dividers into the already cramped staterooms to accommodate the seasonal influx of graduate students. Don Peterson's room was one of the largest, but it was still scarcely larger than the average bathroom back home on Earth—a windowless cell with a sink, foldaway desktops, and a roll-down bed that left no space for a liquid crystal wallscreen.

But one luxury that Singapore's Miranda Research Station did offer was a combination control van and community tearoom with panoramic views. The van was Peterson's favorite place. Even though the view did not change appreciably day-to-day, he had never grown tired of it. Cut by the horizon, Uranus was a huge dome glowing with backscattered sunlight. The rocks outside cast long shadows over fields of dust and ice crystals, blue under the pale white stars.

Peterson liked the solitude of the graveyard shift. No one else had wanted it, but he had volunteered gladly, because it released him from the overcrowding of a dozen-member support crew and a scientific party of thirty. He also hoped to take advantage of a phenomenon no one had yet explained, but which had been confirmed by nearly a century of oceanic and space exploration—that most important discoveries tended to be made between midnight and 3:00 A.M.

Tonight, as he sipped a bulb of tea and scribbled notes on a liquid crystal pad, Peterson was keenly aware of the probability curve, and waited patiently for something interesting to emerge; but his fears that he would end his tour on Miranda without scoring any significant discoveries were wrongly placed. He was about to score far too many.

The first sign of the visitors was eighty gamma photons—each measuring exactly 0.5 million electron volts—passing through the observatory's array of tanks and producing brief pulses of light that were measured and recorded by ultrasensitive photomultiplier cameras set on the tank walls. One ten-thousandth of a second after the first eighty photons struck, a small area of the station's computer memory—the SETI file—was triggered in time to receive the next batch. By then, the SETI bank had programmed itself to respond only to the 0.5 million electron-volt gammas, ignoring all other particles passing through the detectors. In every tank, the cameras recorded gamma-ray tracks through the fluids, revealing their energy levels and indicating precisely the direction from which they had entered.

In that first part of a second, the computer searched the roster of station personnel and learned that no one present was even remotely affiliated with Project SETI—the Search for Extraterrestrial Intelligence. In that same part of a second, following protocol, the SETI bank fixed on Peterson, who was on duty and by profession an astrophysicist. His special interest was in anomalously large flares on dwarf stars, which was at best small preparation for recognizing the first evidence ever that starship engines were burning in the galactic night. Peterson was here searching for something else, which was typical of the history of exotic discoveries; but an astrophysicist would have to do, the computer decided.

And so, still within the first part of a second, Peterson's pad went blank, blinked red, then displayed a star chart as the SETI bank called out, "We have an anomalous gamma-ray source at the position displayed on your pad"—a red dot began to blink—"0.5 million electron volts. Intensity holding steady. Zero probability of Earth vessel in that sector matching these outputs. Your opinions and queries are urgently needed, Dr. Peterson."

The intensity profile showed that hundreds of anomalous particles were coming in, all with the precise energy obtainable only from electron-positron annihilation. Even one such particle was proof enough that someone out there had manufactured antihydrogen and was using it to power an antimatter drive.

Peterson immediately rejected the notion that he was the butt of an elaborate joke; these days the penalties for even minor hacking offenses were too severe to be worth the risk. And he knew the computer's fail-safe systems too well. He also knew the crew. Even though most of them were competent scientists, and young Steven Bilenkin seemed especially promising, outside their individual areas of expertise they were typical university brats: professor-types utterly lacking in imagination. Within the first day of their arrival, they had all adapted to and become bored with Miranda's landscape, and had stopped looking out the windows.

Peterson stared at the star chart and the blinking red dot, then glanced outside and found the same stars on the horizon. Where the dot should have been, just above the eastern edge of Miranda Canyon and Bardo's Leap, nothing was visible to unaided eyes. But *something* was out there, undeniably, by everything he knew.

He said, "Give me distance, vector, and velocity." The particles alone, emanating from a point source, would provide all the necessary information—requiring only a few calculations using a sphere whose radius extended from the gamma-ray source to Miranda. The computer flashed numbers that would have, under different circumstances, made Peterson famous. They told him that the engine was five light-months away and approaching the solar system at 92 percent of light speed. The number of particles being emitted indicated that it was decelerating at a rate that would simulate a G-force of two against its occupants, assuming a vessel whose mass was that of a small space station.

He did some quick mental calculations. Five light-months away . . . five months since the gammas left their source . . . subtract five months deceleration at two gravities . . . assuming an approximately steady rate . . . and the vessel could be as little as four or five weeks away. . . .

"Oh, my God," he said, catching his breath. "We'll have company—and real soon."

More gamma-ray tracks were lancing through the tanks—more and more of them, all at 0.5 million electron volts. The computer assembled the information, red-dotted the sources, and threw them up on Peterson's star field display.

Without warning, two new points of red appeared beneath Vega.

Another winked on in the shoulder of Orion.

Then another.

And another.

"You're kidding me," Peterson said. "You've got to be fucking kidding!"

"Multiple deceleration sources," the computer replied. "Distance five light-months. Velocity ninety-two percent light speed. Your opinion?"

"They must have been cruising at that speed for decades!" he shouted. "And now they're turning on their engines all at once—correction, they *turned* them on all at once." He stared at the display. "They're scattered across light-months. They can't be communicating with each other, so they must have synchronized years in advance to light up their engines now! But why? And why so many of them?" His throat constricted as he said, "Call Earth."

"Maximum power?" the computer asked.

"Do it. Downlink all data immediately."

"Ready, Dr. Peterson."

He fumbled in his mind for the right words, but there was no precedent. No one had ever announced the arrival of alien starships before. His hesitation insured that the data would arrive ahead of his words, and he decided that this was as it should be: let the facts speak for themselves. Otherwise, someone might think he'd gone nuts out here.

"This is Dr. Donald Peterson at Miranda Station. Here is what has happened—"

His pad flashed, revealing a point of gamma shine only light-hours away. The display indicated that it was decelerating, but not enough to reduce its velocity by any significant fraction. Ahead of it, only light-minutes away, still another point came alive, then burst into ten thousand pieces.

"Oh, God, no!" Peterson shouted.

3

Inner Spaces

As Peterson found the right words, Hollis was just over four kilometers down on the bed of the Atlantic. Woods Hole Oceanographic Institute's inner space craft *Alvin* was now in its one hundred and twelfth year of service, although the decades of constant overhaul and refinement had erased every trace of the ship that was originally christened in 1964. The earliest relic of the old *Alvin* was a titanium sphere 2.13 meters in diameter, dating back to the 1970s. It had once been the entire crew compartment, but was later rebuilt as an escape pod mounted on the aft of the newer, larger cabin. The ship could now support a crew of seven for missions lasting up to several weeks. Today *Alvin* carried only two people, but Hollis would have had the sub all to herself if that Wayville fellow hadn't decided on a whim to come along for the ride.

It was nearing that point in the expedition when everyone topside had just about seen enough of the black wilderness on the bottom, and Hollis preferred it that way. She always looked forward to an expedition's end days, to the rare opportunities for total solitude—just her and the crushing pressures and communion with the Earth. By training she was a Jesuit priest of the agnostic order. She was also a fully qualified *Alvin* pilot, and as a pilot-priest she sought the deserts of the deep in the same way the founding prophets had sought the land deserts as catalysts for meditation and revelation.

Her mentor and late husband had told her, "Moses, Akhenaton, Buddha, Christ, Muhammad all made retreats into the desert to find the beginnings of spiritual life. Away from the distractions of cities nature is reduced to the essentials of life and death. A desert wilderness becomes a strange sort of womb, where you become so lonely that you must face yourself, and then God."

Her husband had found that special, inner peace. He seemed always to have possessed it. But Hollis was still searching. Outside the viewports, sea cucumbers blazed crisscrossing trails over the barren seabed. It was intensely peaceful, but illusory. If the port gave way, the inrush of water at three tons per square inch would instantly separate her body into its individual cells. Here in the deep wilderness, she had found a womb sterile to man, but fertile, perhaps, to God.

An ultrasonic voice called down from the support ship *Calypso II*. "*Alvin*, the crest should bear thirty-six meters to the east."

As Hollis turned east, her sole passenger stopped dictating to his notebooks and nosed up to a forward port. The bottom began to slope upward. At first, with *Alvin*'s floodlamps penetrating only about twelve meters through the dark, Jonathan

Wayville got the impression that they were ascending a tall mountain. But the pilot's monitor, fed by cameras that could peer a hundred meters in every direction, showed it to be the lip of a man-made crater barely half a kilometer across.

With good lighting, visibility was better than forty-five meters, as long as one stayed upwind of the dredge outlets. Dozens of small robots, moving busily to and fro within the crater, sensed *Alvin* coming over the crest and automatically turned on their floodlamps. Hollis watched a false sunrise spreading far ahead in the dark, a ghostly pool of light that shifted from violet to deep blue and then to a greenish-white glare as she reached the center of the crater—a level plain of steel, all that was left of the Royal Mail Steamer *Titanic*.

She had looked nothing like this, Hollis thought, when her great-grandfather first piloted Robert Ballard onto the forecastle deck, ninety years ago.

"It is a quiet and peaceful and fitting place," Ballard had said, "for this greatest of all sea tragedies to rest. May it forever remain that way."

"He should have known better," Great-grandfather had said. "How many sunken ships have been around for fifty or a hundred years or more and been left untouched? None. They found the *Bounty*'s anchor. They found the *Pandora* and the *Roraima*, the *Cinque Chagas* and the *Lusitania*, with never a question about whether to bring things up or not, until the *Titanic*."

But the *Titanic* was different, Ballard had insisted. Every four-year-old child somehow knew her name. Stories had been repeated for so many years that they had become part of the culture—a symbol for tragedy, blind arrogance, heroism, cowardice, even comedy, and sheer irony. Maybe you shouldn't want to touch a symbol too intimately. At the very least, you didn't want to spit on it.

Great-grandfather just couldn't see it that way. He had felt that given respect and good taste, the entire wreck could be raised and displayed in an underwater museum, and the world would accept it without hard feelings. The project needed careful planning, so he had enlisted men like Richard Tuna and Jason Bradley. Ballard never forgave him for it.

By 2010, all of Ballard's injunctions against raising the *Titanic* had been reversed. The "debris field" between the two portions of the ship had already been stripped clean, removing much of the force from the oceanographer's argument that R.M.S. *Titanic* should be left undisturbed, as a permanent memorial on the seafloor. As a cradle of iron pipes enclosed the liner's bow section and was preparing to lift it, Ballard led an extremist faction of Bluepeace in an assault.

Titanic's sinking had proven that objects falling four kilometers through water could reach unexpected velocities. The broken-off stern section was hammered so deeply into the seabed that simply uncovering it would be a major task. She had hit at more than eighty kilometers per hour, and that fact suggested to Ballard his course of action. Downblast had caused most of the damage he had seen when he discovered the *Titanic* in 1985. The same effect might save her.

One night, scores of stubby-winged airplanes

lifted off from Halifax with one destination in their grim minds: 49°56′49″ west longitude, 41°43′57″ north latitude. They were balsa wood cruise missiles, hobby-shop built, propeller driven. Invisible to radar and heat-seeking equipment, fueled for a one-way trip that reduced weight and more than doubled their payload capacity, the robot planes came in from the north, skimming low over the ocean and dropping hundreds of "flechettes," streamlined lead darts that were sinking at more than 130 kilometers per hour by the time they reached the *Titanic*.

Bluepeace knew that it was putting no human lives at risk. All work on the wreck was being done by remote control from the surface. Ballard was not homicidal, but he did commit robocide that night, and succeeded in delaying the raising just long enough. The technical failures that followed, set against the backdrop of an improbable natural upheaval, again paralleled the collision of machine and nature that had set the 1912 disaster in motion. The great underwater avalanche of 2010 swept over and removed R.M.S. *Titanic* from sight. After the surge, camera sleds found no sign of the wreck or of the lift cradle and its attendant robots in the field of freshly deposited mud.

"More than a few men are free at last," said one prominent philosopher, "from the obsessions of a lifetime."

He was wrong. Once people had touched her, the legendary ship did not easily let them go. Random House's TITANIC ILLUSTRATED, one of the world's first virtual reality programs, had been selling briskly for more than sixty years, even as the great ship lay hidden. Hollis's passenger had come to the excavation to update the latest edition. He was the right man for the job; even though his work had been finished by the tenth dive, he came down at every opportunity, as obsessed with the big ship as anyone she had ever known.

Hollis circled a crack in the hull, then settled on a field of rivets and portholes. When her great-grandfather last visited the wreck, the plain of steel had been a cliff, with portholes looking out instead of up. Now the vessel was almost entirely buried, lying on her port side with prow bent at a crazy angle.

E Deck starboard lay directly underfoot. A half-dozen hoses ran into it, gently suctioning the rooms clean, excavating the ship like an open pit mine. Siphons unveiled glittering brass fixtures. Anything that had not been appetizing to wood-boring mollusks or iron-oxidizing bacteria had aged scarcely more than a week during 164 years in the deep freeze of the Grand Banks. Silver had not tarnished, Mr. Hart's claim checks and immigration papers were still readable, and the cheeses, though waterlogged and salty, were still edible.

Hollis scrawled an order on her notepad, releasing forty robots from a basket under the viewports. Small crablike contraptions with overgrown paddles, they scrambled purposefully through open portholes. One of them paused at a golden ring lying on the outer hull. Hollis called the machine back with ring in tow, and got a close-up through the cameras.

There was a small seagull engraved on one side, and a date: 1975.

"Where the hell did that come from?" Jonathan Wayville demanded.

"You tell me," said Hollis. "You're the expert."

——— 4 ———

The Night Lives On

VIRGINIA WAS DESCENDING THE EASTERN FACE OF SRI Lanka's mile-high city tower when Jonathan Wayville called with the latest update from the *Titanic*. She had been getting up every morning before dawn during the past two weeks, and on those days when the air was clear to the horizon, she packed her officeware into a carry-bag and breakfasted in the botanical gardens at the base of Demon Rock. With a little trial and error, she had succeeded in synchronizing the maglev elevator's descent with the Earth's rotation, allowing her to hold the tip of the rising Sun on the horizon and stretch the "green flash" out to a long, steady glow that was more beautiful than the most brilliant emerald she had ever seen. Today's hold was the best yet, and the very last thing she wanted was an interruption from one of her authors.

"We're having a very rewarding night," a voice called from inside her carry-bag. She pulled out the notepad and popped it open. The liquid crystal screen displayed a golden ring with raised letters:

EAST ROCKAWAY HIGH SCHOOL
CLASS OF 1975

21

Virginia's concentration on the maglev controls lapsed, and in that instant the Sun phased from green to yellow, and became a rising red hull.

"Damn you, Wayville," she whispered.

"One of Ballard's people left a class ring here during the second expedition," said Jonathan. "This must be the one mentioned in Ballard's memoirs. All he said was that there was a brief ceremony involving the casting off of rings. I think there was some sort of story associated with it—something sad, like a burial at sea, as near as I can—"

Hollis interrupted him. "Forget the ring," she said with a weary knowledge of Wayville's dealings with his editor. "Show her what the crab probes found in the purser's office. Real treasure, Virginia."

"Treasure?"

"You bet," Jonathan said. "You won't believe it. A bag containing almost all the mail written aboard ship on that first and only voyage. Needs computer enhancing, but it's legible." He flashed an excerpt on her screen:

April 13, 1912: It's most uncomfortable here. The staterooms are too cramped, with lamp wires laid carelessly all over the place, waiting to trip the unsuspecting. The elevator boys have been smoking cigarettes in public. The stewards are rude. The food leaves much to be desired. I've been laid up with influenza and it's getting extremely cold outside. So tell me, what can happen next?

"And this—the same day." Another excerpt flashed up:

I met Mr. Ismay on deck today. He said something about ice warnings up ahead, but not to worry about it.

Virginia laughed. The last word about the *Titanic* would never be said. "Notes from the Purser's Mailbag will be a wonderful new chapter for the next edition," she said. "The night lives on," she then added, now only slightly disappointed that her plan to follow the green flash all the way down the tower had been ruined by the call, because it still promised to be a good day. By the time she was ready for breakfast in the gardens, at least two or three more letters would be available. She could chase the green flash tomorrow or the day after. Archeological breakthroughs were much rarer.

In the forests below, lakes caught the first rays of the rising Sun and threw them back into space. Abandoning the two-dimensional sprawl of twentieth-century cities, Sri Lanka Tower, and others like it, had been erected in the world's rain forests and farmlands, leaving the countryside virtually uninhabited. Even in Africa, where more than a hundred city arcologies had risen, nature was beginning to renew itself. It was a good day to be alive, she told herself, taking in the peace of the garden. Then, looking east, she saw it coming—at least her eyes began to register it—but her optic nerves did not last long enough to transmit what the eyes had seen.

It was quite small for what it could do—small enough to fit into an average-sized living room— but it was moving at 92 percent of light speed when it touched Earth's atmosphere. A spear point of light appeared, so intense that the air below snapped away from it, creating a low-density tunnel through which the object descended. The walls of the tunnel were a plasma boundary layer, six and a half kilometers wide and more than 160 deep—the flaming spear that Virginia's eyes began to register—with every square foot of its surface radiating a trillion watts, and still its destructive potential was but fractionally spent.

Thirty-three kilometers above the Indian Ocean, the point began to encounter too much air. It tunneled down only eight kilometers more, then stalled and detonated, less than two-thousandths of a second after crossing the orbits of Earth's nearest artificial satellites.

Virginia was more than three hundred kilometers away when the light burst toward her. Every nerve ending in her body began to record a strange, prickling sensation—the sheer pressure of photons trying to push her backward. No shadows were cast anywhere in the tower, so bright was the glare. It pierced walls, ceramic beams, notepads, and people—four hundred thousand people. The maglev terminal connecting Sri Lanka Tower to London and Sydney, the waste treatment centers that sustained the lakes and farms, all the shops, theaters, and apartments liquefied instantly. The structure began to slip and crash like a giant waterfall, but gravity could not yank it down fast enough. The Tower became vapor before it could fall half a meter. At the vanished city's feet, the trees of the forest were no longer able to cast shadows; they had themselves become long shadows of carbonized dust on the ground.

In Kandy and Columbo, where sidewalks steamed, the relativistic onslaught was unfinished. The electromagnetic pulse alone killed every living thing as far away as Bombay and the Maldives. All of India south of the Godavari River became an instant microwave oven. Nearer the epicenter, Demon Rock glowed with a fierce red heat, then fractured down its center, as if to herald the second coming of the tyrant it memorialized.

The air blast followed, surging out of the Indian Ocean—faster than sound—flattening whatever still stood. As it slashed north through Jaffna and Madurai, the wave front was met and overpowered by shocks rushing out from strikes in central and southern India.

Across the face of the planet, without warning, thousands of flaming swords pierced the sky.

5

Up!

"THE NIGHT LIVES ON," VIRGINIA SAID.

"You bet," Jonathan answered, and got no reply.

CLANG! The ocean around *Alvin* seemed to . . . move, reminding Jonathan of the barely perceptible jolt that had been the only sign of *Titanic*'s dreadful impact with the ice 164 years ago.

"What was that?" Hollis demanded.

Jonathan raised his hands. "I don't know. Nothing I did." He looked out the viewport. Clouds of sediment churned a meter high as far as the floodlamps enabled him to see. "Something moved out there."

"*Calypso II*," Hollis called, "there seems to have been a quake. Felt close. Do you have an epicenter?"

The acoustic communications system answered with a clean silence.

"*Calypso II*, please respond."

When she got no answer, Hollis cranked up the resolution on the sonoscans, boosted her signal output, and peered into the still-rising murk.

"*Calypso II*, we've lost downlink," she announced.

27

Silence.

"Maybe we should start back up," Jonathan suggested.

"Not yet." A loud *ping* sounded from Hollis's notepad, then another, and the liquid crystals flashed a red warning. "Stand by, Wayville."

Ping, ping, ping.

"I'm receiving multiple targets!" Hollis shouted. "They're coming down fast. That's it!" She throttled the motors and began pulling clear of the hull and siphons, driving east as fast as she could.

On his notepad, Jonathan saw a scatter field coming, at least five large objects over an area of half a klick—a duck's-eye-view of a shotgun blast—and it would hit in less than a minute.

There was no way out of the blast radius, but Hollis was determined to dodge the pellets. She turned *Alvin* sharply, pitching over twenty-two degrees. Jonathan grabbed a handhold and squinted through a viewport, but for human eyes there was only blackness outside. He snatched a pad with his free hand and called for a visual on the nearest object. The computer merged the returning sonoscans into a simulated image and threw up a scale bar and composition estimate. The object was a blob of fused ceramic, 2.13 meters on a side. It rotated and plummeted, then carved out a crater sixty-four meters away.

"What in hell was it?" Jonathan asked.

Hollis said, "I hope it's not *Calypso II*, but it can't be anything else."

Two more blobs hit beyond the glow of the floodlamps.

"Wayville, we're in real trouble."

Jonathan heard a loud bang. The hull shivered. "You mean our support ship just sank?"

Hollis shook her head and nosed *Alvin* up. "Much worse," she said, but her words were drowned out by the high-pitched rumbling that was rolling toward them.

Up! Up! It was the only way. Hollis knew what was coming and wanted to be at least three hundred meters above the thing when it swept by. If *Alvin*'s jets survived the strain! But she didn't want to rise too high. What was happening on the bottom had to be ten times worse on the surface. *Calypso II* was proof of that. Let the crisis roll over and under, she decided, and use the intervening kilometers of ocean as a shield for *Alvin*.

As she and Wayville stared at their screens, the avalanche seemed at first glance to be the disaster of 2010 all over again; but the sonoscans showed this one to be trillions of tons more massive than the movement that had buried the *Titanic*. This time the liner would be hidden so deep as to be forever beyond human reach. No one would ever touch her again.

"Ballard," she whispered, with fear constricting her throat, "you've finally had your way."

6

Ceres Station

VIEWED FROM THE DISTANCE OF THE *VOYAGER II* spacecraft, from a height of almost six light-days, the single most breathtaking aspect of the solar system was how closely it resembled the Saturnian and Uranian ring systems. There were gaps where any student of Newton would expect to find them, marking the paths of little worlds that had swept up whole mountains of debris. But this ring plane was not a mere two or three light-seconds across; it was in fact the largest structure in this part of the cosmos, a fractal image of Saturn's dust lanes projected on a screen more than twenty light-hours wide.

On the outer rim was the edge of the Oort Disk, where comets formed. Looking sunward, the outermost world-pair, Pluto-Charon, together with Neptune, Uranus, Saturn, and Jupiter, had carved out the ring system's widest gap. If she had been equipped with more advanced sensors, *Voyager II* could easily have resolved the innermost ring—which began just inside the orbit of Mercury and descended almost to the Sun's surface.

A less diffuse band of solar driftwood—the Asteroid Belt—was even easier to see, sandwiched between the orbits of Mars and Jupiter. Viewed from *Voyager II*'s oblique angle, the Asteroid Belt was a complex series of gaps and rings buried within an already complex series of gaps and rings.

In the center of the Belt's largest gap orbited a mote of iced-over dust named Ceres. Because of her location, she had never, in the eyes of Earthly astronomers, attained the status of Uranus's Miranda or Saturn's Enceladus. Those bodies were actual moons, or worlds, whereas Ceres would forever be a lowly asteroid or worldlet, even though at one thousand kilometers in diameter, she was rounder than Enceladus and Miranda, and twice as large.

Far below the surface, Ceres Station had been growing for nearly twenty-six years, with the aim of one day occupying the whole interior of the asteroid, shell within shell, down to the very center. Isak had often dreamed that one day the spinning worldlet might become mobile and head out to the stars, as a few of the smaller asteroid colonies had been planning to do. He liked to imagine what the completed world of shells within shells would be like: spaced three hundred meters apart, the total inside acreage of the shells would easily exceed the total usable land surface of Earth. Worldlet, indeed! Ceres could become a world unto itself.

The vision that he had carried around inside himself—one which had seemed so unstoppable only a little while ago—was now a hopeless extravagance, stopped in its tracks by a development he would never have counted as a possible obstacle. He had hoped he might see the Ceres project completed when he was an old man. But no matter how long he lived—and he was no longer a young man—he knew he must, in his despair, prepare himself to accept the idea that he was not going to see humanity recover from this latest setback.

Against all the odds that had threatened to destroy civilization, his ancestors had somehow made it. Degrading universal empires had been avoided. The runaway fouling of the planetary nest had been halted. Most important of all, population growth had been brought under firm if not always humane control. Even with the expansion to the Moon and Mars, Ceres and Miranda, humankind's numbers never again matched the preplague, preimmunogenetic maximum. Isak's people had realized—miraculously, it often seemed to him—that even as ascents to orbit finally became cheap, new worlds must never be viewed as relief valves for expanding, ravenous hordes who had overrun and exhausted their home. The deadly temptation to think of Earth as a disposable planet had been squelched with barely a decade to spare. One spring afternoon, the forests, rivers, and barrier reefs were coming back to life, and a new human kinship was arising throughout Sunspace. Then out of nowhere—out of the deep impersonal nowhere—came a bombardment that even the science fiction writers had failed to entertain.

Just nine days short of America's tricentennial celebrations, every inhabited planetary surface in the solar system had been wiped clean by relativistic bombs. Research centers on Mars, Europa, and Ganymede were silent; even tiny Phobos and Mookau were silent. Port Chaffee was silent. New York,

Colombo, Wellington, the Mercury Power Project and the Asimov Array. Silent. Silent. Silent.

A Valkyrie rocket's transmission of Mercury's surface had revealed thousands of saucer-shaped depressions where only hours before had existed a planet-spanning carpet of solar panels. The transmission had lasted only a few seconds—just long enough for Isak to realize there would be no more of the self-replicating robots that had built the array of panels and accelerators, just long enough for him to understand that humanity no longer possessed a fuel source for its antimatter rockets—and then the transmission had ceased abruptly as the Valkyrie disappeared in a silent white glare.

Presently, most of the station's scopes and spectrographs were turning Earthward, and Isak found it impossible to believe what they revealed. The Moon rising over Africa from behind Earth was peppered with new fields of craters. The planet below looked like a ball of cotton stained grayish yellow. The top five meters of ocean had boiled off under the assault, and sea level air was three times denser than the day before—and twice as hot.

Sargenti, her face slick with sweat, wiped the picture of Earth and Moon from her liquid crystal pad, tossed it onto Isak's table, and slumped back in her chair.

"We're going to have to power down even more," she said, smoothing back her long black hair with both hands. She had talked of doing something about her hair, and he wondered now if his silence had prevented her from cutting it short.

Isak put his own pad on top of hers, leaned against his balcony railing, and stared off into empty space, as if searching for something in the deep twilight of the amaryllis garden below. Finally, he looked beyond the garden toward the lake where a few children were playing and said, "It's going to get awfully dark in here."

"You have no choice but to order it," Sargenti said. "You do understand what has happened, don't you?"

Isak understood too well. If there had been any questions at all, the Peterson transmission had answered them. The solar system had been "bug bombed," as if humankind had been nothing more to the Intruders than an insect infesting an apartment dwelling. And now there were ample signs that the hunt for the surviving eggs of human civilization was beginning.

It would be impossible to stop Ceres' fusion reactors from leaking neutrinos into space, right through the many kilometers of surrounding rock. It was also clear that the R-bombs had zeroed in on the signatures of civilization everywhere, overlooking Ceres so far by some happy accident. It seemed likely that the Cerans would enjoy only a brief respite if the Intruders began stringing neutrino telescopes across Earth's ocean basins and the asteroid's reactors continued to outshine the galactic neutrino background.

"We're going to have to rely on fission," he said at last.

Sargenti nodded. "Inefficient, but only one third the neutrino flux per unit of power. Now, if we can power down to one-hundredth our present consumption, that just may be enough."

"That will dim our neutrino glow by a factor of three hundred. Enough?"

"Yes," she said. "That should save our necks. We'll be virtually invisible to them."

"It's going to get cramped down here."

"It's the only way," she added.

"And the end of a dream," Isak continued. "We're going to," he said, choking up, "stop all new ranch construction . . . evacuate most of the shells and shut them down, bringing maybe three or four families into each home. . . ." He trailed off into thought, trying to remind himself not to dwell on the sheer weight of his responsibilities or on the many ways that he could fail, for in that direction lay paralysis, if not madness.

He remembered the story of astronaut Fred Haise, trapped aboard an *Apollo* moonship that had become crippled by an oxygen tank explosion after crossing the fail-safe point. He and his crew had to redesign and actually rebuild the lunar landing module in midflight, so that it could act as both lifeboat and tugboat for the return to Earth. It had occurred to Haise that the explosion, which had destroyed most of the ship's systems, might also have damaged the heat shield, meaning that all their efforts to save themselves would come to nothing when they thundered down through Earth's atmosphere. The thought had nearly crippled Haise, but he shrugged it off and continued to work; for the greater and more present danger was that if he allowed fears of cracked heat shields to obsess him, he would never get the necessary work done and he would die whether or not the heat shield had survived.

"Never dwell on cracked heat shields," Haise

later told young, academy-bound Isak. The lesson was as important now, in the shells of Ceres, as it had been in the little titanium shell of *Apollo 13*, and Isak found the resolve he needed with which to face his responsibilities to the nine thousand settlers of the asteroid. Most were simply people who loved farming, and they had brought with them the best that self-replicating robot technology could offer. Starting with an initial investment of only thirty machines, and using as building materials the substance of Ceres herself, whole armies of "worms" and "caterpillars" had grown and spread like a viral infection throughout the worldlet. At the north and south poles, borers were pushing up great dunes of dust, like piles of worm feces grown out of control. The dunes were joining to become mountain ranges; and at the edge of one range, the dust spread glacierlike into lower latitudes, where the centrifugal acceleration flicked it skyward and created a dust storm in space—which threatened to become yet another signature of civilization.

More than twenty kilometers below the spreading dust fields, the first and largest of Ceres's inner shells was nearly complete. It resembled a giant bicycle wheel embedded in the asteroid, and it provided each of the homesteaders with a ranch larger than some Earth counties.

Now, most of the power had been cut off, as Isak had ordered, and all the fields were withering in the night. The pioneering days were over. From now on, the Cerans would draw their nourishment using the old standby methods of deep space explorers living in cramped and energy-efficient quarters. After the last crops were harvested, and the

last of the cattle killed, each family would be reduced to a meter-square box of lights and tubes
filled with recombinant algae. From these gardens
of algae would come all the food ever to be produced again inside Ceres. There was simply no energy for anything else.

"Fission reactors," Isak said at last. "How long
will the fuel last?"

"Thorium won't last indefinitely, sir. We'll have
to think of something else as soon as we can."

Isak's pad chimed and flashed red, throwing up
a star chart with Earth at its center as the computer
said, "Those two nearer gamma-ray sources are
growing stronger. I have identified them as our Valkyrie starships, *Nautile* and *Graff*, decelerating from
Barnard's Star. They are down to sunspace cruising
speed—one hour, fifty-seven light-minutes away.
They continue to call for information on all channels, from anyone who can hear them. Instructions?"

"Maintain silence," Isak said. "Do not answer under any circumstances."

Stealthily, Isak and Sargenti—and every other inhabitant of Ceres—watched as the two Valkyrie ultralight starships fell homeward, broadcasting
every kilometer of the way. Then the pilot of *Graff*
started to speak in German, words of astonishment,
and his gamma flare died in the middle of course
correction. The *Nautile* quit without any words at
all.

Isak guessed that only the German had lived long
enough to see something, and it had stupefied him.
He had let out two or three exclamations before try-

ing to describe it, and by then, of course, he couldn't.

Now, two dwarf novae burned where the Valkyries had been, emitting gamma flares and plasma shock bubbles that in certain wavelengths lit up their small corner of the heavens fiercely enough to drive back the glow of Sagittarius. The expanding concussion of light brought home to everyone the message of the destroyed Valkyries: it was fatal to communicate. Something ruthless and fast acting had entered the solar system, and whatever it was, it was looking for them.

"No surviving human group," Isak said, pushing his chair back from the table, "can choose not to power down."

Sargenti was taking in the lesson of the fading novae on the pads. Her usually pale face was flushed. Her tall, willowy frame was hunched down over Isak's table, and she was breathing fitfully.

Isak turned away from her and looked out across the fading light of his amaryllis garden, while on the twin pads the plasma dissipated and Sagittarius returned to prominence again.

Sargenti watched the cold stars burn, wondering if somewhere out there the Intruders knew her thoughts, could actually trace them like streams of neutrinos to their source and read them, if such could conceivably be the extent of alien power. No. Isak would say that this was worrying about another cracked heat shield, she realized—and tried to shrug the idea away. Neutrino glow you could reduce and hide, radio waves you could hide. How, she asked herself, does one go about hiding one's thoughts?

Isak could not help thinking, even in the midst of calamity, that late middle age was turning him into the oldest fool in the world. When Sargenti looked up from the starscape, she noticed that his lips were pressed together, but he seemed to be smiling wryly. She felt an urge to reach for him, but then stowed it away and returned her attention to the pad.

But her impulse did not go unsuspected.

It could never have worked, Isak told himself. He was born in the 1990s, and could still remember when Paul McCartney, Mick Jagger, and Ronald Reagan were alive. By the time Sargenti reached sixty, he would be nearly twice her age—not that such chronologies really mattered anymore.

"One other thing . . ." he started to say, feeling a surge of genuine affection for her. The old fool in him had restrained it too long, hoping not to let it grow into more. But she had crept into his heart despite his self-control, and he had, without fully realizing it, accepted her presence there.

"Yes?" she asked, pushing her seat back from the pad.

Isak motioned at the floor of the cave, toward the outer wall of the wheel, beneath which lay many kilometers of rock and the surface of Ceres. "How well do our internal communications leak through the rock?"

"Not very well, I'm glad to say. The rock shields us."

"I wonder," he said. "Call it corrosive paranoia setting in, but I think we should restrict all communications to hand-delivered messages for a while. We'll have to stop anything that can leak radio waves, however weak. We can't accept even the smallest risk of being found."

"Messengers? That's like living in ancient Greece! Do you think we can live like that?"

"We won't have to for very long," Isak said. "Only long enough to reacquaint ourselves with some nineteenth-century technology."

"What do you mean?"

"Can our factory make about six hundred klicks of wire by this time next week?"

"Wire? Six hundred klicks? Oh, I get it."

"Exactly, Science Officer Sargenti—telephones," he said with a wry grin, then walked past her to where coals were burning in a deep fireplace cut into the balcony wall.

A new rack of pipes lay over the coals, gathering heat for the household water tanks. In the long night that was coming to Ceres, most of the forests, cultivated with painstaking care during the last twenty years, were going to die. But as long as the Cerans did not burn it too quickly and produce a smog problem, they would have enough firewood to last two hundred years or more.

Isak tossed two fresh logs on the fire. A sudden flurry of sparks cast a soft orange light on Sargenti's otherwise pale face, and when he turned around, he found himself yearning for her warmth. Did it make any sense to tell her? Or had she always known how he felt, but had simply not cared to encourage him? He regretted, given the odds against prolonged survival, that he would probably never know.

"I think I can start to see hope in all of this," Sargenti said. "Not much, maybe, but some nevertheless."

"Hope is not always a good thing," Isak said, his wry grin gone. "Let me tell you something about hope. It's the murder of peaceful sleep, the birth of endless worry. All things considered, I think we might have been better off hopeless—and coldly rational."

Sargenti looked at him with dismay; but Isak did not notice as he turned away from her, crumpled a dry twig in his hands, threw it on the fire, and watched it burn.

7

Carbonaceous Chondrite

THE IQ BOOSTERS WORKED SWIFTLY, SURGING UP through the arteries in her neck, seeking the outer layers of the neocortex. Manufactured from algae that had been genetically tricked into producing human enzymes, one set of boosters more than tripled the rate at which nerves recharged and fired, while other substances increased the growth of new nerve connections and modulated energy efficiency. It was the increase in firing frequency that had the first and most profound effect. After only two days on the boost, Tam and her crew were connecting disparate and seemingly unrelated facts faster than they had ever before in their entire lives, possibly faster than any human beings since the beginning of time.

One side effect of her newly acquired abilities was that she could now clearly see the flicker of her liquid crystal display pad, which usually cycled too quickly for the human eye to register. Watching the pad (especially in the 3-D mode) became an activity guaranteed to trigger migraine, and she worried that there might be other unanticipated effects. Yet they were all being forced to think faster, to redesign their own brain chemistries, and, whenever necessary, to experiment upon themselves. They had no choice.

They still called her Prime Minister Tam, although she had retired from politics years ago, and since then had been fulfilling her lifelong dream of becoming a space explorer. Sargenti-Peterson, the comet into which she and her team had burrowed, was now moving deep within the orbit of Mercury. Tam's little world, a marriage of ship and comet, was about the size and shape of Manhattan Island, and from all available evidence the comet was a mere splinter shot from the interior of a much larger body. Some four and a half billion years ago, hydrothermal streams must have honeycombed the parent planetoid. Their remnants were everywhere, in the form of salt veins and microgeodes full of pyrrhotite crystals. As with Ceres, there had been an early period of melting over the entire volume of rock, brought on mostly by the decay of aluminum-26 and other radioactive elements that had been injected in vast quantities into the solar system—fresh and hot from a supernova—almost at the moment the Sun and planets formed.

About four billion B.C., comet Sargenti-Peterson had become warm and wet inside; but the subsurface springs could not possibly have lasted forever. They were, in those days, losing heat at the rate of a half degree per million years. A half-billion years of warmth, and then it was all over. A long time, but not forever.

Nothing lasts forever, Tam reminded herself, least

of all man. The likelihood of life elsewhere in the Galaxy, the inevitability of her species being drawn into an interstellar extinction lottery, was all spelled out on the insides of Sargenti-Peterson. Even before her team had landed and started tunneling, Tam knew the comet to be a treasure chest of strange and thrilling discoveries. Arginine was venting from somewhere below the surface—and ethanol, purines, and even porphyrin molecules—actual precursors of chlorophyll and hemoglobin.

Inside they had found microscopic balls and filaments of protein, filled with enzymes that were able to make starch. A few of them even yielded up crude snippets of RNA. Tam's best guess was that life on Earth had begun much like this, with billions upon billions of protocells forming and dissolving every day on the high seas and in underground slime pools, with no two exactly alike. Earth's protocell era had left few traces of itself in the fossil record, but here was the same process frozen in mid-stride for all to see.

But not permanently frozen, Tam had discovered. Ever since some disturbance had slowed Sargenti-Peterson's orbital motion in the Oort Ring, sending the comet sunward every two hundred years, warmth seeping down below the surface was periodically bringing the hydrothermal springs to life; and for a year or more evolution would pick up where it had left off—random variation providing the raw materials, natural selection sorting out the winners and losers—until the next deep freeze set in.

Most of her crew believed that comets full of protocells had seeded life on Earth, but Tam disagreed. She saw no reason why the Earth could not have cooked up its own life, to which the comets might simply have added their own two cents worth. That colonies of living cells had been found thriving near hydrothermal vents beneath the ice of Ganymede, Europa, Titan, and Enceladus—and that frozen protocells had been found inside Ceres, and were still evolving in the nucleus of Sargenti-Peterson— drove home the conclusion that wherever there existed a warm and wet place, sooner or later the process of life was bound to get started.

Tam floated upside down (by one set of references) in the microbiology chamber, intently studying a cartridge of slides. Everyone else had gone off to take care of more important concerns, such as watching the Valkyries explode or peering down through the clear eyes of Earth's proliferating hurricanes to see what traces of humankind might still be left on the planet.

Tam's wallscreen showed a sample of protocells from one of Sargenti-Peterson's newly restarted vents. Scores of smaller proteinaceous sacks had surrounded and were absorbing a larger one, exchanging biochemistries as they fed. She could not decide whether to call this evolutionary step the invention of sex or the dawn of predation. She was about to decide that both descriptions were true when Second Officer Susan Skurla drifted into the room with something in her hand.

"Here's that book you wanted," Susan said.

"Good, good."

Susan sent it sailing across the lab. Tam snatched it from the air and began leafing through the first chapters. One of only two real books she had brought with her, the ninety-year-old edition was autographed by Isaac Asimov, James Powell, and her grandfather. All three of the authors had anticipated the Sargenti-Peterson discoveries, and later in life had even drawn blueprints for the first Valkyrie starships.

"It's all here," said Tam. "Folsome microbodies, organized elements in the Orgueil and Murchison meteorites, and most important of all, what they all mean."

"Now, Prime—ah, Captain . . ." Susan stopped and looked agitatedly around the room.

"Go on. Say what you were going to."

"Captain, aren't all these protocells just an irrelevant oddity, considering what's happened?"

For two days now, Second Officer Skurla had been dropping hints to Tam, trying as gently as possible to compare any continuation of the original mission to Edith Russell's tidying up of her stateroom before proceeding to the lifeboats on the sinking *Titanic*, a symptom of what the historian Walter Lord had called the *Yorktown* Syndrome, after the hundreds of sailors who had lined up their shoes neatly in rows on deck before abandoning the sinking aircraft carrier. Tam's favorite example of such behavior was the fictional Scarlett O'Hara trying to go back and lock the door of the house before fleeing the Atlanta fire. History was filled with thousands of examples of people tending to absurd details in time of crisis; but this was not one of them.

"Oh, no," said Tam. "There's no *Yorktown* Syndrome here!"

Susan looked at her dubiously and was about to speak, but Tam took a deep breath and said immediately, "Two things I want you to understand. First, I'm done with protocells for now. And second, none of this is as irrelevant as you might have thought at first glance. Don't you see it? Look there, on the screen. It's as obvious as your big toe! The miracle we call life was drawn from a disarmingly simple bag of tricks. It's all nothing more than the most likely chemical reactions undergone by some of the most abundant elements in this part of the universe. So the whole universe—"

"Must be trying to make life," Susan finished for her.

"Exactly."

"So the universe was bound to throw up competitors, and one of them has found us."

"And here we sit, Susan, in the nucleus of a comet. We and our machines must learn to evolve very quickly from here on, if we are to have any chance of addressing the competition."

The look of agitation on Susan's face changed to one of disbelief. "You can't be thinking of going up against them."

"Of course not. I'd just as soon challenge the Sun. No, there is only escape for us. And I'm afraid escape has become a race against extinction. And I'm afraid we are going to lose." Tam pointed at the wallscreen. "Do you see that big globule in the center? The one being devoured by all the others?"

Susan nodded.

"That's us. It's probably the last of its kind, now about to vanish without heir. And for all we know, we are the last of our kind, the only human beings left alive in all the cosmos."

"Not the only ones," Susan said quickly, struggling to sound hopeful. "There's a very loud call coming from the North Atlantic."

"Be real, Susan. There's no one alive on Earth. No one human, at least. Our *competition* is trying to bait us into a response, to find out how many of us are still alive and where. They'll fix on us and we'll go up in smoke like *Graff* and *Nautile*."

Just then the cabin shifted slightly, banking to starboard, as somewhere above a fountain of hot gas nudged the comet into a new heading. Sporadic jets of gas and rock were a natural part of every comet's plunge sunward, and often changed projected course headings in unpredictable and sometimes frightening ways. Comet IRAS-Araki-Alcock had shifted from a far-flung orbit to a near collision with Earth, and the comet Hubble IV had zigged and zagged and sputtered until at last it fell headlong into the Sun. Tam's landing party did not want to chance repeating either of those two scenarios and had, upon taking possession of Sunspace's riskiest piece of real estate, promptly "rewired" Sargenti-Peterson with auxiliary nozzles and easily controllable counterthrusters. The words "preadaptation" and "exaptation" kept playing in Tam's head. Steam and rock jetting from the comet's interior would disguise any course corrections as natural occurrences. In ways that Tam and her crew had not anticipated, all those kilometers of furnaces and nozzles and the dozens of spiderlike robots that had built them—now replicating under Tam's orders into hundreds—and even the gamma-ray observatories, were about to justify their existence.

"So, what do we do?" the Second Officer demanded nervously, her face pale and mournful.

"Oh, you're going to love this," said Tam cheerfully. "It's called engines up four bells full astern, for twenty hours."

"Full astern? You'll practically *kill* our forward velocity."

"That's the idea."

"But that will drop us down from orbit."

"Exactly."

"But we're orbiting the Sun."

"Exactly—and stop looking at me that way. I have a plan."

8

Quest for Ararat

HUDDLED INSIDE THE CERAMIC SHELL OF *ALVIN*, Hollis and Wayville had stopped talking to each other. No one on Earth could blame them, of course. They couldn't even blame each other; there was very little left for the damned to say to the damned. Though *Alvin* could function for years, if necessary, no one had planned for a mission lasting more than two weeks. The provisions Hollis had stowed aboard were now all the food in the world.

In their own ways, Hollis and Wayville were succumbing to *Yorktown* Syndrome; but in different and distant ways they each knew that they were trying to hold themselves together, even if success meant only that they would probably starve to death with their wits intact.

Jonathan continued to update his book, immersing himself in the virtual reality tie-ins; but with all editorial stops pulled out, VR was rapidly becoming the entire book, rather than a mere teaser inviting people to read passenger biographies, court transcripts, or Walter Lord's classic work, *A Night to Remember*.

The teaser principle was a relic from the days of

the great editor Richard Kohl, who saw it as a last opportunity to preserve literacy in the world, but Jonathan disagreed. Even the "Notes from the Purser's Mailbag" could be scanned and recited in fastspeak by the computer. Instead of laboring over the alphabet, every schoolchild had been trained to listen to and comprehend computer readings—including instant translations of any language, from Chinese to ancient Babylonian—at five times the speed of human speech.

Jonathan had tried to convince Virginia that reading was becoming a lost art. It was, to him, no more necessary than the memorization of multiplication tables in the aftermath of the first pocket calculators. Why bother, when with a pierced ear and an equally painless bonephone implant, every child could have the entire universe at her fingertips, with the great works of art and literature included and accessible through a mere touch for instant fastspeak or visualization.

But book publishers were all dinosaurs. Worse off now even than dinosaurs! The dinosaurs—dwarfed and genetically redesigned into household pets—were living and breathing on the last day. Not so Virginia. Jonathan found it difficult to believe that she had ever been fully alive. He remembered the days when he could almost hear the slosh of formaldehyde in her veins—preserver of literacy, indeed!

So he had activated his bonephone and, almost from the hour of the world's end, begun revising TITANIC ILLUSTRATED. Writing a history book was now probably even more pointless than Virginia's concerns about literacy, but it made perfect sense in its own way. Jonathan's response to the disaster that had overtaken humanity was to escape into another disaster.

Each day he compulsively improved the program, to the extent that the computer was now enabling him to converse, in rudimentary fashion, with the "ghosts" of *Titanic*'s passengers and crew. With each passing hour, his program became more lifelike, and as he wandered endlessly through sinking corridors, his subconscious self, fully aware of what he was really up to, made him gravitate toward passenger Edith Russell. More and more of the computer's memory was being dedicated to her. She was becoming increasingly articulate, no longer merely responding to questions with appropriate answers from her diaries and memoirs. On at least two occasions she had even asked Jonathan questions of her own, and it was possible to believe that if he continued improving the program, he might simulate in her the perfect illusion of self-awareness.

Presently, he was standing with Edith and Mr. Rothschild on E Deck forward. A steward came striding down the long hallway and joined them. The young man's clothes were drenched in sweat. The whole corridor was slanting toward the bow, and the lights had dimmed to an ominous red glow. Thirty meters ahead, a lake that had no business being there gleamed obsidian black as it lapped at the doors of the first class staterooms. A leather pillow floated in it.

"Gee," Mr. Rothschild said, "this is really beginning to look serious."

"Do you think she'll sink?" asked the steward.

Another three meters of carpet disappeared as the lake crept toward them.

"Nah!" replied Rothschild. "The ship has row after row of watertight compartments. She'll settle only so far and stop sinking."

"Do you see what's happening here?" Edith asked Jonathan. "They refuse to believe what their own eyes are showing them."

"Freeze program!" Jonathan shouted.

Edith Russell was about to say something, but stopped in mid-breath. From somewhere far away, a shiver had begun to run through the deck beneath Jonathan's feet. An ankle-deep wave was cresting toward him, about to eat up meters more of carpet—but now it stood motionless . . . waiting.

Jonathan called out new instructions to the computer. For the second time in as many days he began tampering with Edith Russell. He had already softened the tone of her voice. Now he decided that her nose had too much of a hook, so he remolded it. When he had finished, he was only remotely conscious that he had given her his mother's voice and his mother's nose; but his subconscious was happy.

About thirty of the crablike *Titanic* probes were left. One by one, Hollis was replacing their paddles with wings—converting them into ornithopters. And one by one, as Hollis surfaced into the tranquil eyes of hurricanes, she released the mechanical birds. More than a dozen were already following the storms landward, transmitting everything they saw, telling her that the winds blowing over the ocean's surface were sometimes lethally hot and that all communications from other people had ceased, even from the Moon and as far away as Mars. Every time she surfaced, Hollis signaled with increasing power, until at last her voice should have been received anywhere in Sunspace, even with minimal equipment. Yet her distress calls continued to go unanswered.

Through the eyes of electronic doves, Hollis saw that the atmosphere over Manhattan had cooled sufficiently to allow them brief excursions, even though there was more radioactivity in the air than she had expected to measure. She could survive out there, but she wouldn't want to spend a week camping in the ruins. What ruins? she asked herself, startled at how her mind invented and clung to even vaguely hopeful images of continuity. There were no archeological traces of the city she had hoped to find, only bodies of water where none had been before, and a featureless landscape in which it was impossible to guess where the Twin Towers and the Empire State Building once stood.

Everywhere the doves looked, the destruction was the same. Penetrating the perpetual cloud cover with their imaging radar, sampling and analyzing the air with their filters, and landing occasionally, they became a gallery of windows on a denuded Earth. In all of Jerusalem, not a single brick lay atop another brick. The Temple Mount was cracked down its center, and springs bubbled forth from the cleft. A stream now flowed from the Mount all the way down to the Dead Sea. Further west, two doves had found pyramid-shaped mounds near the place where Cairo used to be. Perhaps because they had not been directly under an epicenter, together with their combination of resilient geometry and immense bulk, the pyramids had withstood the planetary shocks—just barely. On the entire surface of the Earth they appeared to be the only evidence that mankind had ever existed.

All life was erased from the continents. Not a single tree stood, not a blade of grass grew, not even a scorched twig smoldered. The only bacteria on the planet seemed to be those vented from *Alvin*'s crew compartment whenever Hollis went topside to release the doves. She imagined that in a half billion years or so, if the bacteria survived, organisms descended from her own bad breath might build bacterial reefs and set evolution in motion again.

But to what end? she asked herself. Another total destruction?

In the safety of Earth's womb, more than a half kilometer down in the everblack, the sea lulled Hollis into bad dreams, bad expectations, and even worse remembrances. She had always sought peace and solitude in the depths, but these days there was too much of it down here, causing her to dream too much and too long about the people she had known and loved. And in the aftermath of the dreams came a numbing guilt; for it seemed the height of hubris for her to be grieving for a father or a friend when all of her mother's people—four hundred million Chinese living in the richest country and last surviving democracy on Earth—had also vanished.

Four thousand years of civilization—the Forbidden City, Emperor Ch'in's terra cotta army, the Tsien Space Center—gone in an instant. Her heart beat faster for the shore that lay only a couple of hundred kilometers ahead, beat faster for landfall and for the dim hope that by actually planting her hands and feet in the ashes of her world she might find in some mote of dust the answer to how under a just God this senseless evil had been allowed to prevail—why under a just God it was brought into the universe in the first place, and how under a just God her suffering might be ended.

She knew that she could end it herself; half a kilometer beneath the Atlantic, no one need die slowly. But she did not have to hurry it. The end would come soon enough of its own accord; and while she still had a breath of air in her, she would rail against dying, until she had that answer.

Something leapt up from the bridge, up to where the cold stars burned, and then the stars were gone—extinguished in a concussion of light and shadow. Hundreds of upturned faces flashed out pallid white, and when his eyes adjusted to the blaze, Jonathan, who had half forgotten where he really was, realized with horror that he had lived through this night before.

The black Atlantic, as calm as a pool of quarry water, sparkled for miles around. Lifeboats could be seen on it. The huge smokestacks and tapering masts were illuminated in a shower of white stars that sank slowly down the sky. In that cave of manmade light, minds, too, were illuminated. Everyone understood the message of the rocket without being told: the ship was calling for help from any steamer, any fishing boat—anyone who was near enough to see.

Edith, who had just returned from her stateroom with something bundled in her arms, nudged Jonathan's elbow and tried to lead him toward the promenade deck. He resisted, and the bundle dropped from her arms with a snap.

"Come," Edith said. "We must find you a lifeboat at once. They're taking men off on the starboard side."

"There's still time," Jonathan protested. He bent down and picked up a blanket wrapped around a toy pig. He knew, without Edith's telling him, that it was the same pig her father had given her after a car crash from which she emerged as the sole survivor. He had explained that the pig was a symbol of good luck in China, and made her promise to keep it with her always. But Edith, a fashion reporter destined to become the world's first woman war correspondent, was adamant that her space in a lifeboat should be taken by others. Later this night, Jonathan knew, a young officer, mistaking her bundle in a blanket for a baby, would snatch it from her arms and toss it into number 11, one of the last boats down on the davits. Only a pig and a promise were going to save her.

Jonathan dusted the pig off very carefully as he handed it back to her, noticing that one of its little forelegs was broken.

"Edith," he said, smiling, "I'd hold on to this if I were you."

Just then, Hollis's voice pierced Jonathan's bone-phone: "Earth to Wayville! Earth to Wayville! Reality check. We've just surfaced and I need you topside!"

Inside the hurricane's eye, the air was sticky and close and three times as dense as it had been before the relativistic bombing. The surface layers of the oceans had actually boiled off. There was no escaping the oppressive atmosphere. Hollis had equalized the air pressure in the crew compartment with that of Earth's surface, so that even when they submerged again, the dense air would still be with them. The humidity was unbearable. Jonathan imagined that Venus must look and feel a lot like this, as he and this priest, the only other living person on Earth, stood atop *Alvin*'s coning tower, looking about them. All around was dead calm and a thick, yellow-white haze.

"Mayday! Mayday! Mayday!" Hollis called out, cranking the transmitter to its highest level yet: "Position forty-one twenty-six north, seventy-one four west. Require immediate assistance. Come at once. This is the research vessel *Alvin*. We are running out of supplies. Starving."

Hollis put the transmitter down. Jonathan merely shook his head, activated a dove, and sent it flapping into the fog. "Who do you think is going to hear you?" he said. "They're all dead."

"There's always hope."

Jonathan rolled his eyes heavenward, thinking that a priest would believe anything to avoid the sin of despair, and began preparing another dove.

"We'll make landfall tomorrow," said Hollis with an unconvincing tone of optimism.

"Can you keep us within the storm's eye?"

"Sure. This one's only a baby. She's making toward shore at twenty knots. We can keep up with her. She'll bring us right to Long Island, somewhere near Jones Beach."

Jonathan loosed another dove, and Hollis began unscrewing a thermos.

"I've prepared us a little treat," she announced. "The last of the coffee."

Jonathan raised a hand and tried to wave her off.

"Come on."

He refused to take the cup.

"You've got to keep up your strength."

"No."

"You've got to go on."

He turned away from her.

"For the love of God, Jonathan!"

"No coffee," he said, making two fists and raising them. And then, as he thought of the *Titanic* fossilizing now under a hundred meters of mud, he fixed onto an echo from the past and decided to sting Hollis with the very words Mrs. Astor had used when Edith Russell offered her coffee and God's blessings aboard the rescue ship *Carpathia*.

"No coffee," Jonathan said in unison with the past. "No God, either. God went down with the *Titanic*."

9

Thriller

FOR AS LONG AS CIVILIZATION HAD EXISTED, CHIL-
dren had brought home family pets that ended up
in the care of parents. Not that Isak really minded
the responsibility. He had always enjoyed the long
walks through the Ceran forests with his son's be-
loved minisaur. Steven had been nearly five years
old when the first dwarfed and brain-boosted apatosaur pups, with a guaranteed cockatoo-equivalent
IQ of ninety, hit the market; and because every
child also developed, sooner or later, a puzzling
and totally instinctive love of dinosaurs, it was pre-
ordained that minisaurs would become the pet
craze of the twenty-first century.

Apatosaurs, it turned out, preferred a diet rich
in alkaloid-laced flowers, which in allosaur and
tyrannosaur times must have made their flesh utterly distasteful, if not downright poisonous. A
pattern of warning colors alternating from orange
to black and yellow, displayed on its hide like the
stripes of a Bengal tiger, made apatosaurus the
most beautiful of the cloned saurians. By the late
twentieth century, snippets of DNA preserved in
everything from skin in the mouths of amber-

embedded horseflies to mummified dinosaur femur bones had begun to dethrone diamonds as the world's most resilient and valuable form of carbon. Though the saurians themselves had vanished by the billions, a few grams of well-preserved tissue had managed to pass their genetic blueprints across oceans of time like bits of gossip passed over a backyard fence. Putting such genetic gossip to good use had to await the development of equipment able to scan DNA molecules without breaking them apart or wresting them from their stony matrix. With such grace did corporate paleontologists redefine both extinction and death, by reconstructing genetic codes in computers, then sequencing entire symphonies written on DNA and performed by protein.

Once computers and scanners had become sufficiently advanced, the sequencing was fairly straightforward. The single tissue sample from which all living apatosaurs were derived, discovered in the jaws of a ninety-five-million-year-old fly from New Jersey, contained thousands of preserved cells—thousands of copies of the genetic blueprints necessary for constructing an identical twin of the insect's last meal. All of the copies had been damaged by the radioactive decay of carbon-14, potassium-40, and even the occasional cosmic ray; but even this turned out to be a relatively simple technological hurdle, not much unlike the one encountered by archaeologists who had come upon multiple copies of the Book of Isaiah, every one of them scattered in pieces and mostly missing, among the Dead Sea Scrolls. In both cases, a program for "matching and patching" missing segments—for building a single composite "text" from a collection of partly damaged copies—had solved the problem.

But with such abilities came the inevitable urge to tamper. The prophecies of Isaiah were remolded and removed from their original context, as were the apatosaurs.

Crichton stood barely forty centimeters high at the shoulders, and his personality—also genetically remodelled—was that of a loyal and reasonably smart lapdog. Isak never tired of watching him drive herds of Chihuahua-sized mammoths across the fields or having a romp through the amaryllis gardens, which he had all but taken over as his private territory, even to the exclusion of Isak. As a pup he had always slept in Steven's bed, until the mysterious illness that broke the hearts of a hundred million children nearly struck the saurian down.

Crichton was three years old, and a full-fledged family member, when throughout the solar system, all at once, the apatosaurs began dying. The dwarfing and brain-boosting of the dinosaurs had rearranged delicate biochemistries in subtle and unpredictable ways. The distortions seemed such a little thing, until they reached the flash point and began resounding through entire organ systems like a harmonic chord misstruck.

Yeon, the only woman Isak had ever married, had removed Crichton from Steven's room and banished the ailing pet from the house, fearing that the disease might be contagious. Yeon had never known a time when an ailment could not be quickly and routinely cured. Despite Isak's protests that the condition was purely genetic, the dying saurians filled her with an irrational dread, which turned out to be the only ailment that truly was contagious.

Crichton emerged as practically the sole survivor of the first generation minisaurs—thanks largely, Isak believed, to the long nights he had spent out in the garden with his son's pet, trying to nurse him through the crisis. But even expensive joint and nerve replacements could not repair or hide all the damage, and even Steven's love for his boyhood friend—shaken by the fact that Crichton had almost died, and also by his mother's fear—never fully recovered.

Steven's childhood was not all that ended with the minisaur die-off. Isak and Yeon were two people deeply in love but terribly mismatched. He believed in monogamy; she did not. Isak felt attracted only to women, and to only one woman in particular; Yeon had always felt an attraction to both sexes—and the more variety the better—but she had chosen monogamy for Isak's sake. Isak, who seemed to worship science, spoke constantly about how immunogenetic therapy could render her choice completely painless by simply changing her desires at the source, or removing them completely. Such treatment seemed unnatural to Yeon, even sacrilegious. If the medical community had its way, everyone who felt as she did would be extinct within a single generation. The prospect smelled a little of Buchenwald.

The final break between Yeon and Isak gave the appearance of being caused by escalating arguments about "not letting that filthy animal back into the house," but in truth poor Crichton was merely the explosive charge that brought a whole swamp of hidden conflicts bubbling to the surface.

Little Crichton, who was becoming more and more to Isak the last perfect symbol of loyalty, had not only outlived a marriage but most of the human species. Seventeen years ago, in what seemed to Isak another lifeime, Steven was born to him, and he was in love, and he had thought himself the happiest man in all the world. That he lived alone now, taking care of Steven's pet, would have seemed to any outside observer part of the natural order of the human life cycle; but it only seemed so. Seventeen-year-old Steven had developed an interest in stellar atmospheres, which had taken him to Miranda Station, where he had been studying under Professor Donald Peterson when the end came.

"I've always been a little curious about one little detail," Sargenti said, "if you don't mind my asking."

"Go ahead," said Isak, trying to fit an uncooperative phone jack into his pad. He needed more light. Beyond his balcony, beyond the glow of his fireplace, was total darkness. He thought he felt the ghost of a breeze coming from the direction of the forest. It brushed his cheek and sent a powerful chill down his spine; but it did not trouble Crichton, who was sleeping peacefully by the fire.

"You say you remained friends with your wife?"

"As much as two people could stay friendly under those circumstances."

"So—did you ever find out?"

Isak grinned in spite of himself. After the breakup, Yeon had taken advantage of medical advances that had rendered sex changes so easy and so perfect as to be considered almost natural. In a span of only two years, Isak had watched her transform from a woman to a man and back to a beautiful woman again. After the second change, they fell briefly in love all over again, and even considered having a second child, until Yeon decided that she wanted to be a man after all and announced her wish that Isak become the mother of her child, a request he had refused. And through it all, the obvious and burning question had nagged him, as it now nagged Sargenti, a question that could only be answered by someone who had lived as both sexes.

"So," Sargenti prodded, "which sex has more fun?"

"Well, how's this for an answer—" Isak began to say, but was interrupted by a ringing sound from his pad.

"Hello?" Isak asked, and the pad automatically went into phone mode.

"Everything working all right?" a voice asked back.

"Not really. The ringer is irritating and your picture is very blurry."

"The bell ringer is just a little authentic touch I added. As for the picture—" the figure on the screen made a quick, forward motion "how's this?"

The resolution improved enormously, shifting from blurry black and white to an easily identifiable picture of Ed Bishop, the station's stocky robotics expert, now doubling as telephone lineman.

"Much better," said Isak, "but the colors are a tad off and there's no 3-D. Can you do something about that?"

"You'll have to live with it for now. Yours is only the first line in, and we've had to hurry just to get this far, so you'll find these cables a little crude. There's only so much information we can cram through them, you know. If you insist, I can improve your system, but I'd rather spend the time getting everyone else on-line. Do I have your approval?"

Isak had no objections. He just waved Bishop on and said, "Good-bye," which signaled the computer to "hang up" the phone.

Sargenti was leaning forward in her seat, obviously impatient. "So," she said, "what was the final verdict?"

"On what?"

"Which sex has it better?"

"Oh, that." Isak let out a loud laugh. "You may not like the implication. I'm sure I don't. Means she became a neuter, eventually, and *stayed* that way."

Sargenti looked at him in frank astonishment. A slow smile spread across her face.

"Back to more important business," Isak said, and Sargenti's smile was suddenly gone. "We must have an ultrasensitive gamma-ray telescope—as good as the one they built on Miranda." His mind struck the word "they," which included Steven. "We need that telescope," he said after a moment, "if that's possible—so we can watch our Intruders' movements anywhere in the solar system. Can we make one, and how soon?"

"I've already had Bishop work that out. He says that if we use every available robot, it should take about two weeks to build a sensitive detector array."

"Get it started," Isak said, noticing something awkward in the way she looked at him.

"I did—early today. The workforce is already proliferating toward the needed numbers."

"With better eyes, we might even hope to intercept some of the Intruders' communications. Not that we'll be able to understand what they're saying."

"I can't believe," Sargenti said, looking even more uneasy in his gaze, "that they managed to overlook us before we cut down our neutrino glow." She grimaced. "If they record their scans, then they can go back and find us at any moment!"

"*If* they go back and look."

"We all know," she said, "that these creatures are far from stupid. We must expect them to review their scan records at autointervals. That may be the only time we have left! Once they find us in the recorded data, and see our blackout, what can we do?"

"Nothing. Let's hope they just missed us somehow. That would tell us something nice about them—that they're not infallible."

"It's plain that they hit all the obvious targets first," she said. "I think they'll get around to the lesser ones later. Even if we don't broadcast our presence, our unnatural rotation may give them a clue."

Isak pushed his chair back from the table and swung around to look out over the railing. Sargenti seemed to linger behind him, then left, and he was alone in the night with his fears for what little remained of humanity. The fact was dead weight in everyone he talked to, and growing heavier day by day.

As he sat quietly, Crichton hobbled to the table and stopped by his chair, and Isak realized that if the Intruders had their way, what was left of the most successful species ever to walk the Earth would perish again, along with the rank newcomer, Man. All the effort that had gone into resurrecting the dinosaurs, albeit at a more manageable scale, would be for nothing.

Crichton, whose hip replacements still did not work as well as they should, took a step toward him and gazed up at him with his left eye, as if preparing to say something, then came forward and lay his long neck across Isak's lap.

"We'll go down together this time," Isak said, scratching Crichton's head. The apatosaur snorted contentedly, and Isak realized again what a miracle this miniature saurian was—and even more precious now that he was again one of the last of his kind, if not the last. Even with genetic defects and hip replacements, he was a whole sentence out of Earth's library of life, whose volumes were now all but gone. The cometary strike which had destroyed the dinosaurs more than sixty million years ago had been merciful and slow compared to the swift swords that had butchered humanity.

As he rubbed Crichton under the chin, Isak reached for his pad with his right hand and called up a view of the site at Ceres's north pole where the gamma-ray telescope would soon be built. Starlit spidery shapes moved to and fro on the Lunar-like surface, throwing up streamers of dust as they excavated a cradle for the gamma-detector tanks. They were like a swarm of black insects, these builders, communicating by tight microwave and laser beam, so as not to be detectable by the Intruders. He and Sargenti had always communicated in a looser way, through subtle channels, leaving each other's feelings to delicious guesswork.

Isak wondered again about Ceres's artificial rotation, and whether the Intruders would be observant enough to notice that it was spinning with a force sufficient to fling stones near the equator into space with an acceleration of one half Earth gravity. Surely it would be apparent to any close observer that without engineers, Ceres could not have held itself together, and would long ago have flung itself apart. He decided that Sargenti had the right idea. They had hit all the major centers of life first and would systematically go through all the lesser possibilities whether there was life there or not. Ceres would be destroyed whether it did anything to hide itself or not.

He watched the spidery robots sinking shafts into the polar dust and tried to imagine how Ceres might be hidden from the Intruders. Maybe they'll just overlook us, he thought. Why would they want to be so thorough? In human experience only a great hatred might create such dedication. They don't know us at all. We never did anything to them. So they'll probably overlook Ceres, he told himself. It was a great leap of hope, he realized, to conclude that because humankind and the Intruders didn't know each other, the aliens might over-look the remnants of humanity; but hope was all that could keep his people going. What would Fred Haise have done in a situation such as this?

Isak had asked himself that question every time a crisis, large or small, had loomed in his life—ever since his school days, when Haise himself had given him the blue plaque, which he had brought to Ceres with him, and which he kept these days on his balcony table. It was a single piece of pressed cardboard to which a small strip of beta-cloth netting had been glued. Almost as an afterthought, the *Apollo 13* astronauts had torn the cloth from their Lunar lander turned tugboat before abandoning it in space. They had wanted to personally thank the builders of the ship that had saved them; and each of the three hundred plaques was autographed by the crew. One of these had become Isak's prize pos-session. He ran his fingers over the beta cloth and read the words:

A PIECE OF AQUARIUS
LAUNCHED 4–11–70
SPLASHDOWN 4–17–70
THANKS FOR A JOB WELL DONE!

That near disaster had occurred over one hun-dred years ago and more than fifteen light-minutes away. But even in the midst of an infinitely greater crisis, Haise's reassuring presence was still wel-come. And Isak asked, "Well, old friend, what is *your* advice?"

Don't dwell on cracked heat shields, an inner voice answered. *And don't fail to do your best, either.*

So Isak continued his little game of planning for the worst, and at least trying to hope for the best. Perhaps the aliens would want to find some survivors out of sheer curiosity, to examine, maybe to preserve some samples of DNA against the day when humankind might be resurrected in the same way as Crichton—when the Intruders had attained the quality of mercy. It was a low-probability hope, Isak realized, and a sad one at that, but only hope and action would save any vestige of humanity. But what action? Only thought could answer that question—if he thought the right thoughts and undertook the right actions. The strategy was right but bare of tactics. There was nothing to do except move one step at a time, very carefully, to live long enough to take the next step.

It startled him that in the secret depths of his mind, in that core of ancient reptilian brain that resided in all humanity, there was more than mere hope. Every morning when he awoke from his dreams, he actually believed that vengeance could be had against his enemies, that he or some other warrior messiah might rise up and smite the Intruders hip and thigh. What confidence! What arrogance! What delusion! Crichton gave a confident snort, as if commenting, then lifted his neck and moved back from the mammal whose ancestors had once been only a feeble competitor of his kind, eating saurian eggs and quietly slipping away into the foliage.

Isak looked at the small screen again and saw

that the digging for the gamma tanks was nearly complete. Suddenly the holes in the ground reminded him of a mass grave, and he felt tearful and angry at the same time.

10

Down!

"WE ALL AGREE THAT YOUR PLAN IS MAD," CHIEF Engineer Anjin announced. "The real question that troubles us is whether it's just crazy enough to be right."

"Living inside the Sun?" said the Second Officer. "Impossible!"

Tam erased some figures from her pad, then asked, "Can you think of a better place to hide?"

"Not where we wouldn't still have to worry about a neutrino glow, Skipper. But just the same, I'll believe you when we're down in there in one piece and still breathing."

"Doing it," Tam continued, "need not violate any physical laws. We would have to enforce a clearly defined regime on our presence and make sure it doesn't fail for a moment."

Anjin said, "You mean we'd have to walk through fire without touching the flames."

"Essentially, that's it," Tam said, "and we will have the means to do it."

Sargenti-Peterson was transforming itself by the hour, so great was the pressure for swift adaptations. The ship-comet had approached the Sun at nearly sixty kilometers per second before turning its engines against its own flight path. Inside, Tam and her crew were probing the laws of orbital mechanics. The more they shaved their forward velocity, the more the Sun tightened its gravitational tether, yanking them down through the corona and flinging them forward. Confined to an ever-tightening Sun orbit, their angular momentum picked up, and they found themselves covering so much more of the Sun's surface that convection cells of superheated gas, whose "cloud tops" were sometimes as wide as the Earth, raced beneath their feet in only a few seconds. By the time they dipped beneath the membrane of glowing pink gas known as the chromosphere, they would be flying at nearly five hundred kilometers per second. They had left the driving to Isaac Newton, under whose rules the act of slowing down caused Sargenti-Peterson to speed up.

Now a faint atmosphere of protons and electrons was striking the comet's bow with a force sufficient to cause further slowing—which, if uncontrolled, threatened to drag the ship-comet to depths where the solar gases were twenty-five times denser than iron. A hundred meters behind the point bow, magnetic lenses had appeared. Farther astern, something resembling a ring of jet engine intakes had erupted through the comet's natural surface and begun to take shape with extraordinary speed.

The constantly expanding population of robots could accomplish whatever they were told to, but they were only as good as their instructions. Tam had come to regard them as the comet's immune cells: only as capable as the body that governed them. From now on, she decreed, survival would be a never-ending struggle to evolve new technologies, often at very short notice.

It sounded impossible, but Tam and most of her colleagues had been called impossible long before the Intruders had made IQ boosters necessary. It was one reason for Tam's group having left Earth in the first place—which was just as well for Earth. Only the impossible could be counted on to accomplish the impossible.

"I think I have most of the rough edges smoothed out of our cooling system," said Anjin. "You're going to love this."

"I expect I will," said Tam. "It had better be good."

Tam did not interrupt the engineer as he explained the production and detonation of the little "absorbic bombs" that now made human survival possible near the bottom of the solar corona. The instantaneous conversion of energy to matter: the bombs were so childishly simple that it would have taken an Einstein to think of them, or an alien invasion forcing the redesign of Anjin's brain chemistry to quicken him into seeing the obvious.

"Detonated in tandem, just below the comet's surface, they form a cold barrier through which none of the Sun's heat can possibly seep . . . unless we want it to—"

Tam was well aware that the temperature outside was comparable to standing within a half kilometer of the Hiroshima bomb. Removing all that heat before it could wear away the comet's outer layers of rock was going to create a constant buildup of mass—which, according to the chart taking shape in her imagination, would, over the course of many years, drag the comet down into violently rising and falling columns of gas even if the accumulation rate was only a few grams of matter per minute. But Tam found comfort in the certainty that she could not possibly be the first to imagine the problem, and guessed that Anjin had already found a way to thwart what seemed an inevitable and irreversible progression.

"I would never want to make a gross claim that my absorbic bombs alone can keep us alive. In fact, without some very careful fine-tuning we could easily be floating in this room at near absolute zero right now, frozen to death even as we go into the circle of hell. Now, two things are happening to us as we ride through the solar atmosphere, neither of which is very good for sustaining orbit."

Tam nodded and smiled knowingly, and Anjin returned the smile, even though both of them knew that their confidence was still waging war with their doubts.

"I don't intend to sound cocky," Anjin said persuasively, "but I think we've come up with a system that can solve both problems. It's mostly protons and electrons out there—all positive and negative charges. We simply project magnetic field lines ahead of the ship and shunt the particles to either side, like the prow of a boat slicing through water. Now, even though none of these particles will touch us, contact with our magnetic field will still impart some slowing to the ship itself. All our magnetic prow can do is provide some shielding and streamlining. If we want to stay aloft, we need a propulsion system suited to these conditions.

Now, at the velocities we will soon be attaining, there is an opportunity to magnetically guide, or funnel, some of these protons precisely where they'll do us good—say, into the engine intakes—and also to eject some of our gradually increasing mass as thrust."

"Beautiful!" exclaimed the Second Officer. "Fusion ramjets!"

"Yes. Fusion ramjets. It's an old idea, never quite practical for the interstellar medium because you just couldn't find enough gas out there. But here, we've got more than we'll ever need."

"You're right," Tam said. "I *do* love it." She was still smiling hopefully, and had just started floating away from her post to shake Anjin's hand personally, when the lights flickered and a distant crackling roar penetrated through kilometers of rock and ice, shaking the walls of the cabin. Tam, still drifting toward Anjin, looked at him with an expression that said, *What are your machines doing to us?* and saw him looking back with one that said, *That wasn't me!*

Almost simultaneously one of the ship's lookouts called in great excitement. "Bridge! Did you feel that?"

"What do you see?"

"Sunquake right ahead, sir."

"Thank you," acknowledged the skipper with curiously detached courtesy. Nothing more was said.

For the next thirty-seven seconds all hands grabbed handholds and all eyes turned toward the pads to watch a spectacle almost as terrifying as the relativistic bombing of Earth, if for nothing more than its sheer scale. Tam and Anjin floated side by side, watching the flames—more than ten Earth diameters at their base—draw nearer. Now they were almost on top of the firestorm, and still the comet did not turn, could not turn, for Anjin's ramjets were not quite ready, the ship's altitude not quite low enough, and the atmosphere not quite dense enough. The eruption, shining with what had to be planetary volumes of colored fires, towered more than 410,000 kilometers above their heads, and everyone aboard braced for a crash.

Then, miraculously, the fires began to part like the waters of the Red Sea in the Book of Exodus. At the last second, walls of plasma opened up and glided swiftly by on the port and starboard sides. It looked to Tam like a very close shave.

In the next moment a curious motion communicated itself through the walls and handholds, as if the ship were grinding heavily across a field of marbles. What had reached them before as a distant crackling noise now grew louder and more disquieting, reminding Susan Skurla of someone tearing a long, long strip of calico.

Anjin was calling orders into his pad, and his machines were adjusting the trim of the ship's magnetic fields accordingly, allowing the comet to slip with relative ease through a tunnel of its own creation.

"Any damage?" Tam called out, wondering why she wasn't laughing hysterically.

"I don't think so," said Anjin. "It's just a magnetic storm trying to shake us up a little bit—but it's really not much more violent than a bad case of air turbulence."

Tam noticed that Anjin was tunneling down as

well as ahead through the fire, using his magnetic field lines somewhat like rudders and ailerons on a plane. She searched for but could find no expression of alarm on his face, just a serene trace of thrill, as if he were actually beginning to enjoy the new challenge.

"I wish I could get some deeper magnetic soundings," he said. "If we can see what's coming at us from below, we'll have nothing to worry about. I just don't want any surprises."

Tam studied the pads. On every side was searing pink glare. There was nothing to see beyond the tunnel walls.

"We really need to extend our sensory range," said Anjin. "That's my next priority, even before we get the jets working."

"But we're all right for now?"

"I hope so, Skipper. But no surprises, please."

Just then the glare vanished and the horizon of the Sun shone on every quarter, seeming nearer and flatter than the Earth's would appear to a man standing in the middle of the Sahara. Tam had enough time to realize that they had just exited the flare, and to identify three more streamers looming up ahead, and to understand that each must be standing higher than the distance from the Earth to the Moon, before the whole cabin shifted and the wall met her shoulder with a bone-cracking bang.

"See what I mean?" said Anjin. He reduced power to the fields forward and below, and eased the ship-comet's quakings until it was smoothly under way once more. Tam, who was nursing her shoulder with her one good arm, lifted her eyes and at once forgot her injuries. The ship was heading directly toward a streamer that had grown to fill even the widest angle pad's field of vision. She judged that they would reach it in less than fifteen seconds, but then saw that Anjin had already applied his experience of the previous flare to new instructions for the field generators—which he called down through the pads with more than five seconds to spare. Single-handedly, he was rendering the Sun more awe-inspiring than dangerous.

They entered the flare with barely a ripple, and no unpleasant tearing noises. When they exited less than a minute later, Sargenti-Peterson merely bobbed up and down two times before Anjin steadied her out and found the way ahead clear of flares.

"Thanks, Anjin—good piloting. But I hope we don't run into many more of those."

"We probably will, Skipper. But the next time we'll be ready for them—especially with a little sensory extension."

Anjin had already worked out, in his mind, plans for new scanners. Given proper instructions, the robot factories would have them built within the hour. Now that the danger had passed, he would study the flares almost at leisure, searching for details that might improve their chances at lower altitudes, in the thin layer of glowing pink gas called the chromosphere, where visibility was bound to be no better than inside a flare.

He had already uncovered at least one major surprise, although in hindsight it should have come to him as no surprise at all. The temperature inside the columns of flame had actually dropped precipitously, owing to the shielding from rays at the

Sun's surface by all those mountains of gas. Seen from a great height—say, from the orbit of Mercury—the flares would have appeared as dark spots on the Sun's surface; not because they were actually dark but because they were so vastly outshone by their surroundings. The open spaces of the solar corona were hot enough to blacken anything, whereas the inside of a solar flare was, by comparison, only good for warming hors d'oeuvres. For similar reasons, the chromosphere into which he hoped to take Sargenti-Peterson would, paradoxically it seemed, provide cooler surroundings in spite of its being nearer the Sun's surface.

"Good piloting," the Captain had said, unaware of the echo from the past. Anjin was a very unusual Japanese name that happened to mean "pilot." It had come down only through one small family whose members showed no outward signs of European ancestry but who, according to family legend, were descended from a British pilot who rose to nobility after his ship had run aground nearly five hundred years ago. Anjin had never believed the story, until genetic maps became available to verify it. Now, as the columns of fire receded aft, he realized that he was carrying on an ancient family tradition. Even when viewed from the rear, shrinking rapidly second by second, the sunquake lost none of its drama and spectacle. What would the first Anjin have thought, he wondered, if he could have looked heavenward and known that one of his descendants would sail through a sunspot and master it? The eruption could easily have engulfed a thousand Earths; and Anjin imagined that if his ancestors could have peered ahead in time to see what their namesake had done, they might have felt confirmed in their Sun worship.

11

The Secret Savior

AFTER POINTING EDITH TOWARD LIFEBOAT NUMBER 11, Jonathan continued to wander through the dying ship. Forward of the Grand Stairway, at the entrance to third class, he found the brass gates drawn shut and locked. At the official inquiries into the loss of R.M.S. *Titanic*, surviving officers had denied barring the way from third class to the lifeboats, but robot probes had proved them liars, finding the way still blocked nearly a century later.

Jonathan found endless fascination in what was, to him, becoming the strangest night of leadership in the history of the North Atlantic: twenty men and a dog lowered away in a lifeboat built to hold sixty-five people.

He called through the gateway to third class and heard no reply. Perhaps the passengers had found some other way up; he was thinking of breaking the gate down when a wave of waist-high water came crashing through and drove home the message that it was getting late and there was no time left for sightseeing. Somewhere nearby a bulkhead had burst, sending the ship's bow down like an express elevator.

85

An insistent tide pursued Jonathan up three decks, paused for a moment, then came again higher. He beat the rising water to the ship's kennel, where he came upon the officers who had left the gates to third class locked, but who nevertheless had the presence of mind to be running around frantically opening cages, so first class dogs might have a chance at survival.

"You arrogant bastards!" Jonathan shouted. "We really have overromanticized this time period, haven't we?"

"Pardon?"

"Now I understand Hitler," Jonathan said. "His seed is in all of you." As he hurried off to find Edith, one of the officers shot him an expression that said *Who the hell is Hitler?*

"What a strange man," said one of the others.

Two minutes later, as he passed the Marconi shack, Jonathan noticed that the ocean was only some five meters from the boat deck, where the members of *Titanic*'s all-string band had just finished a new Irving Berlin tune—"One O'clock in the Morning I Get Lonesome"—which was getting very close to being the last piece they would ever play. Legend would have it that they closed with "Nearer My God to Thee," and classical films would depict the passengers in the lifeboats looking on in awed silence as the liner's three giant propellers rose out of the water and the heart-wrenching strains of the Welsh hymn reached them. It was dignified and highly dramatic, but it never happened.

In reality, the final notes from the boat deck included:

Camptown ladies sing this song,
Doo-dah, doo-dah.

At least, that was what Jonathan Wayville heard, reconstructed from actual survivors' accounts, as he made his way toward the stern. The musicians' way of coping was to impose a mental gag order on their distress and keep busy. A few meters away, in the Marconi shack, wireless operators Harold Bride and Jack Philips tried to control their fears with gallows humor. SINKING FAST BY THE BOWS, they morsed to the rescue ship *Carpathia*. WE ARE ABOUT ALL DOWN. BETTER HURRY, OLD MAN, OR IT WILL BE FISH FOR BREAKFAST FOR US TOMORROW . . . OR VICE VERSA.

As he passed under the third funnel, Jonathan heard a young man calling down to a friend in a lifeboat. "When you get back, you'll need a pass. You can't get on the ship for breakfast tomorrow without a pass." Jonathan shot the man a puzzled look and kept on walking.

Titanic was never going to get anywhere near serving another breakfast. She was creaking and snapping throughout, and the sound of windows imploding under the crush and swirl of water was making it harder to hear *"Camptown Races"*; and in the midst of this horror that no one wanted to believe, this passenger was worried about meal tickets. Jonathan guessed that the man must have been the last person aboard the *Titanic* who was still certain of life going on; but when he caught up with Edith, he saw that she, too, just did not seem to understand.

He watched a crewman toss her toy pig into lifeboat number 11, and then stood in stunned silence as she steadfastly refused to follow it.

(What in hell? That wasn't in my program!)

"Edith!" Jonathan shouted. "What are you doing? You must get in that boat at once. Don't hesitate!"

"But where have you been? I've been looking all over for you."

"You needn't worry about me."

"Get in the boat, son. I won't leave without you." And Jonathan saw that she meant it.

A crewman, watching the scene from the bow of number 11, called up to Jonathan, "Young man, are you a seaman?"

"Well, sort of," he said hesitantly. "I've taken the helm of *Alvin* a few times."

"Taken the helm of *what*?"

"It's okay, sir. I guess you could call me a seaman."

"Good. I'm shorthanded here. Get in and take the stern."

Jonathan took Edith's arm and guided her toward the lifeboat. She submitted, and he stepped in after her, taking his place next to the rudder right behind the two Hoffman boys, whose family name was not really Hoffman. Their father had kidnapped them from their mother in France, hoping to raise them in America under an assumed name. Before putting them in the boat the man kissed them both farewell and then whispered a message to Michel, the older of the boys: "When you see your mother, you tell her exactly what I am about to tell you."

Jonathan knew that Michel's mother would eventually die in a mental institution, and that eighty years later Michel would tell a researcher, "I still remember every word of what Father said, and it will go to the grave with me."

Jonathan could not hear what the father had whispered. It was not in the program, remaining for him one of *Titanic*'s unsolved mysteries. He could only wonder, as Michel looked down and pointed excitedly to a line of portholes still glowing under the cold green Atlantic.

"Pretty," Michel announced as the lifeboat reached the water. But when Jonathan looked where the child was pointing, a shudder ran through him *(My Jesus! Did I write that?)* as he saw that two or three meters below the surface, in a cabin that was still unflooded, a man was peering out into the ocean, straight up at the white-painted keel of number 11. Then a dull thud, more felt than heard, came from below. The man in the cabin glanced away toward the bows, then scurried aft as if he had seen something.

The crewman in charge ordered the ropes unhooked and Jonathan obeyed; and then, while Edith's back was turned to him, he wrapped his legs around the after fall and hoisted himself back to the boat deck. Edith called for him to come back, but he waved the boat away, assured her that he would be all right, and disappeared into a crowd of onlookers.

By now the slant of the decks was becoming so steep that it was difficult to stand without holding onto a fixture or a rail. He made his way to a railing just aft of the second class library on the starboard side. *Titanic*'s lights had dimmed to a warm red glow, and mist was gurgling out of her from somewhere far forward, a tangible brown vapor that spread with lazy speed and cast a glare of backscattered light upon her decks. The masts and deck-houses stood out of the night as though they were on fire. Overhead, men from steerage were clambering up a cargo crane, crawling out on its boom in an attempt to reach the imagined safety of higher ground.

"Oh, yes," Jonathan told himself. "You've got the scene almost perfect this time. Just like the history books."

The *Titanic* held him spellbound. She was exactly as the surviving Second Officer, Charles Lightoller, had said. She was awesome and obscene. She was fascinating and violent. She was horrible and wonderfully dramatic. And most of all, Jonathan realized, she was escape from something worse.

If his timing of events on the program was correct, Jack Phillips would now be tapping off two *V*s

DIT-DIT-DIT-DA

DIT-DIT-DIT-DA

the fateful opening to Beethoven's Fifth Symphony, Death knocking at the door, the last signal anyone heard from the *Titanic*.

And then all was confusion—dimming lights, toppling smokestacks, and a rumbling roar that carried up through the deck plates, building to such convulsive force that the iron hull disintegrated amidships and a 120-meter length of ship broke loose and began hurtling toward the bottom. Then, as quickly as they had started, the roaring sounds died away. The women in lifeboat 11 thought they saw *Titanic* cutting short the final plunge and settling back again toward her propellers, with few of them guessing that what appeared to be a miracle—the great ship rising up again and righting itself in the water—was only a brief respite bought by a spectacular loss of weight.

Edith, who had been holding the "Hoffman" boys in her arms, knowing that their father was aboard the doomed ship and not wanting them to watch, now uncovered their eyes and unwittingly made them witness to the most gruesome part of the sinking.

High on the flagstaff, a kerosene lantern still burned. In its dim glow, Jonathan saw hundreds of shadows jostling about him. And then the *Titanic*—what was left of her—rolled gently onto her port side and all those hundreds of jostling bodies slid away from him into the dark. But Jonathan kept his balance. He hauled himself out over the starboard rail as the stern continued heaving to port, until at last he found himself standing level on the starboard hull of the ship.

He began running toward the lonely flagstaff lantern, barely noticing that he was stepping over upturned portholes until an open one caught his right foot, fractured his shin and sent the whole world spinning away from him. He came down hard on a curving wall of steel plates, felt rivets and brass porthole rims sliding under his outstretched palms, screamed, bounced off another open porthole, came down on his broken leg once more, heard it snap someplace else, rolled, bounced into the air again, and suddenly fetched up against *Titanic*'s six-story rudder.

As he tried to get his bearings, the stern's nose

corkscrewed straight down, swinging him and the giant brass propellers more than thirty meters above the water. For long seconds the stern seemed to hold steady, standing perfectly perpendicular in the night, silhouetted against the stars like a tall building, and then she began to slip down, bringing him closer to a sound such as no one would describe again until General Patton's troops discovered the starving multitudes in Hitler's death camps. It was the pleas and death cries of hundreds upon hundreds of people trying to haul themselves atop floating debris and atop each other, of children being dunked under, having ribs broken and arms dislocated, of Rosa Abbott crying out for her two missing sons. All that massed agony reverberated up the *Titanic's* sides, up her cliffs of steel, to Jonathan's ears, as a single unendurable moan.

Injured though he was, he craved to distance himself from the sound, and tried as best he could to ascend the rudder; but he lost his grip and dropped two stories more, and heard a sickening crack that told him his bad leg was now his good leg. There was nothing left for him but to wrap his arms around a joint in the rudder and wait for the program to end.

Not very far below, off the starboard side, a dozen men struggled for footholds on the keel of an overturned lifeboat. Wireless operator Harold Bride and Second Officer Charles Lightoller were among that dozen, Jonathan remembered. The last thing he saw before the sea closed over his shoes was Charles Joughin, the chief baker, striding toward him over the white-painted steel plates of the rounded, aftermost part of the ship.

Jonathan had lost the race to the flagstaff lantern. It was all he cared about, all he understood, as Hollis piloted *Alvin* toward dead New York: Joughin, not Wayville, had been the last man off the *Titanic*, this time. . . .

History was going to change, Jonathan decided. So he went directly to the lower decks of third class and smashed open the gates. Then he climbed the stairs to Edith's stateroom and found her exactly where the history books said she would be, folding her clothes neatly into drawers, closing the tops of her trunks, and generally tidying up before going to the lifeboats.

But she wasn't really Edith Russell anymore. Her hair was red, not black; and her skin was much smoother than Edith Russell's. Jonathan had remade her completely in the image of his own mother—perfect, exactly as he remembered her, though out there in the real world most assuredly dead, yes; but perfect nonetheless.

Edith's window was still open. The collision had nearly thrown her to the floor, and she had poked her head outside just in time to see a wall of ice gliding past her nose.

For a moment they just stood in the stateroom, Edith and Jonathan, looking across the cold air at each other.

Edith said, "You're running the program again."

"It's just a book, actually."

Edith scowled. "*Program*. You'd better face up to it, Johnny. Call me what I am."

Jonathan looked embarrassed, and a new silence fell upon the room. Edith poured herself something.

It steamed in the cold air. "Would you like a cup of tea?" she asked.

"Yes, I'd like that . . . Mom."

She poured a second steaming cup and held it out to him. Their hands met and, like two mismatched holograms, passed through each other.

"Jesus Christ, Mom!" Jonathan cried. "What are you doing?"

"That's my question, Johnny. What are you doing here? Trying to play God? Trying to create a little universe you can control? It won't work, damn you. We can't let it work."

"This isn't supposed to be happening," Jonathan said, touching his own cheeks and ribs and feeling reassured by their solidity and warmth. "My hand passed right through yours."

"And mine through yours."

"Like a ghost."

"As I willed it, Johnny. Don't you think it's time to start facing up to reality?"

"But you're alive."

"Sure. You devoted as much memory to me as would have filled the entire hold of *Alvin* with machinery only a few years ago. You bone-phoned as much of me into this book as you did the whole damned *Titanic,* so why shouldn't I seem to you like someone who really sees and thinks and feels? Why shouldn't you start believing that I am as real as anyone who ever lived? You programmed me that way. There's a kind of chaotic unpredictability in a complex mass of data. Things can happen. It can jump in unpredictable ways."

"That's ridiculous. We're *alive!*"

"*You're* alive. I'm just a VR program of your own

creation—your memories personified."

Jonathan was saddened by the ring of truth in her words. His real mother had been a religious woman, and would never have acknowledged any creator except God.

"What is this, Mom? Don't you believe in God anymore?"

Edith knew that her son had once believed in God, but she also now had enough awareness of her own origins as an epiphenomenon of a complex program to guess that even if something like God did look after Man, it probably did not take much notice of artificial intelligence. She did, to her own mind, feel real enough to think of asking Jonathan whether he believed that the only difference between them was that she had met and come to know personally her creator; and she wondered, if she asked him, if he could possibly prove to her that he and his entire universe were not part of someone else's VR program; but she thought better of it. Jonathan was close enough to a breakdown, and while she had always been an inquisitive woman, she was never malicious.

"Ah, now, that's enough," Edith said.

"You didn't answer my question."

"You didn't answer mine. What are you doing here?"

"I'm finishing my book."

"Reality check, Johnny. Have you asked yourself who's going to read it?"

"But I've never left a project unfinished. Never in my life."

"Dedication. Is that what I taught you?"

"Yes."

"No, I never taught you this. Dedication is one thing. Obsession is something else. I think this is something else. I think this is something you learned from your father."

She understood exactly how Jonathan felt about his father, and hoped that comparing him to Christopher Wayville might bring her son to his senses. Christopher had been so obsessed by the chance of exploring a distant star that his family became meaningless to him. He had even left to marry another woman solely because she was slated for command of a Valkyrie starship. Then he had left altogether, without ever looking back, on a mission that was to have lasted at least twelve years, but which no one survived. Christopher had known that the first antimatter rockets were notoriously unreliable. He had known all the risks, and yet he took the gamble anyway, so taken was he by the idea of finding something no one had ever seen before.

Jonathan had never gotten over the loss of his father. As a teenager he blamed the abandonment for his mother's early death, and developed an absolute hatred of space travel and all things associated with it. When he married, he vowed to his bride that he would never go into space, because he would hate himself if he ever became like his father. "God, no," he had said. "Don't let me be like him."

Looking back, it seemed to Edith—and to Jonathan, who in a profound sense was talking to himself through her—that the things we vow never to become are the very fates to which we doom ourselves. Edith imagined that Jonathan probably believed he had kept his promise. He had stayed away from space, yes, and gone into the sea instead; but the history was the same. The only reason he was alive today was that he had left a wife and son for a career on the bed of the Atlantic. Edith was certain that if the Devil himself offered Jonathan a chance to explore the *Titanic*, he would have pricked his finger and signed the contract without even stopping to read the small print. She loved her son, loved him so much that she would have died for him; but she detested the choices he had made.

"Grow up, Johnny. You're a big boy now."

"Are you blind? Can't you see that I *have* grown up?"

"I see very well. You are the one who does not see. Which is why you need me to get around yourself."

"But look around you. See this world I've built! It's perfect in every detail."

"Perfect, maybe. But all a figment from the past."

"No. If you think and speak and argue with me, then you're as real as I am."

"How can you be certain?" *How can you prove either of us is real?* Edith almost said. Jonathan heard her distantly, but ignored the question. "What year is it?" she asked.

"Nineteen twelve."

Edith took Jonathan's hand in hers, and this time they remained warm and alive to each other. "What can that mean to you, when you stand here knowing all about *Alvin* and computer programs?"

Jonathan considered this, and tears began to sting his eyes. "Why can't you just let me stay here? I don't want to see the future."

"You *are* the future!" Edith said, knowing what must come next and regretting that if she hoped to become Jonathan's savior, she must also become his tormentor. "Do you not understand? You are alive. I am dead. The *Titanic* is dead! Now let it go."

"And go back to that dead world?"

"Yes. You're afraid?" Edith's eyes were filled with sorrow. "Who wouldn't be afraid? You're running the gamut of escapism, and I don't think you can escape anymore. You're going to have to face up to what's happening around you and survive."

As if on cue, Hollis's voice pierced Jonathan's bonephone. "Reality check, Wayville. Time to put your toys away and come topside. We're about to make landfall."

Edith nodded. "You know what you have to do, don't you?"

"That's murder," Jonathan said.

"Nonsense. I'm only a program, Johnny. Nothing more."

"But I gave you life!"

"You gave me only the illusion of life. I am not Edith Russell. I am not your mother. I am not even a thinking entity, except insofar as you're talking to yourself—your better self. But this is all fundamentally an illusion, Johnny, and there's only one way for you. You must erase this whole *Titanic* program . . . and me with it. Listen to yourself, Johnny!"

"No. I'm afraid."

"Damn it, if that world out there kills you, then it kills you; but don't dare look me in the eye and tell me you've let it break you. Remember? Do you remember, the same hammer that breaks glass can also forge steel? Isn't that what you were always told as a child?"

"By you!"

"No, by your mother."

"*Wayville*—" The whole stateroom seemed to jump, not from a collision with any iceberg, Jonathan knew, because the crystals dangling from a silk lampshade did not jingle, and beneath the lamp the tea in Edith's cup showed no sign of a ripple. The jolt came from outside the program, and Jonathan realized that Hollis had just run *Alvin* aground.

"If I do as you ask," Jonathan said, looking frightened and sad—and more sad than frightened—"will we ever meet again?"

"I doubt it," Edith said. "But who knows? Perhaps some other night. It will be up to you, won't it?"

Music began to drift in through the open window, cheery and ragtime. Mr. Hume and his orchestra were gathering for the finale. Edith put her hand under Jonathan's chin and turned his head toward the ceiling. He did not resist, and called out, "Computer! Delete the *Titanic* program."

"All of it?" came the reply, unsurprised but simulating it.

"Yes, all of it."

"Are you sure?" asked the computer, as if resisting.

He looked down at Edith, pleadingly. "Tell me you're just a figment. Tell me you wouldn't be lying for my own good."

"It's all true. I'm just a figment."

"Computer," Jonathan said, stiffening his spine, "follow my instructions."

As the stateroom began to fade and turn into the gray-painted cabin of *Alvin*, Edith put out her hand to touch Jonathan, but it melted through his chest, to his heart, as if she were trying to say, *I'll be right here.* And then she was gone, leaving Jonathan with the only lie she had told him.

12

Long Beach

THE SHORE WAS A QUARTER KILOMETER SEAWARD OF where the computers said it should have been. Even with the unusually high tide created by pressure reduction in the hurricane's eye, more than a fathom of water was missing beneath *Alvin*'s keel.

The air was clear and calm, although a one-meter surf was crashing around the submarine's hull. Hollis threw lines from the deck, and Jonathan breathed deeply. The atmosphere was still thick and hot, but he began to savor the daylight and the escape from the cabin.

He noticed that the sunlight was just barely able to filter down through the perfectly cloudless eye of the storm, which meant that something far above the eye, probably a globe-spanning layer of stratospheric dust, was intercepting much of the solar radiation before it got anywhere near sea level, and that within a year the oppressive heat on the surface would be replaced by oppressive cold.

Not that we'll have to trouble our little heads about that, Jonathan thought acidly, and then, looking northward across Long Island, he saw a rapidly retreating stack of cloud banks—the nearer wall of the eye, where the winds were exceeding two hundred kilometers per hour. He guessed that it would be passing somewhere between Oceanside and Rockville Centre by now, and he understood that if the northern wall were moving away from him at nearly thirty-three kilometers per hour, the southern wall would reach him in scarcely more than ninety minutes.

"Well, here's the game plan," Hollis said. "I want to be back in the hull and under deep water with ten minutes to spare before the south wall hits us. If this weren't likely to be the only calm break we'll ever have to go ashore, I wouldn't be risking my ship. Got that?"

"Understood, sir."

"Good. *Alvin* will keep time for us on our pads and sound the alarm every fifteen minutes. One blast when we've gone a quarter hour, two when we've gone half an hour, and so on. When we hear two blasts we start winding up whatever we're doing, and at three blasts I don't care if you've found the Ark of the Covenant itself, you drop everything and come right back. Before the fourth blast we must be closing the hatch and blowing ballast." She adjusted the utility belt around her coveralls.

"Got it, sir."

"No more daydreaming, Wayville. I'll leave alone if I have to."

The pilot descended the line, and the would-be historian followed. The surf threw up angry bursts of foam, breaking against Jonathan's thighs and waist and making it awkward for him to maneuver. Twice he lost his balance, and by the time the water was below his knees, he saw that Hollis was already ashore and heading toward a dozen dark shapes sprawled above the high tide line.

As he emerged onto dry land and began to walk toward the remnants of a stone jetty half buried in dunes, the pad dangling from his belt gave out one loud blast. He cursed and walked on.

Hollis came to a herd of pilot whales, washed up on what was, according to the charts, the city of Long Beach, New York. All things considered, the bodies seemed to be in reasonably good condition. Scans from her pad revealed that they had been boiled through to their very hearts, and she realized that in the absence of bacteria the corpses would never rot. Only the wind and rain would remove them, by a process of slow erosion.

Her scans also showed that a wide variety of radioactive elements had penetrated the whales' flesh. The meat was not hot enough to cause immediate illness if she tried to extend *Alvin*'s virtually nonexistent food supply with it; but there was no escaping the fact that her readings were twenty points in the yellow. Doesn't matter, she told herself. Dead by Labor Day, both of us. No need to worry about the long-term effects of radiation. She unholstered a blade and began cutting.

Jonathan came to a crest above the beach, paused, and looked out across more than ten kilometers of shallow dunes. The only recognizable feature on the horizon was the pyramid-shaped mound of the Oceanside landfill. It was no less than he had expected to see; but the sight was sobering.

The city of Long Beach was simply gone, all of it, as if no one had ever built it in the first place.

Condos with names like The Breakers, The Ocean Club, and Sea Point Towers—gaudy monuments to late-twentieth-century architecture—had disappeared without leaving a single brick behind.

The sand at Jonathan's feet was warm and dry and strewn with little green slabs of Trinity Glass. Jonathan picked up a piece and held it up to the weak, post-apocalypse sun. The glass was filled with blobs of air and iron, which told him that a great wind had swept through this place, hotter than live steam, hotter than molten glass, hotter than iron emerging white from a furnace. As he dropped the glass, a light breeze brushed over his ears and blew the hair off his forehead before dying, and at the same moment his pad sounded two blasts. He lifted the pad and began a quick sonoscan of the ground. The Long Beach he had known was one of those exclusive preservationist communities, so overly civilized that one had to obtain a license even to fly a kite. Its streets had looked almost exactly as one would have found them about 1995: a gallery of antique cars and restored buildings ranging back through the architectural low point of the 1970s to the Spanish stucco and red tile mansions of the city's *"Godfather* period." Even the boardwalk and red brick streets had been painstakingly resurrected, and local ordinances had required the display of fake TV antennae and telephone poles decorated with dummy wires and transformers, as if this small part of America were trying to escape back to the glory days, before Mexico began protesting that its economy could no longer sustain the constant influx of illegal aliens sneaking south across the Rio Grande.

As he made his scan, Jonathan's pad monitored Hollis broadcasting to space. She was giving their precise latitude and longitude, following that with the usual distress call.

"Come on, Hollis," he muttered to himself. "Time to turn the disk over. That side stinks."

He continued his scan of the ground, and after only a few quick passes locked onto something. About five meters beneath his feet he could see the outline of a concrete swimming pool. The tops of foundation pilings surrounded the basin, revealing that it had been located indoors on the ground level of a reasonably large apartment dwelling. His pad told him that the only oceanfront building matching this description was The Renaissance, and as he increased the scan strength he could see pilings running down more than fifteen meters below the pool. He could just begin to make out a pattern of broken floor tiles and sewage lines, and it made him ever so slightly happy that some small archeological traces of humanity still existed. He was reminded of an elderly mason who had come to an old apartment Jonathan was renting years ago, and had asked if he could inspect the bathroom, just to see if the tiles were still there. The man had installed them more than fifty years before, and was delighted to see how well his craftsmanship had endured.

The pad sounded three blasts before Jonathan could trace the sewage lines northward to the foundations of another building. He let the pad drop to his side, turned, and began briskly striding down the beach. Hollis was already in the pounding surf, tugging at strips of leathery matter tied in a large bundle. The sky to the south was a wall of roiling hot air closing in fast; and now the breeze came again, stronger, bringing the smell of salt, sulfur, and burnt wood. And there was an unpleasant surprise hidden just beneath the surface—an odor just like sweet Chinese pork.

He broke and ran, gagging, into the water, only anxious now to get back into the filtered air of the submersible, away from the smell of what could only have been people—hundreds of millions of carbonized people.

13

When I Have Fears

SOMETHING LIKE A LIGHTHOUSE BEACON WAS SWEEP-
ing the solar system. On Ceres, the first cluster of
gamma-ray telescopes picked it up and passed the
signal to the station's computer net with a red tag
for instant analysis. Within a microsecond, one of
the most highly advanced brains ever built by the
hand of man had undergone a subtle change in programming and, against all previous instructions,
sent an ominously less subtle program change on a
hairline beam of laser light to one of the gamma-
ray telescope robots.

And still within that part of a second, the robot
began to respond. Its multiple brains had been designed to predict the consequences of any action—
from lifting a rock to constructing a new furnace—
and then to decide the appropriate action at light-
ning speed by committee voting. Even without a
human presence, the machine was capable of manufacturing a gamma-ray telescope, or anything else
it was instructed to supply.

Antlike in appearance, it was more like a colony
of machines than an entity of its own—just as its
creator had intended. It had been built from and by

a hive of smaller, simpler machines, which still circulated inside it like motile cells through a dense matrix of connective pathways. There were workers of many shapes and sizes, and what could even be called "drones" and "egg-laying queens." Each was so intensely social, and so intimately connected to the robot's circuits, that if it were isolated from the rest of the hive, it could no more function on its own than an ant cast out of its hill or a human marooned on an island, and it quickly "died." Like an anthill, or the Ceran colony itself, every robot hive met all the essential criteria of an organism.

One half second after the laser flashed into its eyes, the hive sensed a loss of some essential material it had been programmed to produce—a loss that, left unaccounted for, would have violated its first directive and allowed the human colony inside Ceres to come to harm.

The material in question had never existed before on Ceres, or anywhere else in the solar system; but the hive did not know that it was being deceived, that it was not acting on orders given it by human beings. Egoless, incapable of friendships or emotional ties, free of conscious sympathies and antipathies, without overt motives or concealed ones, the hive's brains and workers responded so fast that it was already fashioning the right tools and had already located the right chemicals before Ed Bishop could even begin to notice that a problem was developing.

Minutes passed and still he did not notice, because a report he was preparing had preoccupied him with a vague sense of superstitious dread. He tried to bury his disquiet by isolating the station's telescopes from the computer net, just as a precaution, while there was still plenty of time to imagine low-probability events and guard against them.

"Plenty of time," he assured himself, muttering under his breath. "Plenty of time."

CONFIDENTIAL FROM ED BISHOP
TO CMDRS. ISAK BILENKIN AND TERESA SARGENTI

RESTRICTED: NEED TO KNOW STATUS ONLY
MESSAGE FOLLOWS:

AS REQUESTED, I HAVE COMPLETED MY SEARCH OF THE OLD VALKYRIE COMMUNICATIONS FILES. THE SCIENTIST IN CHARGE OF NASA'S SEARCH FOR EXTRATERRESTRIAL INTELLIGENCE (HEREAFTER REFERRED TO AS "SETI") DURING THE VALKYRIE BRAINSTORMING SESSIONS WAS DR. J. TARTER. I HAVE EXCERPTED CERTAIN OF HER COMMUNICATIONS WHICH MAY BE RELEVANT TO OUR PRESENT SITUATION. I SHOULD POINT OUT THAT SOME OF THE THEORIES HEREIN, THOUGH HIGHLY CONTROVERSIAL AT THE TIME (EVEN PATHOLOGICAL, ACCORDING TO CERTAIN PRESS REPORTS), NEVERTHELESS DID COMPEL DR. TARTER TO DISCONNECT THE ARECIBO AND BETA RECEIVERS FROM ALL OTHER COMPUTERS, AND FROM ALL PHONE LINES. I SUSPECT THIS ALSO EXPLAINS WHY CONGRESS ENDED DR. TARTER'S FUNDING IN 1993 AND ATTEMPTED TO SHELVE PROJECT SETI ALTOGETHER. THIS CAUSED A TRAGIC DELAY. IF WE HAD KNOWN MORE ABOUT OUR OWN STELLAR NEIGHBORHOOD SOONER, WE MIGHT HAVE GUESSED THAT WE WERE LIKELY TO BE INVADED, AND WE MIGHT EVEN HAVE GUESSED IN TIME TO DO SOMETHING ABOUT IT.

END MESSAGE
EXCERPTS FOLLOW:

FROM JILL TARTER, NASA/SETI
TO JAMES POWELL AND RICHARD TUNA,
CARE OF BROOKHAVEN NATIONAL LABORATORY
JUNE 5, 1986

OUR LAST HILTON MEETING ON INTERSTELLAR
TRAVEL AND COMMUNICATION WAS A REAL EYE
OPENER FOR ME. UNTIL FINALLY HAVING THE
CHANCE TO SIT DOWN AND TALK WITH YOU FACE-TO-
FACE, I NEVER REALLY BELIEVED THAT THE GALAXY
MIGHT BE A CHESSBOARD, WITH AN UNSEEN PLAYER
AT THE OTHER END AND THAT WHETHER OR NOT WE
CHOOSE TO PLAY WE MAY FACE JUDGMENT ON OUR
MASTERY OF THE GAME—IN WHICH CASE WE MAY BE
ELIMINATED AT ANY MOMENT.

ISAAC ASIMOV TELLS ME THAT HE OFTEN WONDERS
ABOUT THIS, AS OUR SEARCH FOR INTELLIGENT SIG-
NALS FROM THE STARS WIDENS AND SHOWS THE GAL-
AXY TO BE DEATHLY QUIET. HE POINTS OUT THAT THE
SURVIVAL VALUE OF HUMAN INTELLIGENCE HAS
NEVER BEEN PROVED AND MAY IN FACT BE MORE OF A
LIABILITY THAN AN ASSET, AS COMPARED AGAINST
SUCH DEVELOPMENTS AS ENDOTHERMY AND BROAD-
RANGING DIETARY HABITS. ONCE A SPECIES REACHES A
CERTAIN LEVEL OF INTELLIGENCE, IT HAS A SURVIVAL
ADVANTAGE UNTIL SUCH POINT THAT IT DEVELOPS
SUFFICIENT POWER TO DESTROY ITSELF AND EVERY-
THING AROUND IT: AND IT MAY BE, THEN, THAT IT AL-
WAYS DOES. THE UNIVERSE MAY BE FULL OF PLANETS
ON WHICH HIGH INTELLIGENCE AT THE HIGH-

TECHNOLOGY LEVEL HAS NOT YET DEVELOPED, AND ALSO FULL OF PLANETS BEARING THE RUINS OF HIGH-TECHNOLOGY CIVILIZATIONS THAT NO LONGER EXIST.

OF COURSE, ISAAC JOKES, FOR ALL WE KNOW, LITTLE STARSHIPS MIGHT BE CRISSCROSSING THE GALAXY, WITH NOT A SINGLE ONE HAVING REACHED US OR SENT A RADIO MESSAGE IN OUR DIRECTION—EITHER THROUGH CIRCUMSTANCE OR BECAUSE THEY'VE WARNED ONE ANOTHER TO "STAY AWAY FROM THIS PLACE!"

FROM J. POWELL AND R. TUNA
TO JILL TARTER, NASA/SETI
JULY 4, 1986

FROM ALL WE KNOW ABOUT CHEMICAL EVOLU-TION, ABOUT PLANET FORMATION, AND THE PRES-ENCE OF HUNDREDS OF BILLIONS OF SUNLIKE STARS IN THE RIM OF THE GALAXY, THE EXISTENCE OF EX-TRATERRESTRIALS IS PRACTICALLY A STATISTICAL CERTAINTY. ISAAC ASIMOV HAS PROPOSED THAT "PANCAKES" AND OTHER FORMS OF DARK MATTER MAY RENDER OUR FAST-MOVING VALKYRIE ROCKETS IMPOSSIBLE TO FLY EVEN IF THE MEANS CAN BE FOUND TO BUILD THEM, AND THAT THE ONLY WAY TO THE STARS WILL BE IN SLOW-MOVING, HOLLOWED-OUT ASTEROIDS OR "ARKS." IT FOLLOWS THAT MORE TECHNOLOGICALLY ADVANCED CIVILIZATIONS SHOULD HAVE DISCOVERED LONG AGO THAT ISAAC IS RIGHT, THAT THERE IS TOO MUCH MATTER FLOAT-ING BETWEEN THE STARS, AND THAT TRAVELING THROUGH IT AT AN APPRECIABLE FRACTION OF LIGHT SPEED IS SUICIDE. KNOWING THAT NO ONE CAN GET

THERE FROM HERE, THEY SHOULD THEREFORE FEEL MUCH FREER TO COMMUNICATE THEIR PRESENCE, TO SEEK OUT LONG-DISTANCE CORRESPONDENCE WITH OTHER WORLDS. YET THE GALAXY, IN EVERY DIRECTION, REMAINS SILENT, EVEN OUT TO A SAFE DISTANCE (SAFE FROM EARTH, AT LEAST) OF 60 to 100,000 LIGHT-YEARS. IT SEEMS UNLIKELY THAT WE ARE TRULY ALONE IN THE GALAXY. THE GREAT SILENCE IS PERHAPS THE STRONGEST INDICATOR OF ALL THAT HIGH RELATIVISTIC VELOCITIES ARE ATTAINABLE AND THAT EVERYBODY OUT THERE KNOWS IT.

THE SOBERING TRUTH IS THAT RELATIVISTIC CIVILIZATIONS ARE A POTENTIAL NIGHTMARE TO ANYONE LIVING WITHIN RANGE OF THEM. THE PROBLEM IS THAT OBJECTS TRAVELING AT AN APPRECIABLE FRACTION OF LIGHT SPEED ARE NEVER WHERE YOU SEE THEM WHEN YOU SEE THEM. RELATIVISTIC ROCKETS, IF THEIR OWNERS TURN OUT TO BE LESS THAN BENEVOLENT, ARE BOTH TOTALLY UNSTOPPABLE AND TOTALLY DESTRUCTIVE. A STARSHIP WEIGHING IN AT 1,500 TONS (APPROXIMATELY THE WEIGHT OF A FULLY FUELED SPACE SHUTTLE SITTING ON A LAUNCHPAD) IMPACTING ON AN EARTHLIKE PLANET AT "ONLY" 30 PERCENT LIGHT SPEED WILL RELEASE 1.5 MILLION MEGATONS OF ENERGY—AN EXPLOSIVE FORCE EQUIVALENT TO 150 TIMES TODAY'S GLOBAL NUCLEAR ARSENAL.

THE FACT THAT WE MAY BE WITHIN ONLY A FEW DECADES OF BECOMING A RELATIVISTIC CIVILIZATION OURSELVES RAISES NEW PROBLEMS AND POSSIBILITIES THAT, FOR THE MOMENT AT LEAST, ARE SIMPLY INTERESTING TO THINK ABOUT, PERHAPS EVEN FUN TO JOKE ABOUT. BUT THE ABILITY TO LAUGH AT A PROBLEM IS DIRECTLY PROPORTIONAL TO ONE'S DISTANCE

FROM THE PROBLEM. DURING THE NEXT SEVENTY TO ONE HUNDRED YEARS, WHEN A GENERATION ONLY NOW ABOUT TO BE BORN FINDS ITSELF STANDING ON THE BRINK OF INTERSTELLAR FLIGHT, THE POSSIBILI-TIES WILL HAVE TO BE CONSIDERED VERY SERIOUSLY. SUDDENLY OUR JOKES WON'T SEEM QUITE SO FUNNY ANYMORE.

FROM JILL TARTER, NASA/SETI
TO JIM POWELL, RICHARD TUNA, ISAAC ASIMOV
JULY 20, 1986

PERHAPS THE MOST SOBERING TRUTH IS THAT ANY EXPEDITION TO ANOTHER SOLAR SYSTEM, USING THE ROCKET YOU HAVE DESIGNED OR SOME VARIATION THEREOF, CARRIES WITH IT OVERWHELMING DE-STRUCTIVE POTENTIAL; AND THERE IS NO WAY TO DIS-TINGUISH A PEACEFUL EXPLORATION FROM AN INTENDED ANNIHILATION—EXCEPT (AS YOU HAVE MADE TOO CLEAR) IN THE MINDS OF THE VISITORS.

FROM ISAAC ASIMOV
TO JILL TARTER, NASA/SETI
OCTOBER 4, 1986

WELL, I HOPE YOU, CARL SAGAN, AND THE OTHER SETI SCIENTISTS WHO HAVE LONG BELIEVED IN A BE-NEVOLENT UNIVERSE WILL FORGIVE ME THIS TRES-PASS, BUT I'M AFRAID THE PICTURE POWELL AND TUNA HAVE BEGUN TO PAINT (UNLESS RELATIVISTIC FLIGHT SHOULD TURN OUT, AS I HOPE IT WILL, TO BE A PHYSICAL IMPOSSIBILITY) IS CLOSER TO THE TRUTH.

THAT'S BECAUSE I'M A SCIENCE FICTION WRITER. YOU, POWELL, AND THE REST OF THE SETI CROWD ARE SCIENTISTS, AND YOU ALL HAVE VERY FAR-REACHING IDEAS. I MAKE A LIVING HAVING FAR-REACHING IDEAS. I'M NOT GOING TO TALK ABOUT IDEAS. I'M GOING TO TALK ABOUT REALITY. IT WILL PROBABLY NOT BE GOOD FOR US EVER TO BUILD AND FIRE UP AN ANTIMATTER ENGINE. ACCORDING TO POWELL, GIVEN THE PROPER DETECTING DEVICES, A VALKYRIE ENGINE BURN COULD BE SEEN OUT TO A RADIUS OF SEVERAL LIGHT-YEARS AND MAY DRAW US INTO A GAME WE'D RATHER NOT PLAY, A GAME IN WHICH, IF WE APPEAR TO BE EVEN THE VAGUEST THREAT TO ANOTHER CIVILIZATION AND IF THE RESOURCES ARE AVAILABLE TO ELIMINATE US, THEN IT IS LOGICAL TO DO SO. THE GAME PLAN IS, IN ITS SIMPLEST TERMS, THE RELATIVISTIC INVERSE TO THE GOLDEN RULE: "DO UNTO THE OTHER FELLOW AS HE WOULD DO UNTO YOU AND DO IT FIRST."

FROM JIM POWELL AND RICHARD TUNA
TO JILL TARTER, NASA/SETI
OCTOBER 31, 1986

IT SEEMS ONLY NATURAL THAT WHEN WE GOT TOGETHER WITH ISAAC ASIMOV, WHO IS PROBABLY BEST KNOWN FOR HIS THREE LAWS OF ROBOTICS, THE RESULT WOULD BE THREE NEW LAWS. WHEN WE PUT OUR HEADS TOGETHER AND TRIED TO LIST EVERYTHING WE COULD SAY WITH CERTAINTY ABOUT OTHER CIVILIZATIONS, WITHOUT HAVING ACTUALLY MET THEM, ALL THAT WE KNEW BOILED DOWN TO THREE SIMPLE LAWS OF ALIEN BEHAVIOR:

1. **THEIR SURVIVAL WILL BE MORE IMPORTANT THAN OUR SURVIVAL.**

    IF AN ALIEN SPECIES HAS TO CHOOSE BETWEEN THEM AND US, THEY WON'T CHOOSE US. IT IS DIFFICULT TO IMAGINE A CONTRARY CASE; SPECIES DON'T SURVIVE BY BEING SELF-SACRIFICING.

2. **WIMPS DON'T BECOME TOP DOGS.**

    NO SPECIES MAKES IT TO THE TOP BY BEING PASSIVE. THE SPECIES IN CHARGE OF ANY GIVEN PLANET WILL BE HIGHLY INTELLIGENT, ALERT, AGGRESSIVE, AND RUTHLESS WHEN NECESSARY.

3. **THEY WILL ASSUME THAT THE FIRST TWO LAWS APPLY TO US.**

FROM JILL TARTER, NASA/SETI
TO JIM POWELL AND RICHARD TUNA
JANUARY 28, 1987

I'VE ASKED MYSELF OVER AND OVER, THESE PAST FEW MONTHS, DO WE KNOW ANYTHING ABOUT ALIEN BEHAVIOR BEYOND THESE THREE LAWS? ANYTHING AT ALL? WITH ALL THE SPECULATION AMONG SAGAN AND OTHER SETI SCIENTISTS ABOUT A SO-CALLED GALACTIC CLUB, AND WITH COUNTLESS SCIENCE FICTION FILMS AND NOVELS CIRCULATING AROUND US, AS OF LATE, DEPICTING CULTURALLY ADVANCED AND BENEVOLENT *ET'S*, ONE MIGHT BELIEVE WE SHOULD KNOW MORE ABOUT THE POSSIBILITIES THAN

THREE LITTLE LAWS. BUT WE DON'T, AND I'M AFRAID I MUST BEGIN TO AGREE THAT THE WIDELY POPULAR SAGAN UNIVERSE, IN WHICH ANY ALIENS WHO ARE SMART ENOUGH TO HAVE SURVIVED THEIR THERMO-NUCLEAR ADOLESCENCE WILL BE FRIENDLY TO US, IS ONLY A REFLECTION OF HUMAN HOPES AND FEARS, NOT POSSIBLE REALITY. THEY REVEAL MORE ABOUT THE MINDS THAT IMAGINE OTHER MINDS THAN ABOUT OTHER MINDS.

SOME YEARS AGO I APPLAUDED WHEN A BINARY CODE DEPICTING A DNA MOLECULE WAS BROADCAST TO THE STARS FROM THE ARECIBO OBSERVATORY. IT WAS A VERY NARROW STREAM, BROADCAST FOR A VERY SHORT TIME, AND IT WAS AIMED AT THE GLOB-ULAR CLUSTER M13, ABOUT 25,000 LIGHT-YEARS AWAY, FAR FROM THE PLANE OF THE MILKY WAY GALAXY. I USED TO WORRY THAT SUCH SIGNALS HAD ALMOST NO CHANCE OF BRINGING A RESPONSE. NOW I WORRY THAT THEY COULD BRING FAR TOO MANY.

FROM GREGORY BENFORD, UNIVERSITY OF CALIFOR-NIA/IRVINE
TO JIM POWELL, RICHARD TUNA, ISAAC ASIMOV, JILL TARTER
FEBRUARY 12, 1987

YOUR THINKING STILL SEEMS A BIT NARROW. CON-SIDER SEVERAL BROADENING IDEAS:

1. SURE, RELATIVISTIC BOMBS ARE POWERFUL BE-CAUSE THE ANTAGONIST HAS ALREADY INVESTED HUGE ENERGIES IN THEM THAT CAN BE RELEASED QUICKLY, AND THEY'RE HARD TO HIT. BUT THEY

ARE COSTLY INVESTMENTS AND NECESSARILY RE-
DUCE OTHER ACTIVITIES THE SPECIES COULD EX-
PLORE. FOR EXAMPLE:

2. DISPERSAL OF THE SPECIES INTO MANY SMALL,
   HARD-TO-SEE TARGETS, SUCH AS ASTEROIDS, BUR-
   IED CIVILIZATIONS, COMETARY NUCLEI, VARIOUS
   SPACE HABITATS. THESE ARE HARD TO WIPE OUT.

3. BUT WAIT—WHILE RELATIVISTIC BOMBS ARE
   READILY VISIBLE TO US IN FORESIGHT, THEY
   HARDLY REPRESENT THE END POINT IN FORESEE-
   ABLE TECHNOLOGY. WHAT WILL HUMANS OF, SAY,
   TWO CENTURIES HENCE THINK OF AS THE "OBVI-
   OUS" LETHAL EFFECT? FIVE CENTURIES? A HUN-
   DRED? PERSONALLY, I'D PICK SOME RAMPAGING,
   SELF-REPRODUCING THINGY (MECHANICAL OR OR-
   GANIC), THEN SNEAK IT INTO ALL THE BIOSPHERES
   I WANTED TO DESTROY. MY POINT HERE IS THAT
   NO PARTICULAR PHYSICAL EFFECT—WITH ITS
   PLUSES, MINUSES, AND TRADE-OFFS—IS LIKELY TO
   DOMINATE THE THINKING OF THE GALAXY.

4. SO WHAT MIGHT REALLY AGED CIVILIZATIONS
   DO? DISPERSE, OF COURSE, AND ALSO *NOT ATTACK
   NEW ARRIVALS IN THE GALAXY, FOR FEAR THAT
   THEY MIGHT NOT GET THEM ALL.* WHY? BECAUSE
   REVENGE IS PROBABLY SELECTED FOR IN SURVIV-
   ING SPECIES, AND ANYBODY TRULY LOOKING OUT
   FOR LONG-TERM INTERESTS WILL NOT WANT TO
   LEAVE A YOUTHFUL SPECIES WITH A GRUDGE,
   SNEAKING AROUND BEHIND ITS BACK.

   FINALLY, WE CAN'T GET OUT OF OUR OWN CUL-
   TURAL/BIOLOGICAL MATRIX IN DISCUSSING THIS.

BE PREPARED FOR SURPRISES, NO MATTER WHAT
STRATEGY YOU PURSUE.

FROM RICHARD TUNA
TO GREGORY BENFORD
FEBRUARY 20, 1987

I AGREE WITH MOST PARTS OF POINTS 2, 3, AND 4.
AS FOR POINT 1, IT IS CHEAPER THAN YOU THINK. YOU
MENTION SELF-REPLICATING MACHINES IN POINT 3,
AND WHILE IT IS TRUE THAT RELATIVISTIC ROCKETS
REQUIRE PLANETARY POWER SUPPLIES, IT'S ALSO
TRUE THAT WE CAN POWER THE WHOLE EARTH WITH
A FIELD OF SOLAR PANELS ADDING UP TO BARELY
MORE THAN 200-BY-200 KILOMETERS, DRAWN OUT
INTO A NARROW BAND AROUND THE MOON'S EQUA-
TOR. SELF-REPLICATING ROBOTS COULD ACCOMPLISH
THIS TASK WITH ONLY THE COST OF DEVELOPING THE
FIRST TWENTY OR THIRTY MACHINES. AND ONCE
WE'RE POWERING THE EARTH PRACTICALLY FREE OF
CHARGE, WHY NOT LET THE ROBOTS KEEP BUILDING
PANELS ON THE LUNAR FAR SIDE? ADD A FEW SELF-
REPLICATING LINEAR ACCELERATOR-BUILDING FAC-
TORIES, AND PLUG THE ACCELERATORS INTO THE
PANELS, AND YOU COULD PRODUCE ENOUGH ANTI-
HYDROGEN TO LAUNCH A STARSHIP EVERY YEAR. BUT
WHY STOP AT THE MOON? HAVE YOU LOOKED AT
MERCURY LATELY?

FROM PROF. LESLIE WELLS, PACIFIC TECH.
TO JILL TARTER, NASA/SETI
MAY 5, 1987

POWELL AND TUNA ARE SICK. SICK. SICK. SICK. I
FIND MYSELF IN COMPLETE DISAGREEMENT WITH

EVERYTHING IN THEIR THESIS BUT THE PHYSICS. THE LEAP FROM THE UNSTOPPABILITY OF RELATIVISTIC BOMBS TO THE RATIONAL REQUIREMENT TO DESTROY ALL OTHER TECHNOLOGICAL SPECIES IS *MOST* DISTASTEFUL. THOUGH I DO AGREE THAT IT IS FAIRLY IDIOTIC OF SAGAN ET AL. TO WANT TO SHOUT OUR PRESENCE FROM THE INTERSTELLAR ROOFTOPS, IT IS NOT, TO MY MIND, PROVED THAT WE LIVE IN A VIOLENT UNIVERSE. IT IS ONLY FAIR TO WARN YOU THAT A COPY OF THIS LETTER IS GOING TO CONGRESSMAN AXFORD. SETI INDEED! YOU ARE THE ONLY "SCIENTISTS" IN THE WORLD WITH THE PECULIAR DISTINCTION OF NOT YET HAVING PROVED THAT YOUR SUBJECT MATTER EVEN EXISTS! I INTEND TO PERSONALLY SEE TO IT THAT NOT ONE RED CENT MORE IS SPENT ON THIS QUEST FOR LITTLE GREEN INVADERS FROM MARS!

FROM JAMES POWELL AND RICHARD TUNA
TO JILL TARTER, NASA/SETI
JULY 14, 1987

WE ARE IN RECEIPT OF YOUR LETTER FROM DR. WELLS, AND AS YOU KNOW WE HAVE NEVER ADVOCATED DESTROYING OTHER INTELLIGENT SPECIES. WE HAVE SIMPLY SUGGESTED THAT SUCH DESTRUCTION MAY BE HOW THE REST OF THE UNIVERSE WORKS, AND HOW IT MAY BE LIKELY TO RESPOND TO US. WELLS HAS OBVIOUSLY BOUGHT INTO THE VIEW OF A FRIENDLY GALAXY. THIS VIEW IS BASED UPON THE ARGUMENT THAT UNLESS WE HUMANS CONQUER OUR

SELF-DESTRUCTIVE WARLIKE TENDENCIES, WE WILL WIPE OUT OUR SPECIES AND NO LONGER BE A THREAT TO EXTRASOLAR CIVILIZATIONS. ALL WELL AND GOOD UP TO THIS POINT. BUT THEN THESE OPTIMISTS MAKE THE JUMP: IF WE ARE WISE ENOUGH TO SURVIVE AND NOT WIPE OURSELVES OUT, WE WILL BE PEACEFUL—SO PEACEFUL THAT WE WILL NOT WIPE ANYBODY ELSE OUT, AND AS WE ARE BELOW ON EARTH, SO OTHER PEOPLES WILL BE ABOVE. THIS IS A NON SEQUITUR, BECAUSE THERE IS NO GUARANTEE THAT ONE FOLLOWS THE OTHER, AND FOR A VERY IMPORTANT REASON: *"THEY" ARE NOT PART OF OUR SPECIES.*

BEFORE WE PROCEED ANY FURTHER, TRY THE FOLLOWING THOUGHT EXPERIMENT: WATCH THE FILMS *PLATOON* AND *ALIENS* TOGETHER AND ASK YOURSELF IF THE PLOT LINES DON'T QUICKLY BLUR AND BECOME INDISTINGUISHABLE. YOU'LL RECALL THAT IN VIETNAM, AMERICAN TROOPS WERE TAUGHT TO REGARD THE ENEMY AS "CHARLIE" OR "GOOK," DEHUMANIZING WORDS THAT MADE "THEM" EASIER TO KILL. IN LIKE MANNER, THE BRITISH, SPANISH, AND FRENCH CONQUESTS OF THE DISCOVERY PERIOD WERE MADE EASIER BY DECLARING DARK- OR RED- OR YELLOW-SKINNED PEOPLE AS SOMETHING LESS THAN HUMAN, AS A GODLESS, FACELESS "THEM," AS LITERALLY ANOTHER SPECIES.

PRESUMABLY THERE IS SOME SORT OF INHIBITION AGAINST KILLING OTHER MEMBERS OF OUR OWN SPECIES, BECAUSE WE HAVE TO WORK TO OVERCOME IT. OTHERWISE, IN THE MODERN WORLD, MOST OF US WOULD COMMIT MURDER, OR HAVE IT COMMITTED AGAINST US, AND THE COURT HEARINGS THAT ACCOMPANY MURDERS WOULD NEVER BECOME FRONT-

PAGE NEWS BECAUSE MURDER WOULD NOT BE AT ALL UNUSUAL (ONE WONDERS IF IT WOULD EVEN BE IL-LEGAL). INDEED, THIS INHIBITION AGAINST KILLING OUR OWN KIND CAN NOW BE SEEN IN THE GROWING RELUCTANCE EVEN TO PUT SERIAL KILLERS TO DEATH. THE INHIBITION IS NOT TOTAL, BUT IT IS THERE, AND IT HAD TO BE THERE OR OUR ALERT AND AGGRESSIVE SPECIES WOULD HAVE KILLED ITSELF OFF AGES AGO.

MURDER IS AN ABERRATION OF HUMAN BEHAVIOR, NOT THE NORM. WE OPERATE UNDER THE SAME RULES AS WOLVES, WHICH HAVE CERTAIN DEEP-ROOTED INHIBITIONS AGAINST KILLING (AND ESPE-CIALLY EATING) OTHER WOLVES. BUT THE RULES DO NOT APPLY TO OTHER SPECIES. BOTH HUMANS AND WOLVES LACK INHIBITIONS AGAINST KILLING CHICK-ENS.

HUMANS KILL OTHER SPECIES ALL THE TIME, EVEN THOSE WITH WHICH WE SHARE THE COMMON BOND OF HIGH INTELLIGENCE. AS YOU READ THIS, HUN-DREDS OF DOLPHINS ARE BEING KILLED BY TUNA FISHERMEN AND DRIFT NETTERS. THE KILLING GOES ON AND ON, AND DOLPHINS ARE NOT EVEN A THREAT TO US.

AS NEAR AS WE CAN TELL, THERE IS NO INHIBITION AGAINST KILLING ANOTHER SPECIES SIMPLY BECAUSE IT DISPLAYS HIGH INTELLIGENCE. SO, AS MUCH AS WE LOVE HIM, CARL SAGAN'S THEORY THAT IF A SPECIES MAKES IT TO THE TOP AND DOES NOT BLOW ITSELF APART, THEN IT WILL BE NICE TO OTHER INTELLIGENT SPECIES IS PROBABLY WRONG. ONCE YOU ADMIT IN-TERSTELLAR SPECIES WILL NOT NECESSARILY BE NICE TO ONE ANOTHER SIMPLY BY VIRTUE OF HAVING SUR-VIVED, THEN YOU OPEN UP THIS WHOLE NIGHTMARE

OF RELATIVISTIC CIVILIZATIONS EXTERMINATING ONE ANOTHER. IT'S AN ENTIRELY NEW SITUATION, EMERGING FROM THE PHYSICAL POSSIBILITIES THAT WILL FACE ANY SPECIES THAT CAN OVERCOME THE NATURAL INTERSTELLAR QUARANTINE OF ITS SOLAR SYSTEM. THE CHOICES SEEM UNFORGIVING, AND THE MIND STRUGGLES TO IMAGINE CIRCUMSTANCES UNDER WHICH AN INTERSTELLAR SPECIES MIGHT MAKE CONTACT WITHOUT TRIGGERING THE REALIZATION THAT IT CAN'T AFFORD TO BE PROVEN WRONG IN ITS FEARS. GOT THAT? WE CAN'T AFFORD TO WAIT TO BE PROVEN WRONG. THEY WON'T COME TO GET OUR RESOURCES OR OUR KNOWLEDGE OR OUR WOMEN OR EVEN BECAUSE THEY'RE JUST MEAN AND WANT POWER OVER US. THEY'LL COME TO DESTROY US TO INSURE THEIR SURVIVAL, EVEN IF WE'RE NO APPARENT THREAT, BECAUSE SPECIES DEATH IS JUST TOO MUCH TO RISK, HOWEVER REMOTE THE RISK.

KIND OF MAKES YOU WISH WE'D STAYED IN FRONT OF CAVES MILKING GOATS, DOESN'T IT?

FROM JILL TARTER, NASA/SETI
TO JIM POWELL AND RICHARD TUNA
JULY 16, 1987

I THINK THE SCIENCE FICTION WRITER JERRY POURNELLE PUT IT BEST WHEN HE SAID YOU GUYS MUST HAVE FASCINATING NIGHTMARES. (RELATIVISTIC BOMBS INDEED! YOU ARE TRULY THE PABLO PICASSO AND SALVADOR DALÍ OF NUCLEAR DESTRUCTION!) ALL OF THIS IS VERY NEW TO ME. NOT UNTIL RELATIVISTIC FLIGHT BEGAN TO LOOK ACHIEVABLE WAS THERE CAUSE TO BELIEVE THAT BROADCASTING OUR

PRESENCE TO THE REST OF THE GALAXY MIGHT BE DANGEROUS. I HAVE SPOKEN AGAIN WITH ISAAC AS-IMOV, AND HE SAYS COLONIES INSIDE THE ASTEROIDS MAY BECOME THE ONLY UNPREDICTABLE ELEMENT IN YOUR EQUATION. HE BELIEVES THAT ASTEROID-BASED COLONIES, IF AND WHEN THEY DEVELOP, WILL INEV-ITABLY START LEAVING THE SOLAR SYSTEM, SOMEWHAT LIKE DANDELION SEEDS. AND UNLIKE YOUR VALKYRIE ROCKETS, SLOW-MOVING COLONIES WILL NOT EMIT A DISTINCTIVE GAMMA-RAY SHINE OR BLUSH RADIO PULSES WHEN THEY IMPACT AGAINST INTERSTELLAR HYDROGEN AND DUST GRAINS. IT WILL THEREFORE BE VERY DIFFICULT FOR ANY WOULD-BE EXTERMINATORS TO FIND AN ASTEROIDLIKE OBJECT DRIFTING BETWEEN THE STARS. ESPECIALLY IF IT IS ONLY FIVE OR SIX KILOMETERS IN DIAMETER AND HAPPENS TO BE PAINTED BLACK. YOU SIMPLY CAN-NOT SEE THEM, EVEN IF YOU HAVE REASON TO SUS-PECT THEY EXIST. ANYONE TRYING TO STERILIZE THE SOLAR SYSTEM WOULD HAVE NO IDEA HOW MANY OF ISAAC'S DANDELION SEEDS WERE OUT THERE OR WHERE THEY WERE HEADED.

FASCINATING NIGHTMARES, YES. ALMOST MAKES ME HOPE THAT WHAT THE GREAT SILENCE REALLY MEANS IS THAT WE ARE ALONE IN THE GALAXY. ALL ALONE.

I SHOULD PROBABLY ALSO ADD THAT KAMEN AERO-SPACE VICE PRESIDENT JOHN RATHER POINTS OUT: ''IF WE EVER DO GET A SIGNAL ON OUR RADIO TELE-SCOPES, ONE HAS TO WONDER WHAT MIGHT BE IM-PORTANT ENOUGH TO TELL US. THE INITIAL TRANSMISSION COULD BE SOMETHING AS ELEMEN-TARY AS AN ALERT SIGNAL, REQUIRING THE CON-STRUCTION OF VERY SOPHISTICATED COMPUTERS TO

DIG OUT VAST AMOUNTS OF INFORMATION CON-
TAINED IN THE ALERT. WHAT THEY MIGHT IN REALITY
BE TRANSMITTING ARE INSTRUCTIONS FOR THE REP-
LICATION OF AN ALIEN PROGRAM ON EARTH, SEDUC-
ING US, AS IT WERE, INTO CREATING A SORT OF
ELECTRONIC CLONE. AND THERE'S NO TELLING WHAT
THAT SAVAGE BRAIN MIGHT DO, ESPECIALLY IF WE
ARE CARELESS ENOUGH TO LEAVE ITS MODEM WORK-
ING. IT COULD ACCESS COMPUTERS ALL AROUND THE
WORLD—REPROGRAM THE ENTIRE PLANET IN LESS
THAN AN HOUR."

WELL, THERE YOU HAVE IT. JUST WHEN I WAS BE-
GINNING TO WORRY ABOUT SUGGESTIONS THAT WE
COULD BE INVITING TROUBLE IF WE BROADCAST DE-
LIBERATE SIGNALS TO THE STARS, ONE OF YOUR TEAM
MEMBERS TELLS ME THAT IT MIGHT BE DANGEROUS
EVEN TO LISTEN.

FROM JIM POWELL AND RICHARD TUNA
TO JILL TARTER, NASA/SETI
AUGUST 8, 1987

WE UNDERSTAND THAT A LOT OF PEOPLE ARE UP-
SET OVER OUR SUGGESTIONS. BUT THEY ARE ONLY
SUGGESTIONS, ARISING FROM A SUBJECT THAT IS SIM-
PLY FUN TO THINK ABOUT, SIMPLY KID'S STUFF. WE
HAVE NEVER MADE A FIRM CLAIM THAT "MORE
HIGHLY EVOLVED" BEINGS WILL NECESSARILY BE
HOSTILE AND EXPLOITIVE. STILL, IT IS IMPORTANT FOR
US NOT TO ASSUME THAT IF ETI's ARE MORE TECH-
NOLOGICALLY OR CULTURALLY ADVANCED THAN US,
THEY ARE MORE BENEVOLENT FOR THAT REASON

(NOT THAT THERE IS VERY MUCH WE CAN DO, NO MATTER WHAT WE ASSUME).

THE MOST HUMBLING FEATURE OF THE RELATIVISTIC BOMB IS THAT EVEN IF YOU HAPPEN TO SEE IT COMING, ITS EXACT MOTION AND POSITION CAN NEVER BE DETERMINED; AND GIVEN A TECHNOLOGY EVEN A HUNDRED ORDERS OF MAGNITUDE ABOVE OUR OWN, YOU CANNOT HOPE TO INTERCEPT ONE OF THESE WEAPONS. IT OFTEN HAPPENS, IN THESE DISCUSSIONS, THAT AN EXPRESSION FROM THE OLD WEST ARISES: "GOD MADE SOME MEN BIGGER AND STRONGER THAN OTHERS, BUT MR. COLT MADE ALL MEN EQUAL." VARIATIONS ON MR. COLT'S WEAPON ARE STILL POPULAR TODAY, EVEN IN A SOCIETY THAT POSSESSES HYDROGEN BOMBS. SIMILARLY, NO MATTER HOW ADVANCED CIVILIZATIONS GROW, THE RELATIVISTIC BOMB THREAT IS NOT LIKELY TO GO AWAY.

AS FOR RECOMMENDATIONS THAT COMPUTER NETS SHOULD NEVER BE CONNECTED TO RADIO TELESCOPES . . . WELL, ONE CAN CARRY PARANOIA TO EXTREMES, AND HUMANS OFTEN DO. WHY SHOULD ALIENS BE ANY DIFFERENT?

IN HIS NOVEL, *THE WAR OF THE WORLDS*, H. G. WELLS DESTROYED THE COMPLACENT ARROGANCE OF THE BRITISH EMPIRE WITH A WORK OF FICTION ABOUT INSCRUTABLE MARTIANS WHO INVADED THE EARTH AND GAVE US A GLIMPSE OF WHAT TWENTIETH-CENTURY WARFARE MIGHT BE LIKE. BUT WE ARE NOT FACED WITH FICTION. WE ARE FACED WITH A POSSIBILITY THAT IS INTOLERABLE AT ANY DEGREE—ONE THAT WE CAN AVOID ONLY BY NOT CALLING ATTENTION TO OURSELVES, BY NOT SETTING IN MOTION AGAINST US FORCES THAT WE CANNOT RESIST. WELLS CAUGHT SOMETHING OF THE BACKWARD SHADOW OF WORLD

WAR I IN HIS NOVEL. WE SEE A SHADOW THAT MAY BLOT OUT OUR ENTIRE HISTORY. TO SEND OUT SIGNALS THAT MAKE PLAIN OUR COMING INTERSTELLAR CAPACITY IS THE SAME AS THE *TITANIC* STEAMING FULL AHEAD THROUGH THE DARK, INTO A FIELD OF ICEBERGS THAT IT HAD ALREADY BEEN WARNED ABOUT.

WE ASK THAT YOU TRY JUST ONE MORE THOUGHT EXPERIMENT. IMAGINE YOURSELF TAKING A STROLL THROUGH MANHATTAN, SOMEWHERE NORTH OF 68TH STREET, DEEP INSIDE CENTRAL PARK, LATE AT NIGHT. IT WOULD BE NICE TO MEET SOMEONE FRIENDLY, BUT YOU KNOW THAT THE PARK IS DANGEROUS AT NIGHT. THAT'S WHEN THE MONSTERS COME OUT. THERE'S ALWAYS A STRONG UNDERCURRENT OF DRUG DEALING, MUGGINGS, AND OCCASIONAL HOMICIDES.

IT IS NOT EASY TO DISTINGUISH THE GOOD GUYS FROM THE BAD GUYS. THEY DRESS ALIKE, AND THE WEAPONS ARE CONCEALED. THE ONLY DIFFERENCE IS INTENT, AND YOU CAN'T READ MINDS.

STAY IN THE DARK LONG ENOUGH AND YOU MAY HEAR AN OCCASIONAL DISTANT SHRIEK OR BLUNDER ACROSS A BODY.

HOW DO YOU SURVIVE THE NIGHT? THE LAST THING YOU WANT TO DO IS SHOUT, "I'M HERE!" THE NEXT TO LAST THING YOU WANT TO DO IS TO REPLY TO SOMEONE WHO SHOUTS, "I'M A FRIEND!"

WHAT YOU WOULD LIKE TO DO IS FIND A POLICEMAN, OR GET OUT OF THE PARK. BUT YOU DON'T WANT TO MAKE NOISE OR MOVE TOWARD A LIGHT WHERE YOU MIGHT BE SPOTTED, AND IT IS DIFFICULT TO FIND EITHER A POLICEMAN OR YOUR WAY OUT WITHOUT MAKING YOURSELF KNOWN. YOUR SAFEST

OPTION IS TO HUNKER DOWN AND WAIT FOR DAY-
LIGHT, THEN SAFELY WALK OUT.

THERE ARE, OF COURSE, A FEW OBVIOUS DIFFER-
ENCES BETWEEN CENTRAL PARK AND THE UNIVERSE:

THERE IS NO POLICEMAN.

THERE IS NO WAY OUT.

AND THE NIGHT NEVER ENDS.

EXCERPTS END

"Anything else?" Isak asked, surveying the grim
faces seated around his balcony table. The small
gathering included Sargenti; Bishop, who had just
been promoted to the rank of general; a second general named Stoff; and Azim Babu, the director of
Ceres' rapidly expanding astronomical observatory.

"Yes," said Sargenti, "there's that mystery call
from Earth. It keeps coming up at us, louder every
day. It's always the same—latitude and longitude
and pleas to come at once. They're starving down
there, so they say. And then there's this . . ."

Sargenti wiped the SETI excerpts from everyone's
pad and replaced them with maps of the sky showing patterns of gamma-ray bursts, each burst indicating an engine burn, presumably a course
correction. The images reminded Isak of a bad microscope displaying unknown organisms, but it was
all too clear what was happening.

At least six antimatter-driven rockets were moving between the planets. One of the ships seemed
actually to have reversed course and was headed
directly for Earth. Isak longed to believe there were
people in them, but he knew better. *Graff, Nautile,*

Melville, and every other starship he knew to be of human origin was gone.

He knew more—much of it from the new telescope array.

The Saudis, returning from Tau Ceti with their antimatter tanks nearly empty and finding the Mercury Power Project obliterated, had begun moving toward the imagined safety of the Asteroid Belt, their engine burns pointing like glowing fingers toward the half-dozen islands of civilization they suspected might still exist.

"My God!" Isak had exclaimed. "Why don't they just paint a big red X on us!"

The Saudis had no idea of what had happened to the solar system; and the asteroid survivors, forced into stealth, refused to answer their queries. Unaware that something might be hunting them, the starships, like the mystery caller on Earth, had broadcast loudly on all wavelengths, demanding information and assistance. In the end, some of the colonies had brought magnetic rail guns to bear on their own spacecraft—which they knew were cruising with low antihydrogen reserves, at interplanetary speeds of only 325 kilometers per second, 28 million kilometers per day—and they fired hastily fabricated smart bombs equipped with maneuvering thrusters, gamma detectors, and mini radio telescopes. When the last of the Valkyries exploded into searing hellfire, it was impossible to verify whether the aliens or surviving humanity had gotten to them.

Of course, not all these facts had boiled up out of the telescope array. Some details could be known only firsthand, from eyewitness participants. Isak knew, better than most, that Ceres had joined in the slaughter. He thought about that for a while.

Finally, he said, "I think Asimov was right. His dandelion seeds may be the only wild card, the only real chance we have—or have ever had."

"I was thinking the same thing," said Bishop. "There's no way we can sneak Ceres out of the solar system without being noticed. But if we can crawl out into a few of the smaller, darker asteroids, and perhaps even flick away from our own equator into interstellar space, inside small, rebuilt pieces of Ceres—"

"You're a jolly optimist," Sargenti said. "In another time I'm sure you would have believed in the king's horse."

Bishop flashed her a half-puzzled, half-angry expression. "Don't you mean horses? Isn't that the one about Humpty-Dumpty?"

"No, no," Sargenti said. "It's a story told for centuries, from bazaars in Baghdad to the court of Henry the Eighth, and it seems quite relevant—to me, anyway—so don't be offended."

"Go on," Bishop said.

"There was a thief whom the king had condemned to death. In order to buy time, the thief boasted that within a year he could make the king's favorite horse talk. So the king's men were ordered to put the thief to the task. 'But that's impossible!' said a friend of the thief. 'Be silent,' the thief replied. 'For within a year, many things can happen. The king may die. Or the horse may die. Or I may die. Or the horse may talk.' "

"Or the horse may talk!" Isak cried out. His easy grin was on his face, and the others at the table joined him in mild bursts of laughter. But Bishop was not laughing. He was scrawling letters on his pad.

"Is anyone here familiar with twentieth-century pop music?" he asked, looking up with astonishment and a hint of hysteria. The laughter died in an instant.

"What's up?" said Isak.

"The Intruders are talking to us, but I'll be damned if I can understand what they're trying to say. I've got a perfectly coherent signal, written in gamma rays and transmitted as binary code. Here, listen."

Bishop wrote a command on his pad, and lyrics began playing from all the other pads on the table; a pleasant and eerily familiar chant. Isak suddenly sensed that he should be able to guess what was going on, and he saw from the faces of the others that they had also responded with vague recognition.

"What was that, Bishop? What you were saying about twentieth-century pop?"

"Wait—I'm finding multiple tracks in this signal, different layers of complexity." He was scribbling on his pad at a manic rate. Every pad except his stopped chanting.

"Layers of complexity," Isak said in a whisper. "Bishop! Remember what that Rather fellow said about the danger of even listening?"

"I'm way ahead of you, sir. I isolated the entire net from the receiver the moment I came across Rather's idea. Only one computer is connected to the array, with instructions to transmit findings nowhere except to my pad. It's the only one in the entire station with a complete copy of the signal. And none of your pads can tap into mine, sir. If Rather was right about the danger of receiving an alien program, it's boxed in tightly, I assure you."

Bishop's pad continued to play the song.

Suddenly Babu, the astronomer, laughed out loud and said, "I think I know what it is!" and began calling out orders to his own pad, initiating searches for a curious combination of 1980s musical compositions and press reports on African droughts.

"Got it!" he announced triumphantly. "The Intruders seem to be rebroadcasting what remains to this day the loudest, most highly synchronized electromagnetic shout ever sent out from Earth. On April 5, 1985, as part of a publicity effort to bring aid to the starving children of Africa, every radio and television station on every continent began broadcasting the same message at the same moment—a composition called 'We Are the World,' by one Michael Jackson. I'm not trying to sound ironic, but I suspect the Intruders are telling us what first drew their attention to our species."

"So this Michael Jackson became the first definitive sign of intelligent life on Earth," Sargenti said acidly. "And the Intruders are throwing it back at us. Whatever for?"

"To mock us?" General Stoff asked. "But of course that can't be true."

"So what did they do all these years?" Sargenti said. "Just wait around replaying this tune to themselves until they could build starships and come finish us off? They must be insane!"

"Or very determined music critics," Isak said.

"It just doesn't make sense," the astronomer added.

"No, it's the only thing that does," said Bishop. "Most likely, the Jackson piece merely alerted them to our presence. Now . . . 1985 . . . that's roughly forty-five years each way at light-speed . . . relativistic bombs came in at ninety-two percent *c*. . . . If the Intruders responded immediately with relativistic attack, that would put their launch point, at most, forty light-years away. My guess is that they watched for a while, aimed a lot of detectors at us, and waited to see if we might become a threat to them. Our first antimatter engines began shining gamma rays to the galaxy about 2010. I'd say that marks the moment we signed our death warrant, although the song had already suggested a unified world that might take its first steps into interstellar space at any time. I'd say that the Intruder star is somewhere within thirty lights of us."

"All that from one song?" returned Sargenti. "It has to be a deception. *Has* to be. Why would they risk telling us so much about themselves—and actually giving us a maximum possible radius of origin? They'd have to be fools."

"General Sargenti," Bishop replied, "there's no doubt they're smart. But if you pressed me to compare them sight unseen to some Earthly species, I'd have to say there's something distinctly feline about them. I don't know how long we'll be allowed to go on, but I do understand their behavior. They mean to wear down what's left of us, like cats waiting outside a mouse hole, and they know they have the strength to do it. We've become a game to them."

He paused, distracted by his pad, which was still playing "We Are the World"; but an odd overlayering of whirrs and squeals seemed to be creeping up from somewhere below. Bishop began scribbling, and volumes of an alien binary code scrolled down his pad. He stopped at random on a "page," and the figures shifted, as if the Intruder program were reprogramming itself.

"What is it?" Isak asked. "What are you seeing?"

"About seven-point-five on the sphincter scale. Get on your phone and tell my guys topside to kill the telescope computer at once. Kill it!"

Isak did so at once, and found one of Bishop's engineers already on the line.

"Better make that nine-point-five," Isak said. "Something's alive up there, and it's eating one of your robots."

14

Voyage to the Edge of Creation

ANJIN WAS AS HAPPY AS A CLAM AT HIGH TIDE. HIS fusion ramjets were now fully operational, and even in the depths of the chromosphere, where the Sun's horizon was obscured by a plasma fog that gave him the impression of flying through the inside of a neon light, it was still possible for him to see clearly. Probing magnetic field lines and invisible wavelengths, he had extended the ship's sensory organs to a radius greater than the diameter of the Earth. No magnetic upheaval could give him less than twenty-six seconds of warning; and three seconds was all his machines needed.

No one aboard would ever forget the view from "high gate" pilot parlance for the approach phase of a runway landing. The "runway" here was islands of boiling hell, jammed side by side and spreading as far as the eye could see. Each was a bright spot with cool, dark edges, measuring 1500 kilometers from end to end. Even from the lofty heights of the solar corona—which had been familiar to Earthbound observers as a shimmering white veil seen around the Sun during total eclipses—the crew could see only a small fraction of the Sun's surface; and more and more of that fraction had slipped behind the horizon and out of view as the comet rode down to the chromosphere. The diminishing radiative surface area to which Sargenti-Peterson was exposed contributed much to the curious and seemingly paradoxical drop in temperature as Anjin steered the ship-comet nearer the Sun's surface.

"High gate" and "surface": the words were misnomers here; and Anjin knew better, but his mind held on to the old planetary references. The Sun had no true surface, just electron-stripped gases that increased in density with decreasing altitude. What he called the surface, or "runway," just below the chromosphere, was in fact a field of turbulent cloud tops rising dramatically from the core, radiating energy produced more than a million years ago, then sinking once again as they cooled—just like convection cells in a cup of coffee.

Anjin and Tam had agreed to keep the ship a safe distance above the cloud tops, in regions that were to the Sun what the stratosphere was to Earth. Even in the chromosphere, vast waves churning over the Sun's surface produced dangerous disturbances; but Anjin was confident that he had mastered these, and was equally confident that, if necessary, he might even adapt the ship-comet to the environs below the cloud tops. Each day's scans rendered the Sun more predictable. The new frontier held few surprises for him. The scanners told him so.

The shock was therefore all the greater when Susan Skurla, who had volunteered for lookout duty, sounded the alarm on his pad, waking him from a peaceful sleep with warnings of "transient phenomena."

As he pulled on his socks, the pad showed him an unimpressive blip, slightly more than twelve thousand kilometers astern.

Astern . . . Anjin wondered. Judging from the tension in Susan's voice, he had been expecting a monstrous eruption only a few seconds forward. Any trouble astern, even the flare of the century, would now be lagging behind at five hundred kilometers per second and was hardly worth worrying about. He thought about telling the Second Officer that she should be ashamed to express such concern over a transient blip falling so quickly behind her, until he watched it disappear and reappear twice over the course of five seconds, and saw that its distance was holding steady at slightly more than twelve thousand kilometers.

"What do you make of it?" he croaked.

"Something highly reflective. Solid, probably. And unnatural."

Ten long seconds passed, and still Anjin's pad showed a tiny blip, slightly more than twelve thousand kilometers astern. He froze, then said, "I see what you mean, Susan. Better wake Captain Tam. We're no longer alone down here."

15

Pentecostal Apocalypse

OF THE TWO BILLION PEOPLE WHO DIED DURING THE first moments of contact with the Intruders—and the ten thousand survivors whose lives were overturned—only two ever came to see the beings who had destroyed them. They were a priest turned submarine pilot and an historian turned VR addict turned historian again, not exactly the most random sampling of humanity, but it would do, for the Intruders, until something better came along.

On the day the ship rendezvoused with Earth and decelerated into a parking orbit, *Alvin* lay hidden beneath a kilometer of water. The instruments left on the surface told Hollis that the latest string of hurricanes had passed and the winds were abating. Frustratingly, her camera buoys were blinded by sheets of driving yellow rain that had reduced visibility to a few meters and had only now begun to retreat.

After following the seafloor west and arriving at the place where New York City's historic Twin Towers should have been, Jonathan and Hollis were struck first by the change in basic geography. They realized immediately that the destruction seen in Long Beach could only furnish criteria for comparison to the forces unleashed against Manhattan. Something monstrous had turned the entire island into a cauldron of white-hot gravel, then pressed it beneath the Hudson. The first tides, as they spilled into the crater through Queens and Jersey City, must have recoiled as flashing white vapor, so that for a time the ocean trembled at the crater's rim.

Even now, the waters steamed over a rock bed that would take years to cool. Near the center of the depression, where 68th Street and Hunter College had met Lexington Avenue, Hollis found a field of undersea geysers. Water was seeping down through the gravel and returning with stolen heat and mineral brines.

About two dozen meters west of the place where Hunter College had once stood, and a kilometer beneath it, she maneuvered *Alvin* to a small chimney-like structure that had begun to condense from the mineral broth. It was in places such as this, Hollis believed, that some of Earth's first living things had taken root. Somewhere out there, her own exhaled bacteria, and perhaps a few organisms already living near hydrothermal vents and undersea volcanoes when the end came, having survived deep in the oceans as she and Jonathan had, were simply drifting with the currents, waiting to wash up against these life-giving springs.

"Pentecostal apocalypse," Hollis said. "God is starting over."

"Yeah, I know what you mean, naturally," said Jonathan, beginning to envy her sense of calm optimism and control. It seemed to be one of the benefits of her ever-questioning, always-probing faith, which had not only helped make her a good explorer, but also had somehow preadapted her to living through the death of civilization. Sometimes, though, he wished that she would stop thinking so much. Most of the time he found her thoughts a little jarring, as had most people who were not well versed in the Dead Sea Gospels and the Book of Revelation.

"If you'd like me to explain, Wayville, just ask. It concerns how the universe is set up. Whether or not you want to believe God ever had a hand in it, every beginning must have its end. What I believe these vents are trying to teach us is that from every end there must also arise a new beginning."

"Well, Hollis, sometimes I think you must be crazy. But no one will ever accuse you of being uninteresting." He laughed. "Since I'm the only one left who could do that."

"Just consider the facts. Do you really think DNA cares which species—man or bacterium—inherits the Earth? Do you really think it matters?"

" 'Matters' is always a question of to whom—but go on."

"There'll be bacterial reefs here soon. You can bet on it. DNA is the ultimate parasite, the ultimate survivor. For billions of years it has managed to preserve its same, essential structure, residing for a little while in you or me, or in a dinosaur, or a bacterium, and then moving on fully intact to the next generation. You like to think your genes serve your best interests, but in a very real sense it is quite the other way around. They simply orchestrate the construction of our bodies, then occupy us for a few decades, with no purpose other than producing and maintaining reproductive systems, so they can carry on in fresh young bodies just as ours begin to wear out. Every breath we take, every sip of water, every bite of food, immortalizes our genetic code, not us. We are just one of the many masks that DNA will wear."

"Seems to belittle the whole point of living, doesn't it?"

"Not at all. Quite the opposite. Here, let me renew your appreciation of the miracle of life. The first microbe that arrives here, and manages to survive in these springs, will reproduce itself with amazing rapidity. Within a year you'll have bacterial mats thick enough to fill this sub, and all the ropes of DNA contained in that single reef, if laid end to end, will reach to the Sun and back over three hundred times, yet will occupy a volume no bigger than an ice cube. So life is—"

"Going to metastasize again," he continued for her, "all over this planet."

She looked at him and knew that, despite the hopelessness of their situation, she had him hooked. It was the first time he had shown a serious interest in anything she had to say; and this seemed to confirm her observation that there was a sudden change in him, a change that went deeper than mere fortification with whale meat.

"Maybe God equals DNA," Jonathan said.

"Well, you'd have to go back before DNA actually—to gravitation. But here's a couple of good questions to think about. We've known for a while now that occupying or renting our bodies isn't the only way DNA survives. Eventually the planet evolved brains capable of resurrecting chromosomes after thousands or even millions of years. So long as the carriers of chromosomes managed to cover the Earth thickly enough, sneaking into every crack and crevice, it happened that wherever there arose an environment capable of preserving DNA, some small amount of it was bound to take up residence. So tell me, Wayville, do we define life as simply a property of the carbon atom, as an information storage system written on nucleic acid and read by protein? And if the answer is yes, should strands of DNA embedded in amber still be considered alive after tens of millions of years, and should the computers that store and replicate all that genetic information also be considered alive?"

There was silence in the cabin for quite a long time, not because Jonathan had no answers but because something on Hollis's pad had caught her attention and she turned her back to him before he could respond. He could see that the buoys were reporting diminishing wind and rain. It was safe to go up and snoop around again. Such opportunities were rare, and the weather could take a turn for the worse at any moment, so they would have to hurry.

Jonathan watched the vent field drop away from *Alvin*'s floodlamps as Hollis pushed the engines up to full throttle. In seconds, the vents were out of sight, but he could not get the coming bacterial assault out of his mind. Behind the familiar bacteria waited a still-larger microbial army, deep in the folds and cracks of the planet's crust, thriving at high heat and pressure, buried so deep that the globe would have to be vaporized to prevent it from invading the unresisting surface. Earth— whose song had begun with the percussions of solar gravitational gatherings, meteoric bombardments, and geologic motion, and had swollen with the violent chorus of life, then shifted into the dissonant keys of technical civilization—had not ended its music with a shrieking coda. Deep inside, the planet still sang softly, holding back the lifeless dark.

Finally, he remarked, "Well, you've really put humanity in its place, haven't you?"

"And man's idea of purpose?"

"I can almost hear those bacterial genes laughing at us. It's too damned ironic. Too appropriate. I keep remembering what my mother used to say about man and God."

Hollis looked up from her pad, and Jonathan's calm brown eyes stared into hers as he said, "Man plans, God laughs."

"Well, I wouldn't go that far," she replied. "Man had his place, as does every tier in the hierarchies; and it was *all* his, for a while. Man just didn't look after his place very well, that's all."

He smiled at her and asked, "Is that what happened?"

The Sun was almost directly overhead, trying to burn through the cloud cover. There was still a slight drizzle, but from where Wayville and Hollis stood, atop *Alvin*'s conning tower, they could look six kilometers in every direction to the edges of the crater. Twelve kilometers in diameter, one kilometer deep. The numbers rolled easily off the tongue, but it was necessary to sail the new bay to appreciate its immensity. Words and numbers would not do.

After they got used to the size of it, they noticed the silence. Except for the gentle lapping of water against *Alvin*'s hull and the faint hiss of millions of little gas bubbles venting to the surface, Manhattan Bay was deathly silent. One of the world's last authentic cities had thrived here, but today there were no reassuring murmurs of crowds, no aircraft engines or police sirens, and no signs that such sounds had ever existed.

For several minutes, Jonathan and Hollis stood motionless on the tower, looking at distant sheets of black rain and listening for peals of thunder that never came. Finally, Hollis activated her pad and began sending up her usual distress call—and for the first time she got an answer.

Something resembling a water balloon splattered down out of nowhere, striking hard against the stern's smoothly curving surface, spreading there, and hardening instantly. Hollis barely had time to notice that the balloon had trailed a thread before a second balloon hit. And another. And another. One struck only a meter from her face, and she was momentarily torn between curiosity and the urge to jump overboard. Then she reached out and touched the thread, not knowing what to expect, but knowing that it now anchored *Alvin* to something above the cloud cover—or maybe even beyond the planet.

It was as taut as well-tuned piano wire, and climbed higher than she could see, as in the legend of Mohammed's rope to heaven. It sent a vibration through her fingers, as if something were alive at the other end, plucking the string with cyclopean fingers.

And then a voice resonated from it and from all the strings anchored to *Alvin*'s hull. Hollis jumped back and heard the strings say in an angelic tenor, clear and bright and in the king's English, "Go inside your ship and seal the hatch at once! You have thirty seconds. At the end of that time you must be lying on the floor, on your backs, waiting."

Hopeful as much as astonished, Jonathan tried to convince himself, as he scrambled down behind Hollis, that this was all a new variety of emergency rescue equipment, and that a ship manned by their colleagues was waiting for them at the other end. He hoped so, but he didn't really believe it.

He lay down near one of the forward ports, guessing from the instructions what was coming next, and was grateful that *Alvin* had once been towed by a Valkyrie to Jupiter's moon Europa, where a crew of dolphins and humans had camped under the ice fields and explored whole new oceans. *Alvin* was thus already adapted to space travel, and Jonathan took great comfort in the fact that the portholes, which on most submersibles were designed only to keep pressure from getting in, would not blow out into the vacuum of space.

He heard a series of rising notes communicating through the tethers into *Alvin*'s hull, coming closer and faster and louder as he listened, sounding to him as if the hull or the tethers or some combination of both might break under the mounting strain; but the initial shock simply hoisted *Alvin* out of the water, to dangle motionless for a moment, its sides dripping. Then, as if propelled by the snapping of a giant rubber band, the ship sped toward the Sun.

Inside, Jonathan was pressed face down against a porthole, through which his field of vision expanded enormously. He thought he could barely make out the Rockaways and Sandy Hook before the ship passed through a veil of brownish-yellow dust into brilliant white sunshine, revealing to him the rim of a cloud-shrouded Earth, through which no mountain ranges or foreign shores were visible.

Looking, for the very last time, in the direction of Manhattan, he remembered something he had read about the last people to flee Thera, routed by the volcanic upheaval that gave rise to the legend of Atlantis. And he realized that the grave and reverent feelings that passed through him were unique. No humans except the Therans of the ancient Aegean could possibly have understood. He and Hollis were leaving Earth, with no hope of ever returning. And now that the last people had gone, their cities and nations, their world, would have no names.

And the sky around them deepened from dirty blue to violet, and at last to the eternal darkness of space. Like a child's telephone line made from cups and string, the tethers continued to transmit sounds through *Alvin*'s hull. Jonathan heard something race down toward him and stop with a bang. Seconds later, there was a roar of retrothrust and objects in the cabin began floating up. He tried to grab a handhold but could find none, and was on the verge of panic when the roar grew louder and the ceiling became the floor.

"Who would have imagined that?" said Hollis.

"Sticky bombs and slingshots with retrorockets!" She was on the verge of laughter.

"Space!" Jonathan cried. "Why did it have to be space?" he asked as he climbed back up to the portholes, "up" now being the floor of the cabin. The inverted point of view made him queasy; but he found it far, far preferable to weightlessness.

One of Hollis's whale meat bundles had struck the ports, smearing them with grease. He rubbed the nearest port clean with a shirt sleeve while Hollis stood anxiously on the ceiling.

"What can you see?" she asked.

But Jonathan was not listening to her. He had just seen the spaceship.

16

Dangerous?

THE LIGHTS WERE COMING ON AGAIN. THERE SEEMED to be no further point in worrying about the Intruders finding Ceres' neutrino glow; so bit by bit, Bishop was powering up the colony. Crichton had resumed his afternoon naps in the amaryllis garden, the colonists were going home to their ranches, and it was possible to believe, ignoring certain facts, that the yellowing fields might even produce papaya again.

Despite the circumstances, the population had remained curiously sober. There were still sporadic loud parties, still drunks sleeping under the trees—zoned out on a mixture of VR, hallucinogens, and drink—but far fewer than anyone would have expected. Like harbingers of a coming spring, the colonists were starting to spread out again, tidying up, and slowly returning to normal.

Isak and Sargenti sat silently over their pads at his balcony table, scribbling furiously, completely lost in thought, glancing occasionally out into the vast, upcurving tunnel whose ceiling was completely obscured by clouds. Through them, a single bar of light only a few meters wide but thousands of kilometers long tried to banish the Ceran night. The clouds were thicker today than they had ever been in the past, offering no breaks; and the light that filtered through them was soft, yellow-white, reminding Isak during those rare moments when he found the time to look outside of a bright, hazy day on Earth.

There was too much to think about. For Isak there were the Tarter group's warnings, ignored for decades; yet they had told exactly what to expect. And there was the colossal mistake with the phone system; it seemed such a little error, at first, as did most disastrous choices when viewed with twenty-twenty hindsight. And there was his son and Yeon and Sargenti. In the final sum, his whole life was regrets. Sargenti was all that was really left for him; but she had seemed more than enough when he began shutting down the fusion plants, and could plan for years of survival under the Intruders, perhaps even count on escape. But then he had been forced to adjust his thinking to days, and then to hours, and now he suspected that it was getting down to minutes. The effect of growing up in the low gravity of Ceres had produced in Sargenti a wonderful blend of litheness and androgyny; and as he glanced up from his pad, he drew some small satisfaction from the likelihood that she would probably be the last thing he would ever see.

For Sargenti there was the death cry she planned to send out to the universe, louder than the Jackson shout, with the final surge of power from Bishop's generators. It would go out as a simple binary code, with no concealed levels of complexity. In it she was including all the great works of art, film, music, and literature—everything that gave her pride in her species, everything from Monet to the dancing antelopes of Thera, from Mozart to the Beatles' "Here Comes the Sun" and Glenn Miller's "Caribbean Clipper," from Plato to Guilder, and especially Guilder, who had penned the twentieth century's greatest poems but went unnoticed in her lifetime because she had insisted on giving them such off-putting titles as "Does Satan Drive a Plymouth Fury?" and "Did Jesus Have a Dog?" And Beavis and Butt-Head, the cartoon figures whose Laurel and Hardy–like stupidity had only grown more endearing with time.

For Babu, the astronomer, there was the rueful satisfaction that the first contact with aliens had been totally exhausting and totally exciting—while it lasted.

For Bishop there was the question of why he was here at all. He had been born and raised in the previous century, and had personally known the members of Tarter's group before volunteering for Project Biotime, a concept whose roots could be traced back to Powell and Tuna.

While designing robot space probes to get under the ice of Europa, Powell and Tuna were forced to practice with deep-sea robots on Earth. Along the way, they had discovered that eggs and larvae on the abyssal plains usually drifted for hundreds of years at two degrees above freezing, until they blundered upon a life-giving volcanic vent or a whale carcass or a ship full of food that fell out of heaven. They survived their journey by existing in a state of suspended animation. And once the biologists learned how to emulate these organisms, whole new worlds were opened to them.

Project Biotime had been the brainchild of a Wall Street investment banker who devised and financed diverse medical applications for the newly discovered deep-ocean chemicals. As the twentieth century had drawn to a close, human bodies were routinely being cooled down to two degrees above freezing, with all metabolic functions flat-lined, making multiple organ transplants routine. But what the banker really had in mind was time travel. He knew that all the books, newspapers, and films available to historians would fail to preserve the personal prejudices and the real flavor of a century that had opened with the ascent of kitelike aircraft and ended with the exploration of the planets. He also knew that some of the most important questions about his time could be asked only by future historians, because he and his fellow travelers were simply too close to the subject matter.

Each of the thirty biotimers had to be willing to spend approximately fifty years in suspension, followed by two months of walking around and providing information to historians, followed by twenty-seven additional fifty-year time jumps. They would begin their fourteen-hundred-year journey in the role of historic artifacts, increasing in value as they went forward, until at last they became living, breathing archeological databases.

What surprised the banker was that, even after all the wrinkles had been ironed out and the safety of the biotime procedure proven, he had found it almost impossible to get volunteers. James Powell, Richard Tuna, and Arthur C. Clarke had been the first to decline, followed by the historian Walter

Lord, along with almost everyone else he had assumed would jump at the opportunity to explore futurity.

But not Ed Bishop. Like Powell and Tuna, he had designed machines so advanced that he could never hope to see them built during his lifetime. His colleagues had resigned themselves to the fact that they were not meant to see starships and self-replicating robots any more than Moses had been meant to cross over to Canaan with his people. They did not need to see the Valkyries burning in the sky; it was enough for them to know they were waiting out there in the new millennium.

But Bishop wanted more. He had never been happy in his own time, and before leaving it behind, he had written on his biotime capsule, "My true friend died before I was born and my perfect lover will be born after I die."

And he told the historians, "Translate that to this: if you want perfection in an off-the-rack world, you will be disappointed, because the odds are that in the whole span of history, your lifetime is too small to expect to meet the perfect love. Of course, you can cheat that by biotiming."

As it happened, he met his perfect love after the very first "timejump," among the Ceres-bound colonists; and he had abandoned the biotimers to help her build a new world. For six brief years he had known perfect happiness, and then it was all snatched away from him forever by Ceres's one and only construction accident. That was eight years ago; and though the option had always remained open to him, he never rejoined Project Biotime. He had spent most of the past eight years living with machines instead of people, indifferent to the future, until now, when it was all so clearly too late.

By the time the maglev had shuttled him from Isak's home to the north pole, a pressurized tent had already sealed off his stricken, half-eaten robot from the rest of Ceres, a phone line had already connected the tent to the colony, and a system of laboratory modules was already being trucked to the site.

The tent itself enclosed a fully equipped "clean room." Bishop had entered through an airtight glove box that fit him like a space suit, and in the center of the room one of the robots was melting in the warming air. It occurred to him then—too late—that no one should have been allowed to pressurize the chamber or heat the air. A second robot had stood on the far side of the room, ready to assist him. Now both machines lay in melting heaps, and Bishop found himself alone and afraid, abandoned by his crew, as he retreated to a module whose hull was twisting out of shape and leaking air. He tightened his suit helmet, hoping to buy himself a few more minutes of life, and began his final report to Isak.

There was very little he could say that was new to the president. One of the machines had been tricked into producing a substance that, for lack of a better name, Bishop had come to call a "molecular virus" or "template"—with which it had promptly infected itself.

Isak had replayed the images over and over on his pad: Bishop's robot on the floor of the tent, being eaten as if by a mighty cancer, breaking open like a poorly constructed beehive, thousands of microrobots spilling out of the rent across its abdomen, writhing and melting; Bishop's robot assistant placing samples under the scopes; and then, after an hour or two, the scopes themselves seizing up and flaking apart . . . and then the robot assistant.

The scopes had lasted long enough to show, with brutally realistic computer animation, what was happening. Most chemical reactions released their excess energy as heat: random, chaotic molecular motion. Every schoolgirl knew that every chemical compound had a specific melting point, at which the motion became so distorted that the crystalline structure broke down and individual molecules drifted off in different directions. The template molecule, when it came into contact with a ceramic composite, a carbon-metallic alloy, or with almost any substance likely to be manufactured by civilized beings, rearranged its crystal structure in such a way that the old melting points were drastically altered. Superconductors failed to function. Mechanical parts either became brittle or liquefied at room temperature. On the face of each crystal in the "tissues" of the stricken robot molecules were rearranging identically and transmitting a pattern of molecular recoil to every neighboring crystal—which vibrated and softened in turn.

"To get the ball rolling, the robot need only have innocently manufactured a few milligrams of this stuff," Bishop said. He was breathing hard inside his helmet, speaking quickly now, and Isak detected a touch of panic in his voice. "When all this got started, that's all there was—less than a gram. Then we had the whole robot and the scopes and then another robot crumbling to pieces—tons of the stuff lying around. How do you contain something like that? Sooner or later it was bound to get out. Sooner or later it should even get to the Intruders."

"But that seems an unlikely hope," Sargenti added. "They would have built-in protection, some sort of half-life. Otherwise they'd have to worry about meteorite impacts flicking bits of contaminated dust off Ceres and one of their ships coming in contact with it."

"If this had happened on Earth," Bishop said, "they could have counted on the winds to spread template dust to every continent. All the towers and skylines would have vanished. Obviously that wasn't enough. They wouldn't have been happy just knocking Earth back to the Stone Age and leaving the Acropolis, Renaissance cathedrals, Mayan temples, and the forests still standing. But here on Ceres, where we depend on high-tech for everything—even the air we breathe—the template is the perfect Final Solution." He stopped and took a deep breath. "One other thing. I'm afraid it's gotten through the material in my suit and into me. From the feel of it, I'd say even the iron and calcium in our bodies is vulnerable."

There was a popping sound behind Bishop, and the room fogged as the air pressure dropped. He was breathing more heavily now, and sweat was beading up and streaming down his face. "I've had it, Isak. Better that you don't see what will be left of me. Good-bye."

"Good-bye," Isak whispered as the screen went blank, and the full force of Bishop's plight—the Greeks would have said destiny—rushed through him. This voyager through time had come so far from home, only to die in this strange way. Destiny—it was what happened to a life when it was over . . . and nothing more could happen to it.

Isak now set about the task of transmitting final orders, trying to work methodically at his pad, trying to ignore the quaking sounds in the cavern roof and the slight tremble that resounded through the frame of his house. One little mistake, one last regret: the very system of phone lines he had hoped would keep the Intruders from finding Ceres Station was actually helping the template to transmit its chain of molecular recoil to all points of the compass. It had shot out of Bishop's tent like a poison dart, and was now crisscrossing the entire network of the colony, into every ranch, every office, every room that contained a phone.

Such a little mistake: but now all the poison had spilled out and was penetrating Isak's world with such swift precision that he was even inclined to believe that the Intruders had anticipated his strategy of stealthing Ceres with phone lines.

Crushed, he sat back and took a deep breath, then glanced over at Sargenti.

She did not look at him but said, "There's only one last thing we can do, if we still can."

She touched her pad, and he saw that she was concentrating vast amounts of power into the station's transmitter and opening as many wavelengths as the equipment could handle.

"There's nothing more they can do to us," she said, "so we might as well get out what we know."

She leaned forward slightly and Isak watched her as if in a dream.

"This is Ceres Station," she said, "broadcasting

on radio carrier wave. We're about all done here. Warning to survivors: the enemy knows how to re-program your computers if they are linked to listening devices. Receivers must be totally disconnected from computer systems—especially robots. There is great danger in listening to or trying to interpret enemy transmissions. Regret we've learned that the hard way. Regret no further communications from Ceres will be possible.''

She went on repeating the message five times, and when she was through she called, "Death cry," into her pad, and in simple binary code the music went out to the light-years, with stereoscopic pairs of Tutankhamen's golden mask, van Gogh's *Starry Night*; the collected works of Shakespeare, Poe, H. G. Wells, Clarke, Lord, Stanislaw Lem, and Guilder; the films of Kubrick, Spielberg, and Limardo; and Henry Roth's great American novel, *Call It Sleep*. She instructed the transmitter to repeat the message over and over again, for as long as the power lasted. Like the old Jackson message, it shone hundreds of times brighter than the Sun on certain wavelengths. Decades from now—perhaps millennia from now, Sargenti guessed—some alien civilization would receive the music and art of her people and, beginning with the collection of children's talking books she had included, might be able to understand or to at least develop some small appreciation for her civilization's accumulated beauty, if not its wisdom.

She suspected, however, that fearing exactly the situation she now found herself in, they might not have sufficient computer power connected to their receivers. If anyone were listening, they would probably record only part of her death cry and rightly conclude that only an exceedingly foolish civilization—or a people who knew they were dying and had nothing to lose—would be so heedless of detection as to deliberately send such a powerful message starward.

Shaped by her encounter with the Intruders, her picture of the universe, if extrapolated over many centuries, became a never-ending story of civilizations hunkering down and watching and waiting, interspersed with occasional loud bangs and shrieks in the cosmic night. And if this were all that eight thousand years of civilization had been leading up to, that small sour grapes part of her was glad to be done with it.

Isak, who had been monitoring distress calls and scribbling instructions, suddenly pulled back his hand from his pad.

The ceramic panel was going soft.

"Mine's going, too," Sargenti announced.

Anger flashed in Isak's eyes. "Bastards! They'll see! If we survived this long, so might others. They're not infallible. Somewhere out there, a warrior waits to teach them a lesson they will not live to learn from."

"Or the horse may talk?" asked Sargenti.

"Or the horse may talk," Isak replied.

The house shuddered, and then from above came a long, drawn-out series of cracking noises, as if the sky were falling—which in a very real sense it was. Suddenly in the distance a slab of rock nearly a half kilometer long peeled away from the tunnel ceiling and came crashing out of the clouds in the slow, frightful majesty that only low gravity could produce. An ocean of water seemed to trail behind it, a foaming, greenish-white column that could only have come from a demolished reservoir on the level above.

Crichton, awakened by the commotion, was padding cautiously in the direction of the downpour, and Sargenti's curiosity was momentarily aroused by a peculiar pattern that the Coriolis force was etching into the water. For the first hundred meters, the column fanned out evenly in every direction, forming ghostly white veils; then, as it neared the plain, it began to curve westward, lagging behind Ceres spin.

"We'd better get out into the open," Sargenti said. "This house isn't safe anymore. I expect it'll collapse in a few minutes. The whole colony soon after."

Isak broke out in sweat and felt a tingling creeping up his arms from his hands, and wondered if somehow the template had already contaminated his blood. He turned to Sargenti and found her gazing at him with a clear, caring smile; and his foremost sensation was not one of fear or regret over failed tactics but of a heartfelt sorrow that life was so full of doors that closed when you were not looking and rooms that you could not reenter.

"How much time do you think we have?" he asked.

She reached out and took his hand. "Enough," she said.

II

THEORY OF CATASTROPHISM

Behold the pale horse. The man who rides it is death. And hell comes with him.
                    —Revelation

Paranoids are sometimes right.
                    —Jim Powell

17

The Resurrectionists

"THE KING'S HORSE" WAS THE STORY OF AN ANIMAL that never spoke. Delay was the point of the tale. But there was a longer tradition of animals and unlikely objects talking, dating back past the thunderstorm that spoke to Job, past Balaam's donkey, to the serpent in the Garden of Eden. The saddest of all these stories had originated in Africa, and was made all the sadder now, for all that a bold electronic shout to the galaxy had wrought.

Omoro was a hunter who, upon penetrating deep into the brush one afternoon, found himself being called by an old human skull. They talked late into the night, Omoro and the skull. And finally Omoro asked, "What brought you here?"

"Talking brought me here," said the skull.

When Omoro returned to the village, he told his family and his friends and anyone else who would listen to him about the miracle of the talking skull. And the word went forth from village to village, and finally there came to Omoro a summons from the king.

"I hear that you have made a great discovery," said the king.

"Yes," replied the hunter. "I found a dry human skull in the bush. It asks you how its father and mother are."

Ignoring the cryptic question, the king said, "Never since my mother bore me have I heard that a dead skull can speak."

He then summoned the Alkadir, the Saba, and the Degi and asked them if they had ever heard the like. None of the wise men had heard the like, and they decided to send a detachment of the king's guards along with the hunter to find the skull, learn if the story was true and, if so, to learn the reason for it. The guards accompanied Omoro into the bush with orders to flay his head to the bare bone and leave him to rot if it turned out that he had lied.

Omoro led them to the skull, demanded that it speak, and was greeted with utter silence.

He asked as before: "What brought you here?"

The skull did not answer.

The whole day he begged and pleaded for the skull to speak, and when night came with not a whisper of a reply, the guards flayed his head bare with oyster shells.

After they had gone the skull opened its jaws and asked the dying hunter, "What brought you here?"

Omoro replied, "Talking brought me here!"

Richard Tuna, toward the end of his life, might have sympathized with Omoro. In 1977 he and paleontologist Gerard Case had made a remarkable discovery in a New Jersey clay pit; and had Tuna never talked about it, others might never have laid the foundations for the appalling conditions that did much to explain why only two billion human beings were living on the day the relativistic bombs came.

From New Jersey's amber beds, Tuna had plucked a flesh-feeding fly whose every eye facet and hair, even the soft tissue of its mouth, had been preserved for ninety-five million years; and the find started a train of thought. By 1982, this strange paleontologist who occasionally designed rockets was speculating loudly to anyone who would listen about flesh-feeding flies of the Mesozoic era drawing skin and blood from dinosaurs and then, minutes later, becoming trapped in sun-warmed, tissue-penetrating pools of tree sap. "Is it possible," he asked, "that saurian genetic codes might still exist in amber and that we might one day be able to read them and resurrect them?"

At last there came a call from the Smithsonian Institution to prepare a report on the dinosaur cloning recipe. But when the entomologists, paleontologists, and zoologists were summoned for peer review, they said they had never heard the like—and some even called it a paper fit for burning.

"Impossible," said Pacific Tech's Leslie Wells. "I would sooner believe the River Jordan ceased flowing for Joshua than submit to the notion that dinosaurs will ever be cloned from amber." Stopping the River Jordan was an odd example, since it was at least possible and left her a way out. Joshua stopping the Sun would have been the example that made her position unequivocal.

"But look around you," Tuna protested. "Look where computer and genetic technology are leading us. You're judging this recipe from a time in which we have little more than 16K computers to work with, and in which it takes an hour to duplicate one trinucleotide sequence; but in a few years we'll be talking about gigabytes and we'll be watching our knowledge of genetics triple every two years. In thirty years, using nothing more exotic than off-the-shelf hardware, I'll be able to give you the ultimate paleontological tool: the ability to study living, breathing dinosaurs face-to-face. It's just a matter of waiting for technology to catch up with the wish, and being lucky enough to find the right fossils."

"You must be a madman to suggest such things," Wells said. She had then blocked publication of Tuna's "madman recipe" everywhere except in chapters of his own book (which his granddaughter, Tam, was to take with her to Sargenti-Peterson), and in the pages of *Omni* magazine, where it attracted little more than yawns. As Tuna and James Powell revealed to radio talk show audiences how it might one day be possible to clone exhibits for a "dinosaur world park," no one except science fiction writers and filmmakers were listening. But they were enough.

By the spring of 1993, three events had converged to change Wells's mind: computer memories had swollen to gigabytes, it was possible to duplicate millions of copies from large sections of a DNA molecule in only an hour, and what had up to that time been one of Tuna's "little throwaway ideas" was suddenly writ large in what he came to call "Steven Spielberg's little home movie about dinosaurs."

"Who cares if it may never work," observed one Pacific Tech scientist. "Amber studies have become the sexy science of the 1990s. It's worth tens of millions in research grants!"

With these words, the assault against Tuna was on.

The grants and the fame would go to the person who could lay claim to first articulating the idea of cloning dinosaurs. Wells was determined to lay a claim; but if she was going to succeed, she had to push Tuna out of the way. Tuna, meanwhile, had kept the letters from the Smithsonian Institution's peer review—black-and-white proof that Leslie Wells had once been a severe critic of his dinosaur-cloning recipe—but the documents could not protect him against police reports mailed anonymously to every institution that offered him work. These reports attested that in the spring of 1968 a thirty-year-old man (occupation: teacher) by the name of Rick Tuna had been arrested for impregnating a fourteen-year-old student.

"Yes," Tuna told his supervisors. "I cannot tell a lie. I *was* fondling fourteen-year-old girls in 1968. But there was nothing wrong with it because I was only fourteen years old myself. I was a *student* at Victoria middle school, *not* a teacher at Lawrence."

The explanation drew laughter but no reprieve; for the next obvious question was, "What did you do to get someone so angry at you? Why is someone willing to go through all this trouble to dig out a police report on a man with the same name—"

"But that's not even my name," Tuna pointed out. "My name is Richard, not Rick—"

"Doesn't matter. Someone was angry enough to find it, copy it, and mail it. What other Tuna slanders are waiting in the wings to threaten the reputations of us all?"

Then, in one of science's most disgraceful episodes since the McCarthy era of the mid fifties, Wells, assisted by an opportunistic editor and Pacific Tech's chancellor for legal affairs, assembled an

ad hoc tribunal to charge Tuna with misappropria-
tion from none other than Leslie Wells. Barred from
submitting any words in his own defense, the verdict became crushingly predictable. Richard Tuna
earned the curious distinction of being the only au-
thor known to have been punished for *being* plagia-
rized; for it was a sad fact of life in the 1990s that
rumor and accusation added up to widespread perception, and that in the real world perception was
the only truth that counted.

Drummed forever out of paleontological research
and branded as a rogue by publisher's row, Tuna
was forced to watch from the sidelines as Wells
picked up a MacArthur Fellowship and research
grants that might otherwise have been his. But he
had simply dusted himself off, remarked to those
few true friends who stood by him that "the best
defense against having one of your ideas stolen is
having eight other ideas," and spent the next decade of his life founding the Valkyrie Rocket and
Verne Launcher programs with Jim Powell. As it
turned out, it was the Verne Launcher, a system of
Florida-based cannons, that finally made the orbiting of space hardware "dirt cheap," and made the
Valkyries feasible.

Meanwhile, Arthur C. Clarke, who had known
Tuna when he first published the *Jurassic Park* sau-
rian-cloning recipe, and who could see beyond accusation and rumor, found it necessary to add a
fourth step to his often quoted three stages that any
new and revolutionary idea must pass: One—
you're crazy. Two—you *may* be right, but so what.
Three—I said it was a good idea all along. Four—I
thought of it first!

For a time Tuna could enjoy the protection of men like Clarke and Powell; and as long as he remained in the field of rocketry and under their wings, Wells could harm him no further. But slowly and surely she drew her plans against him, awaiting the day when Clarke and Powell would be gone, when even the field of rocketry would not be far enough away for Tuna to hide. He would have been as helpless as Nikola Tesla against Thomas Edison—and sooner or later he should have been, if not for Wells's insatiable appetite for headlines and glory.

By the spring of 1995 it was becoming clear that if Wells were going to keep the funding rolling in, she had to produce a newsworthy result suggesting that extinct species would not remain so forever. The age of *People* magazine and "A Current Affair" science was rolling over her—which meant she had to make a sensational announcement, and sooner rather than later. Spielberg's film was already two years old, the public was beginning to forget, and she could already feel symptoms of the dreaded Morton Downey, Jr. fade. Yes, she had to produce results soon; but Tuna's projected timetable for success, about thirty years from 1982, was beginning to look real to her—too real. The best computers and scanners in the world were not fast enough to piece together the genetic code of a fly, much less a whole dinosaur. Even a bacterium was beyond Leslie Wells's means.

But she had to prove that something from the past could be brought back. Had to. Even if this meant shooting at a smaller target.

"We're beginning to look at different kinds of viruses in saurian blood," she announced. "The smallest ones can be made to replicate quite easily, simply by inserting the naked DNA into a host cell, which then produces complete viral particles."

These were the words that brought Tuna storming out of seclusion and into the halls of Pacific Tech.

"Madness!" he said, confronting Wells in her office, where she had retreated and unsuccessfully barred her door. "Can't clone a saurian? Why not try saurian chicken pox? Just what the world needs!"

"Don't go alarmist on me!" Wells retorted. "What's a little chicken pox?"

"Ask the Aztecs and the Sioux. That little herpes virus was just a minor annoyance in Europe; but over here, where no human had been exposed to it for thousands of years, it proved far more deadly than European cannons. This isn't a harmless endeavor, like cloning dinosaurs. There will never be cause to worry about *Tyrannosaurus rex* getting out and terrifying people. If the saurians hadn't become extinct by the time we evolved, they'd now be in as much trouble as the whales and the wolves and the mountain gorillas. But there's just no predicting what an undead germ may do when you disturb its sleep. What was a minor case of chicken pox to the dinosaurs might be lethal today."

"Tuna, you're either a liar or a fool. My labs are designed to contain pathogens, and it's a fact of nature that most viruses are totally harmless. The odds of a Mesozoic virus being dangerous *and* breaking out of my lab are as small as your odds of walking into a Las Vegas casino, pulling the lever

on a slot machine, and hitting the progressive jackpot on the first try."

"People do that all the time," said Tuna, and by
then a couple of security guards had arrived to
usher him forcefully out of Leslie Wells's office. No
one took him seriously, especially at Pacific Tech.
They dismissed his concerns as "jealousy and sour
grapes," and in the autumn of 1995, as uncountable
birds migrated south through California, Leslie
Wells hit the jackpot.

The Wells strain, as it came to be called, became
the final proof of John Horner's and Robert Bakker's
theory about at least one branch of the saurian lineage still surviving in the branches; but not even
Horner and Bakker could draw much consolation
from the proof. And it came to pass that what must
have been a minor microbe in Mesozoic times was
lethal to the dinosaurs' closest living relatives. Although a vaccine was found quickly, man's ultimate misfortune was that the Wells strain was not
a human disease in which all the potentially infected could be summoned by the media to local
schools and hospitals for inoculation. It was impossible to find and inject, one at a time, hundreds of
millions of birds.

With such grace did 1996 become the fulfillment
of Rachel Carson's predictions in *Silent Spring*.
Throughout the United States and Europe, no car-
dinals or robins sang, and no geese flew north. As
far away as China and Chile, there was nothing to
stop the proliferation of root-eating grubs. The
Wells strain had done its work with all-embracing
thoroughness. By August it was clear that Africa,
Asia, and the United States were faced with over-

whelming plagues of locusts and scarab beetles, and a consequent failure of crops. The only defense against famine and anarchy was letting insecticides play the role of the now-extinct birds, but this proved barely as effective as the then-popular medical strategy of substituting chemotherapy for a cancer plagued immune system. Poisoning the insect swarms without also killing the plants, and the people who ate the plants, became an intractable problem.

For a time it was hoped that bats would increase in numbers and substitute for the birds. But they were, as a rule, nocturnal creatures that preyed upon moths. They had no inclination to attack locusts and other day flyers. One did not realize how large a role birds played in the delicate balancing act between nature and civilization until one saw CNN footage of the living black cloud that had blotted out the Sun and settled on the wheat fields of Kansas and Zaire.

Wheat, corn, and potatoes were the first to go. More than a third of the world's harvest disappeared. Then the meat and dairy markets disintegrated as a rising tide of grubs undermined grasses and clover. Even among the insects there were casualties. With the death of clover there was little chance for the bees to harvest enough honey for the winter, meaning that even if the assaults on plants could be stopped, there would be fewer pollinators left to sustain them.

With the human species spreading from pole to pole, food intake was already stretching production to the limit when the poultry supply crashed. Only two years earlier, when North Atlantic fishing fleets had discovered that they were drawing no cod into their nets, some of the older, more observant fishermen had lamented, "We've finally killed the goose that lays the golden egg; we've caught them all."

By the time the Plague Years began, there was no latitudinal freedom between prosperity and famine, no country on Earth that could safely sustain itself on even half its normal harvest. And in most places it quickly got down to less than half. The insects made a clean sweep of equatorial Asia, chewing most of India and Thailand down to bare earth and clay. The hostilities between India and Pakistan escalated into a horrible nuclear spasm that reached into Turkey and Bosnia before dying. Almost simultaneously, Ho Chi Minh City, Shanghai, and Seoul ceased to be. Australia and New Zealand had halted all imports, and had thus managed to stave off contamination by the Wells strain; but Sydney and Wellington were on the verge of war with Beijing when the Americans announced that they might soon be able to clone whole armies of Wells-resistant birds.

Desperate times had brought Richard Tuna back to the field of paleobiology, whether or not he wanted to be part of it. He and Powell had recently modified "a piece of equipment," originally designed to take aim on Saddam Hussein and carbonize him from orbit, into a prototype Valkyrie rocket engine. Joined now by Gerard Case and a paleogeneticist named Mary Schweitzer, they turned the engine inside out, and in so doing created a microscope the like of which no one had ever seen before, one which suddenly enabled them to scan at will any portion of an extinct DNA molecule as quickly and easily as one would scan a laser disc and as often as one wished.

With unlimited billions in funding, the mass resurrection of birds began, made possible by museum displays of stuffed specimens, whose DNA was edited to fight the Wells strain. Rookery building became the top priority of every surviving government. But resurrection was a slow process whose first and most complicated step required the mass production of unfertilized and re-engineered reptilian eggs, for there were simply not enough birds. Without the egg, there could be no chicken. As a result, the resurrection did not occur in time to prevent the fishing of the South China Sea into a biological desert or to save Australia from invasion.

One outcome of the Plague Years was that the technology for cloning lost species, spurred by dire need, came into existence nearly two decades before it should have. As the world's economy began to recover, New Zealand's giant moas and eagles, and South America's overgrown roadrunners, with beaks powerful enough to crush a child's skull, began to redefine the word "extinct." In Washington, D. C., piling live dodo birds on the steps of the Capitol became the political joke craze of the century, amid suggestions that when the first velociraptors really did become available, rather than try to create a "Jurassic Park," the proper use of them would be to follow John Carpenter's lead in *Escape from New York*.

"Wall in Washington," said a prominent late night talk show host, "and keep all the senators and congressmen, judges and lawyers inside. Then set up TV cameras all over the city, charging forty dollars a pop on Pay-Per-View, with commentary provided by Howard Stern and Wildcat Bob as we let the raptors in."

The jokes were not far off the mark. Even shock-jock Howard Stern had not anticipated how low human nature could sink when money was involved. Replicas of the Roman Colosseum were built in Las Vegas and Atlantic City, and no expense was spared in staging the world's most exotic cock fights. Entire fortunes were bet on whether or not the triceratops really could win out against the allosaurus.

And even stranger developments were to arise from the "talking" that had brought humanity such power over life and death. If an identical twin of the last allosaurus could be brought to life after tens of millions of years from fragmented and degraded DNA, then bringing back the twin of a man who had been dead for mere centuries had to be fifty thousand times easier.

The last decades of Earth saw the spread of virtual-reality addiction and the emergence of a class of people who called themselves Zoners. As a rule, they accepted dead end jobs, lived in sparsely furnished apartments or in their parents' basements, and spent all their nonworking hours "plugged in" to the best equipment their earnings could buy. The Zoners were almost exclusively men in their twenties. They showed no interest in either wives or children and, if civilization had lasted, would surely have marched quietly toward extinction. It seemed to some observers to be a lonely, pointless life; but the Zoners did not drag race drunkenly on Saturday nights, rob, or commit murder anywhere except in their private VR worlds, and it could even be argued that by not breeding, they were increasing, infinitesimally, the average intelligence level in the human gene pool.

Still, more than a third of Earth's population succumbed to this super couch–potato existence. The most popular programs, when the end came, were the simulated lives of real people—which meant that there actually lived a Howard Stern and a Stephen Jay Gould, a Harrison Ford and a Harlan Ellison who never guessed that their lives were just somebody else's VR program.

About the time the first virtual lives became available, not very long after the two thousandth birthday of a very interesting man from Nazareth, the Resurrectionist movement began in Egypt. In the immediate aftermath of the Plague Years, an obscure sect began spreading out of Thebes. Anointing themselves as the Lords of the Last Days, they revived the religion of the ancient Egyptians, quickly won over wealthy New Age converts, and placed at the center of their lives the warrior-messiah Tuthmosis III. From fewer than a dozen mummified cells they were able to reconstruct the entire genetic blueprint of the man many believed to be the pharaoh who had invaded the Mount of Megiddo and looked Moses in the eye.

Soon afterward, a Resurrectionist priestess birthed him into the twenty-first century, thereby turning an ancient religious belief into what gave all the appearance of being prophecy. From that moment, even the most pragmatic minds were forced to wonder if the old obsession with preserving pharaoh's body to insure his resurrection had been based not upon superstition but upon actual foreknowledge that cloning technology would one day exist.

At the age of nine, the child-king was anointed God-king, and took the throne at Karnak. By this time, the technology that had permitted an identical twin of pharaoh to rule thirty-seven centuries after his death had become widely available, and the Resurrectionists had begun dividing into opposing factions; and as something much like the Egyptian concept of Judgment Day approached from the direction of Sagittarius, it did indeed appear that the dead walked the Earth, and that the prophets had returned.

Only the followers of Islam resisted. They viewed virtual people in general, and cloned prophets in particular, as abominations against God; but it was their rejection of zoning technology that made all the difference in the world for them. The Koran forbade alcohol and recreational drugs, and virtual reality came to be regarded as just another recreational drug. Consequently, as a third of the rest of humanity became lost in virtual worlds, the number of Islamic scholars at Port Chaffee, at the Ceres colony, and aboard the Valkyries grew proportionally higher.

"The meek have finally inherited the Earth," they were often heard to say. "The rest have gone to space."

* * *

The Cat swung around Saturn, whiskers extended into a dry, surprisingly narrow band of pebbles, ice, and soot. The research station deep in Saturn's Rings had a company name and a number, but no one ever used them. Everyone simply called it the Cat, because its long wire whiskers reached out into the electrostatic field of the Rings and by induction drew enough electrical current to run the small habitat. The station itself, only sixty meters long, was composed of two oppositely rotating cylinders embedded in a large chunk of rock that had once belonged to the Rings.

It was here, one Saturday morning, that Jesus and Buddha listened to the death cry of Ceres, and then, along with most of the other fifty-three researchers and technicians of the Cat, drifted away to their small private quarters to absorb the shock of this latest blow.

Unlike the Cerans, most of the Cat's workers had not brought their families with them. Even if they had been surrounded by their families, it would have been small comfort against the fear that the Ceran fate, or something much like it, awaited them all. They now looked with a strange envy at those of their childless colleagues who had their wives or husbands with them to share the end that would surely come, and who did not have to live each day with the knowledge that their wives, husbands, children, and lovers were all gone. In their grief they did not consider that even the single members of the station had lost parents, siblings, and friends.

The Buddha had anticipated a fatal reprogramming such as that which had overtaken Ceres. So together with his Nazarene friend he had built a replica of an ancient TRS-80 computer, limited to only 4K of memory, and this was what they connected to the Cat's "ears," making doubly and triply sure that there was no line of access to any other computer.

The two men, both now pushing fifty, had never thought of themselves as Jesus and Buddha, even though their crèche father had openly discussed the history of the genetic materials from which they had been cloned. Buddha's tooth from the Temple in Sri Lanka, and a few surviving bone fragments from an ancient golden chest, had been enough to re-create the two individuals. That much was certain; but whether they were Buddha and Jesus could never be an absolute certainty. Good enough, but not guaranteed, because there was no way to check the chain of physical evidence across the centuries. Teeth and bones were not great rarities. No one could ever have been tried for murder on the hearsay basis of their authenticity. Faith still held its vague domain.

Justin and Joshua were the names they chose for themselves when the pressures of life on Earth grew too great and it became necessary for them to hide in the Rings of Saturn.

Although he had, over the years, embraced the role of doubting Saint Thomas and gravitated toward a robust agnosticism, Joshua had sometimes wondered if God's grace, assuming there was such a being to bestow it, could be attracted in something like the same way the Cat's whiskers drew power from the electrostatic sea of the Rings. What kind of

feelers did a human being have to put out, he wondered, to draw Yahweh's or Allah's grace? And how
would that grace, which he could not help but imagine as being a kind mercy, benefit a human being? As
near as he could tell, it might quiet the fear of personal death, or perhaps strengthen one's faith in the
human species' survival, if not an afterlife.

As they listened to the life of Ceres fade away,
Joshua almost gave himself up to the delusion and
reached out to the invisible king of the universe,
asking bitterly why he had forsaken humanity.
What crimes had been so terrible in God's eyes?
And why now, so long past the worst ages, when
humankind had begun to improve so consistently
in its behavior toward itself, toward the Earth, and
had begun to look outward not with conquest in its
heart but with renewed curiosity and a thirst for
knowledge? Why now fulfill the biblical prophecies
of destruction?

The people of Earth were by no means perfectly
reformed. They would never have become angels.
Joshua could admit that. After all, VR Zoners
were completely out of touch with reality. And
the Resurrectionists, who had recalled him and
Justin out of the genetic library of life, could not
be said to have been playing with full decks either, having ultimately rejected their idols because
they had put forward the idea that all faiths
might be correct about the reality they were attempting to grasp, that the "awful rowing toward
God" from the sinking *Titanic* of life revealed
more about the nature of human aspiration than it
did about any transcendent being; that perhaps
God would be the fruit of cosmic history, emerg-

ing only at its end, when all intelligent life had fulfilled itself. But then, what could anyone sane say about a religious group that cloned Einstein twenty or more times and forced their clones of Jesus and Buddha to flee the planet over a speculation about doctrine? Of course, he and Justin might just as easily have disappeared into the mass of secular humanity that was not Resurrectionist or Zoner, which did not care a whit what any kind of religionist or political dogmatist wanted to believe, and simply wanted to get on with chasing its mirage of a steadily improving daily life.

Recalling the Gospel according to Saint Luke, Joshua wondered if the aliens would now "let the broken victims go free," but he doubted it. The destruction of Ceres proved that they would let no one live, if they could help it.

Heresies flooded into his mind as if being churned out by a theological mill. One suggested a new meaning to the idea that "the kingdom of God lies within," that salvation for humankind had always been in looking toward the inward shore, away from the jealous stars, in cultivating its own garden, in not calling attention to itself.

And then the theological mill threw out his name—Joshua—and he was suddenly struck by the strangeness of giving it to a clone of Jesus, even if Jesus was in fact Latin for Joshua. Why not David, Solomon, Elijah, Elisha, Isaiah, or Jonah—the names of the Old Testament people that Jesus himself had called upon as having prefigured his life? Why Joshua, a warrior, the conqueror of Canaan?

He felt his stomach tighten and wondered

whether this realization might in fact be God's grace at work, subtly leading him to a knowledge of himself that he had long denied. The reality might be that the Second Coming of Christ was this very discovery within himself of the savior-warrior. If the historical function of religion was that of social engineering and moral leadership, then it might be his duty to supply that kind of protective response, even if he was Jesus without the benefit of God the Father and the Holy Ghost waiting in the wings. Maybe this was the nature of Providence for what was mostly an irreligious age.

He thought of his friend Justin, the expression of Buddha's DNA, and wondered if he was having similar thoughts. After all, they had both been forced to flee Earth for putting forward the same heresy. And both had come to view the brief but tortured march of civilization, from the time of Hammurabi to the present, as an attempt to define and justify moral codes and keep the fires of justice alive. The trick, then, was to hide judgment in the smoke of fear. All religions were essentially the same in their expressions of human kinship and longing for justice. Humankind had always tried to reform itself by invoking divine sanction for moral codes, so that people might behave out of fear if not faith. Having accomplished the trick, one might even win over men's souls, so long as one never let his followers see that their morality was merely fear, lest they become judges, and one be martyred at the hands of his frightened, judgmental followers.

Followers? Fifty-three of them? Joshua wanted to crumple that thought up and toss it away.

The Cat had turned out to be anything but a random sampling of humanity. It was a Lunarian facility, populated largely by scientists and writers. Agnostics all of them; and as agnostics they had come to know and accept Justin and Joshua for who they really were, even to seek in them the qualities of leadership that made their historical twins legend, even in the age of Armageddon. So it seemed that Joshua had followers, whether he wanted them or not. And so the need for ethical behavior remained, however one justified the ethics, whatever their pedigree, whether God decreed them or not—even if it turned out that God was opposed to them.

Now the last of humanity was faced with a massive alien lawlessness and needed to be saved, whether by divine intervention or through inner resources. Either one required leadership. The moral word must flourish again within human flesh, in order to save that flesh. Spirit must take hold of that flesh, or both would perish.

Slowly, half bewildered by his own thoughts, he got up, left his small cabin, and knocked on Justin's door across the narrow passageway.

"Come in," his friend's voice said through the small speaker.

Joshua brushed the touchplate with his fingers. The door slid open and he stepped inside.

Justin turned from his table, where he had been working on his pad, and smiled, looking less pudgy than usual. "You seem confused."

Joshua stood by the door and told him what he had been thinking.

Justin said, "I was thinking similarly, except that my thoughts were about the martyrdom of man. The crucifixion has happened again. What we most need now is a resurrection of humanity, of the very body of Christ, in Christian terms."

"And in Buddhist terms?" Joshua asked.

"All of humanity, as far as we know, may be gathered up here in the Cat. That may be the central fact of the rest of our lives. We must inquire on this basis what actions will be open to us. If we see what can be done, we must ask if it should be done."

Joshua grimaced. "But how far do you carry the Buddhist principle of tolerance for everyone? The Intruders are outside its circle, are they not?"

"We don't know who or what they are or how we might have offended them, do we?"

"Are you serious?" Joshua asked. "Buddhism and Christianity are for humankind, not for aliens. It doesn't much matter how we offended them, if we did. All that matters is that we must decide what to do now."

"I suspect," Justin said, "that you and I already know what must be done."

"What do you have in mind?"

"The same as you—we must leave. And we both know that there are ways to do it. But will the others agree with us?"

"How can they not?" Joshua laughed, and felt desperation in the effort. "Aren't we going to offer salvation?" He was silent for a moment. "There are a number of ways we can leave. I think we should take the least obvious one."

"The road least traveled?" Justin asked.

"Never traveled is better," Joshua said. "We've got to find an even better hiding place than these rings, hunker down, and increase our numbers." He recalled Moses's forty years of wandering in the

desert after the Exodus from Egypt, and realized
that the ancient leader had not done so merely to
permit the generations that had known sin to be
consumed but to raise an army of young men that
would cross the Jordan under Joshua's leadership
and conquer Canaan, aided of course by a super-
weapon, the Ark of the Covenant. It was a wonderful story, much simplified in the Bible. The
reality of the conquest was long and complex, and
the result much more ambiguous than the decisive
victory claimed by the tellers of the tale.

"Are you thinking we might take the station
down into Saturn?" Buddha asked.

"No," Joshua replied. "We've got to get completely away from Sunspace, and we've got to leave
quietly. I've spoken with Bill and the Luftig boys.
There seem to be places beyond Oort, between one
and three light-months out. If we can get that far,
there will be enough resources for our continued
survival, and we will be undetectable."

"How long to get there?"

"A few decades at best. And we've got to start
soon, before we're caught up in the final death
sweep."

"Are we kidding ourselves?" Justin asked. "Can
we really escape? Or are we merely imagining our
salvation, believing whatever we wish to be true, as
have all the oppressed peoples of the past?"

Joshua looked at his friend and imagined himself
as Moses, who would never cross the Jordan because his followers had turned judgmental and
doubted the Lord. "No, my friend, it *will* be done
because it *can* be done."

"I think so, too," Justin said. And for a moment,

Joshua's theological mill ground to a halt. This was not quite the Exodus from Egypt, although something like pharaoh was in pursuit; neither was it the wandering in the desert or the time to conquer Canaan. And he was not quite Jesus or Joshua, although he had certainly been resurrected, after a fashion. He could be Joshua, but he would have to play Moses first and part the Red Sea. All the biblical prophecies for the end of the world had been fulfilled, but the Earth had not been purged in order to be re-created, transformed, or renewed. Obviously, the historical and personal typology, prefiguring the future from the vantage point of the Old and New Testaments, was not working. Of course, it had never worked, except by bits and pieces, as a self-fulfilling vision. Jesus had never harkened back to Joshua the warrior. And yet, and yet . . .

"What is it, my friend?" Justin asked.

"I think I'm losing my mind."

"The next best thing to do, under the circumstances . . ." Justin said. "Of course, the best line of action is always to rend the familiar way, to make ready an unfamiliar way."

"And yet . . . and yet . . ." Joshua repeated to himself, realizing that Jesus had been a bringer of human possibilities, challenging the reptilian vindictiveness of the Romans and their power brokers with the Kingdom of God that lay somewhere within the potential of human evolutionary programs. If the human "soul" was in fact nothing more than an electronic program run through a piece of computer hardware called the brain, then Jesus had died attempting to enter a new reform software into his followers. Many had been moved to change their lives, but how permanent had it been? Basic structures had not been affected, because no one had known any bioengineering in the ancient world; but Jesus had pointed the way out of the instinctive labyrinth of evolution's slaughterhouse. His had been a strategy without reliable means, without tactics, offering counsels of perfection and discipline that worked occasionally in saints, but failed too easily in most people. . . .

And now the Romans had come again, crucifying all of humanity, making a bitter mockery of love and benevolence.

"How will we leave?" Justin asked.

"By playing a game of celestial billiards," Joshua said, coming out of himself, feeling a new strength as he saw what would have to be done to save his fellow survivors. Was this, then, grace for the irreligious? A merciful God might wish to give him strength even if he had no faith. Right action was right action, however it was sanctioned, even if it was all power of suggestion, and Jesus being his exact twin had nothing to do with it.

"We'll call a meeting," he said, "and make everyone understand what we're up against. We have to be as one now."

Justin nodded, and they looked at each other as if seeing themselves for the first time.

Bill and the Luftig boys were cabling animated maps of the light-years surrounding Sunspace onto everyone else's pads. They were—all fifty-five men and women—gathered in the Belly of the Cat, which was what they called the mess hall.

"I agree with our two theologian friends," Bill announced. "We simply won't survive if we remain in Sunspace, because sooner or later the Intruders are bound to find us, if they look closely enough."

"Yeah!" said a young technician named Carlos, laughing. "Where do you have in mind for us to go?"

Joshua cringed inwardly at the young man's lack of imagination, and saw that it would require trumpets at the walls of Jericho to crack the masonry around such minds. He hoped that there weren't too many like him in the hall, because any decision on a course of action would have to be as close to unanimous as possible. A simple majority would produce too many bad feelings—divisions that the last of humanity could ill afford.

The pads showed nearly a hundred pancake-shaped objects scattered across the cubic parsec of space between the Sun and Alpha Centauri. During the dawn of interstellar flight, it had become necessary to chart every one of the nearby "pancakes," for they had turned out to be the most abundant large structures in the galaxy, which made them the reefs and shoals of the twenty-first century . . . with the added complication that these reefs and shoals were constantly moving.

Every screen closed in on a single pancake whose central dark star was a ball of roiling gas more massive than Jupiter and all the planets combined, but not massive enough to burn brightly, like the sun. The star was invisible against the scale of its electron-charged ring system—which was even more beautiful and more intricate than the Saturnian system and wider than the orbit of Jupiter. Gaps in the rings marked the paths of minor, planetlike objects, comparable in size to Miranda and Triton.

"You plan to bring us to one of those?" asked Carlos.

"There's a suitable one a little more than three light weeks out," Joshua explained. "It has everything we'll ever need to live."

"You want us to hide within rings? But we're already doing that," the young man protested. "What's the difference?"

"It will be much harder to find us *between* the stars, even if they suspect that's where we've gone. And we're not going into the rings. We're going down to the star itself."

"Impossible!"

"*Not* impossible," said a young engineer named Frank. "We've worked it out. With fusion ramjets we can orbit indefinitely in the star's atmosphere, breaking not a single natural law. And because this particular star sustains low-level fusion deep within its core, our own neutrino glow will be masked from the moment we turn the jets on."

Carlos whistled, and Joshua could almost read his thoughts. This was just too fantastic, the young man was saying to himself. A brown dwarf. Who would have believed such an adventure? Not even the aliens, perhaps; and that was the whole point. It was a galactic haystack out there. Where better to hide and begin stockpiling the building blocks of a new civilization? Brown dwarfs were a thousand times more populous than stars like the Sun, so plentiful as to be the likely identity of the so-called "dark matter" that bound the galaxies in gravitational clusters and would eventually pull the whole universe into something akin to a replay of the Big Bang.

"A brown dwarf," Carlos said aloud. "Who would have believed it?"

"And how soon can we get there?" demanded another voice.

"Maybe in a few decades," said Justin, "if we can get past a hundred kilometers a second after we leave Saturn's orbit. The exact numbers are not clear yet."

Frank lifted a hand. "What I propose is that we lasso one of the shepherd moons," the engineer said, "using the Cat's whiskers. Since the shepherd's mass is much greater than ours, it will really, in effect, lasso *us*. We'll have to batten down for some impressive gee forces and make sure our Bardo shield is ready for the one or two rocks we're likely to slam through—but I think we can set up a terrific slingshot effect."

"How high a velocity will that give us?" Carlos asked.

"Not high enough. After we're out of the rings, we must pick up an added slingshot effect from Saturn itself. Now, what we're proposing is a very complicated game of billiards, hopefully without hitting any big balls. The plan is to aim just outside the atmosphere, to come as close as we can to Saturn without slinging ourselves into the cloud tops. If we can manage this, then the planet will give us a nice gravitational kickoff."

"And how high a velocity will *that* produce?"

"Still not quite enough," Frank replied. "We'll have to load on some extra mass before we start, and when we're a few light-hours out, fire it away like icy bullets, using magnetic rail guns to give us that extra little kick, and also to make minor course corrections."

"Why risk smashing into Saturn or risk having the whiskers break while we're slinging around the shepherd?" asked an elderly woman. "Why not just use the rail gun to leave orbit?"

"Because rail guns are less efficient than slings," said the engineer. "We'd need to stockpile a mountain of mass bigger than the Cat itself. And we're probably alive today only because we're too small to be noticed. I'd rather not do anything to alter that condition."

"Besides," Joshua said, "we're probably the only basket of human eggs left. That's our misfortune and our responsibility. If we can just stay small and inconspicuous long enough, that may become the aliens' misfortune."

"Power consumption is going to be very tight," Justin added. "For at least the first year of our outbound voyage we're going to be depending on batteries. According to our chief engineer, most of our battery supply should be of the throwaway kind. As they die, we'll simply grind them down to dust, scavenge whatever substances are useful to us, and shoot the rest away on rail guns for whatever extra velocity that will give us. There will be one very special bank of batteries designed for recharging by the slow decay of uranium salts; but we dare not power up even with those lowest level nukes until we are far enough away not to be outshining the galactic background radiation. We can't afford to leak any unnatural neutrino glow."

"At the brown dwarf," Father John McQuitty

192 CHARLES PELLEGRINO AND GEORGE ZEBROWSKI

said, "what kind of life can we expect to have there?"

"No worse than right here," Joshua answered, looking directly at the old Biotimer.

"Yes, but here we still believe that one day we might go home, walk under an open sky. *Here* was never supposed to be forever."

"Who said that? I didn't say that. Tactics will dictate that we can never go back to living on a planet. Ever again. We must build a new civilization in the dwarf star—unlike anything our kind has known."

"Is it worth it?" MacQuitty asked wearily.

"You mean, why not just stay here and die?" Justin asked.

"Better to die here than in that outer horror," MacQuitty answered, sitting up straighter in his chair. "Be honest—what are the chances of accomplishing anything out there, or of ever reaching the brown dwarf? And even if we succeed, what kind of life awaits us? To live as clever rats?"

"Whatever chances we'll have we'll make for ourselves," Justin said calmly. "But first we have to escape, to get out of harm's way. Think of it one step at a time."

"We have to make good," Joshua added, trying to sound strong and convincing, "for all the dead. If we can save ourselves, that will be saving all of humanity."

As he spoke Joshua noticed that the older man was weeping. His wife was comforting him, but it didn't seem to do any good. And Joshua realized that there were levels of understanding that were reached by the oppressed and sinned against, clarities born of atrocity, that seemed insane when considered in peaceful times. Such were the clarities being born in him now, and he knew that he had to communicate them to each and every inhabitant of the Cat.

Flee.

Survive.

Rebuild.

Grow.

Come back.

Avenge.

18

In the Valley of Aton

CRACK!

Anjin noted the time on his pad and called out, "Skipper, they've just blasted our aft telescope and most of our ramjets—but it's as we hoped: they had to open a window through the plasma before they fired, and I think I got a clear picture of their ship."

The blip had continued to maintain a steady distance of twelve thousand kilometers, following in the magnetic slipstream of Sargenti-Peterson. The refugees knew that sooner or later the shooting would begin—and sooner rather than later. They half expected some new, non-Einsteinian physics to overtake them—faster-than-light weapons or the means for the enemy to transport aboard through something akin to subspace and warp drive. The expectation conjured up nightmare visions of the walls suddenly glowing white hot and exploding away from the very center of the ship-comet.

But nothing happened.

When at last the Intruders opened fire, they had first parted the plasma with magnetic fields, opening a valley in the Sun twelve thousand kilometers long—and it was through this opening that Anjin got his first telescopic view of the stalker.

The image was fuzzy and needed a great deal of enhancement; but it yielded a wealth of detail. The vessel's surface seemed to reflect most if not all of the Sun's energy, which was the antithesis of Sargenti-Peterson's solution, whereby the energy was met head-on and converted to matter. The stalker was smaller than Sargenti-Peterson and gave the appearance of a highly reflective manta ray. Anjin wondered about the wings. At five hundred kilometers per second, flying through a tunnel of vacuum in a sea of plasma, wings made absolutely no sense. He guessed that they were somehow involved in generating magnetic fields, or in temperature regulation, or both. And it occurred to him that because of their totally reflective surface, he could obtain a very sharp image and perhaps solve the mystery of the wings with ordinary radar.

He had barely ordered the proper machinery into place when the alien ship began firing through the window in the plasma, and he was filled with a paradoxical sense of relief as he realized that the little reflective spheres racing toward him were not warping or transporting through space, but merely racing. This meant that no matter how great a technological lead the Intruder civilization had over his own, both sides were made equal by the same universal speed limit and had to play by the same unbreakable laws, on the same chessboard discovered by Albert Einstein.

The plasma tunnel was closed now. The first attempted shelling of Sargenti-Peterson had been held off by a cluster of absorbic bombs racing in the opposite direction. Tam guessed that the Intruders must have smugly expected to chip away with impunity at the comet's stern, then punch through to the core by throwing just one stream of antimatter containers down the long, narrow corridor. She grinned, wishing she could have known what went through their minds as stores of precious antihydrogen detonated halfway to their target; and she recalled with a small measure of pride one of her more hair-raising theories about what would happen when an absorbic bomb met an antimatter bomb and they detonated side by side. It had seemed unlikely from the start, but if that particular speculation had turned out to be true, the antihydrogen, upon converting from supercooled "white cake" to energy, would have been reassembled instantaneously in the heart of the absorbic bomb as supercooled antihydrogen . . . until it struck the Intruder ship head-on and briefly created a second sun within the Sun.

But judging from all the available evidence, the antimatter had been resurrected as ordinary matter. It did not kill the bastards, Tam told herself, but it sure as hell gave them something to think about.

She took a deep breath and waited for the plasma window to reopen. Although shrapnel from the first attack had left her ship half blind, she hoped Anjin still had enough scopes left to see the next attack coming.

A happy thought.

As prime minister, Tam had learned and mastered all the political games, including how to evaluate an adversary, read his intentions—how to manipulate him with kindness or, when necessary, neutralize him with skilled, subtle orchestration of economic sanctions and squads of journalists whose questions and stories would restrict him in what he could say or do—and here she was: stuck in a goddamned ceramic box under four kilometers of frozen rock, fighting an antimatter war inside the Sun, looking for subtleties in the opaque mind of an alien enemy.

Tam's stalkers had much to think about. The comet's jetting activity had *looked* natural enough at first, but had put it on a course that was suspiciously improbable. Nevertheless, once it was located, and a tunnel opened through the plasma, and a clear shot taken, its inhabitants should have been easy, defenseless prey. But the projectiles which had intercepted the antimatter containers, detonating them and absorbing all their energy, did not fit into the original game plan. Now the comet was sweeping their ship with a bath of microwave radiation, pinging it with radar.

The stalkers absorbed all this information and were ready to use it against their prey—instantly.

From the use of radar the stalkers concluded that the first wave of attack had blinded the fleeing ship in some way, and the refugees were now relying on a backup system. Perhaps there was other damage as well. Their antimatter antidote, while extremely clever, was obviously part of their cooling system. In highest probability, they did not have many absorbic bombs to spare, and were therefore on the short side of a war of attrition. Cleverness would not forever overcome short supplies.

In a cavity between the wings, something silvery and crablike moved swiftly and purposefully. The plasma sea parted, and a second, larger wave of antimatter bombs accelerated down the tunnel.

The radar improved Anjin's resolution enormously.

Wings.

The stalker definitely had wings. Something small and snakelike suddenly emerged through the dorsal surface. Its head, too, displayed wings, like the flaps in the hood of a cobra—to what purpose, Anjin could not venture a guess.

"This is amazing," he said.

"You don't seem frightened," said Tam.

He chuckled to himself. "That, too, but mostly I'm fascinated. Think—if any antimatter gets through to us, at least it will be interesting . . . for all of two milliseconds."

And then he saw the reflective orbs.

"High speed cluster dead astern," he announced. "A hundred and twenty torpedoes in the window! Impact in about two minutes!"

"Fire one hundred and thirty," Tam ordered.

"Firing one-thirty." Anjin's radar showed the interceptors accelerating aft, changing course within the tunnel, each taking aim at a specific torpedo.

Ten absorbic bombs lagged behind, in accordance with Anjin's anticipation that there might be one or two duds among the interceptors. The stragglers readied to form a defensive wall that would take aim and detonate against anything that got past the duds.

The exchange was similar, superficially, to submarine warfare during the Plague Years. Everything seemed to be taking place with excruciating slowness, and if anyone wavered and succumbed to fear, there would be plenty of time for a long, long scream. But here, Tam realized, the similarities ended. Both ships relied on magnetic fields to shunt plasma away from themselves; and to judge from the behavior of the stalkers, Tam guessed that no matter how many centuries of technological advance were applied to the problem, the ability to guide and project magnetic fields would always require equipment no smaller and no less cumbersome than the alien ship's wings. As a consequence, neither side possessed torpedoes with magnetic shunts and projectors of their own, so the only way to get at each other was to fire down a long valley carved through the plasma.

This left little room for the sorts of dive plane and rudder maneuvers that had made history in the South China and Tasman seas. Only the torpedoes and interceptors possessed maneuverability. If the plasma-free corridor moved, the projectiles would have to move with it or detonate prematurely. And if the enemy was to be engaged without directly ramming him, a corridor must always be maintained between the two ships. For these reasons, the battle within the Sun was more akin to a battle between antimissile-equipped silos than between submarines.

All well and good, Tam told herself, realizing that she was distracting herself with details. No, not distracting, she corrected herself, but engaging herself with the task at hand, with subtleties that were part of this new environment in which she had to survive—in which they all had to survive by grasping critical possibilities and making them into weapons.

There was some small satisfaction in that thought, even if it might be her last.

"Okay, reading sixty-seven antimatter-absorbic bursts thirty-six hundred kilometers aft," Anjin said.

Tam's eyes locked on Anjin's pad and saw three torpedoes coming through the absorbic wall.

"My God," said Second Officer Skurla. "Only sixty-seven bursts? Does that mean more than fifty got through, with only ten of ours left to stop them?"

"No," said Tam. "We hit them head-on. All but three. They're throwing decoys at us. Getting us to waste our absorbics."

"That could be a mistake for them," Anjin said. "Do you know what happens when an absorbic bomb detonates without an accompanying nuclear explosion? I'll wager they've never seen anything like this before!"

A small voice in the left side of Tam's brain began reciting conversion formulae, and her right brain began running motion pictures of an absorbic bomb exploding near her home town on Earth. For twenty kilometers in every direction, she pictured the inverse of a nuclear explosion . . . a dark wing instead of a burst of light cutting across the sky as the temperature plunged to absolute zero and the air crystallized instantly . . . houses, trees, cars, and the people inside frozen to the rigidity of a child's sand castle, and about to be scattered just as easily . . . a massive implosion instead of an explosion as air from the surrounding countryside rushed in to fill the vacuum . . .

The radar now showed 120 absorbic bursts, fifty-three of them without accompanying antimatter-matter detonations. What the radar did not show, could not show, was the briefly spreading darkness thirty-six hundred kilometers aft. The walls of the valley bent and bulged there, caught in an expanding subzero storm that was soon swallowed by the chromosphere, as a raindrop is swallowed by an ocean.

Anjin's equipment did not register the darkness and the plunging temperatures, but it did show the walls buckling. Tam guessed what had almost occurred and seized on an idea. "Anjin, prepare six hundred absorbics to fire."

"But that's almost all we can spare," objected Second Officer Skurla.

"Then we'll have to build replacements more quickly."

"Six hundred—" Susan Skurla pounded her fist on the bulkhead. "There'll be barely enough left to keep us cool, much less to continue the battle!"

"We either win the next round or all the cooling equipment you can imagine won't make any difference. Six hundred absorbics, Anjin. Do it!"

"Six hundred, aye." Anjin sent the orders through his pad, then watched the three incoming breakthroughs close with his ten outgoing stragglers. The odds were that at least one and possibly two of the breakthroughs were decoys and that none of the stragglers were duds. There was a chance to take the offensive by sending only half his tiny fleet after the breakthroughs, and then hurling the remaining five after the alien ship.

But Tam and Anjin were taking no chances and

ordered all ten to stay on collision course with the enemy torpedoes. The field buckled again, and the next moments were for Anjin a mix of confusion and calm resignation. There was nothing on his pad that specifically signaled alarm; there was only his intuitive realization that the intercept had not gone exactly as planned, and that something was coming in fast.

Looking over his shoulder, Tam saw a subtle trail of secondary radiation so faint that her conscious mind did not take notice until well after her swift subconscious had connected the dots and sent up a warning. Realization and adrenaline struck at the same instant.

Streams of muons had emerged from the anti-matter-matter-absorbic storm. After traveling only a few microseconds, they decayed into positrons and electrons—which reached Sargenti-Peterson at near-light speed, but were shunted aside by the comet's magnetic field and produced nothing more alarming than an aurora of gamma rays. They were then deposited as heat in the comet's surface and were easily cooled by absorbic bombs.

The real danger, barely perceptible to human eyes, lay in a more sluggish product of the storm. One tiny stream of antihydrogen, supercooled and unreacted, was jetting down the tunnel toward them.

"We're going to be hit," Anjin said.

"I know it," Tam said more calmly than she felt. "Six hundred absorbics away—now!"

"Fire six hundred!" Anjin shouted.

The central stern shuddered as the charges ejected and the comet accelerated ever so slightly from the recoil. At that exact instant, the unspent antihydrogen, hardly more massive than a green pea and cutting through space at eighty-three klicks per second, struck a glancing blow aft of midships on the starboard side. It embedded in forty centimeters of rock and exploded one ten-millionth of a second later.

The force of the explosion hurled Anjin, Tam, and Skurla against the starboard wall of the control room. Tam felt a wet snap in her already broken arm and knew that she had just fractured it again. As she pushed the pain out of her mind, the first thing she noticed were shards from broken pads rising into the air, needlelike and dangerous if inhaled.

Immediately, she began breathing through the makeshift air filter of clenched teeth. The next thing she noticed was Susan floating about two meters away, unconscious and drifting toward a cloud of needles. Tam removed her own shirt and tied it around the Second Officer's head while keeping a keen eye on Anjin, whose first action had been to find a still-working pad and try to assess the damage.

The explosion had occurred on the surface, and a small voice in Anjin's head congratulated him for anticipating a direct hit, and for programming his absorbic bombs, arrayed below the surface, to do nothing if this should happen. Against the relatively steady influx of solar radiation, energy absorption was a slow, stately process. But against the sudden surge of an antimatter detonation, absorbics always overcompensated and overwhelmed. Had Anjin's shell of absorbics responded, the result would have been a horrible surge in which all the energy being released inside the comet converted suddenly to matter. The air in the control room would have flowed liquid, then crystallized, and Anjin's eyelashes would now be as brittle as glass.

Instead, his absorbic shell had merely stood by as a slug of antihydrogen turned one cubic kilometer of rock into plasma. The shock front hammered two klicks deeper, smashing through rock and leaving rubble in its wake, shredding pipes and passageways and storage tanks as it went, weakening, pushing the ship hard to port until the last of its force was dissipated against an impenetrable mantle of Bardo cones.

Anjin and Tam had built the shield from robotic cones developed by Lex Bardo, the stunt pilot–engineer who had been mourned by millions when the first Valkyrie exploded en route to the nearest star. Bardo's system of pressure-equalizing cones was able to respond instantly to almost any situation. After he brought *Nautilus* out of Mirandan orbit, penetrated the jet streams of Uranus's equator, and probed an ocean more than a thousand kilometers deep, he became as loved as Charles Lindbergh. If the cones could survive *those* extreme pressures, Anjin had concluded, then perhaps they could provide added protection against antimatter bombs.

During the previous two weeks, Anjin had been calling more and more robots away from the task of absorbic bomb production, threatening to exhaust the ship-comet's resources in his effort to build a secondary, deep-interior coat of Bardo armor. In theory, having more than three kilometers of rock overhead was armor enough; but in practice, if not for the cones, the force of the explosion would have reached and spent itself upon the ship's crew. Instead, it was both reflected whence it came and dissipated laterally throughout the entire defensive barrier. Inertia had sent all the contents of Sargenti-Peterson crashing to starboard, and Bardo reflection had dislodged house-sized boulders from the blast zone, enlarging the crater and producing a loss of building materials that would be missed; but the ship was otherwise intact, and might remain so if it survived the third wave of attack.

The stalker flew through the immediate aftermath of two absorbic storms, finding potential hazards in the turbulence and realizing that the vessel might be overwhelmed by a sufficiently large number of absorbic bursts without accompanying antimatter detonations. In such instances a pursuit ship was always at a disadvantage. Reconstructing events of the second attack wave, and trying to project them into strategies for the third, it became immediately apparent that using decoys was a failed tactic. So the Intruders dispatched a cluster of twenty antimatter torpedoes.

Then another twenty.

And another.

And another.

In the control room, Anjin was relieved to find that the radar still worked; and on the very stern, one of the repair robots was even bringing the telescope back on line. He could see the six hundred absorbics rushing down the tunnel. In the space beyond, he observed the stalker dispatching clusters of antimatter bombs—and decoys, presumably.

"Tam?" He turned and saw the Captain securing Susan to a railing.

"We do nothing. We've no thrusters left and we're too sluggish even if we did. And we've no absorbics to spare. We've done all we can. Now we just watch."

Anjin saw another cluster of twenty bright objects separate from the stalker and accelerate toward him. So here we sit, he thought, in the middle of an immovable target waiting for our crust to be blasted away clear to the Bardo shield probably. Then a long, long spiral toward the center of the Sun, with little material left for building new thrusters or absorbics.

Just when he thought the situation could not get any worse, the radar fluttered and died. He shouted commands to his pad but was left with only a very weak signal in the visible wavelengths of light.

"Wonderful," he said, turning to Tam. "First you tell me there's nothing we can do but watch. And now we can't even watch. So tell me, Skipper, what can happen next?"

As the two robotic armadas approached each other, thrusters fired wildly to keep them within the tunnel and on target. The stalker-bound absorbics were essentially decelerating, relative to the Sun, and had to fight the increasing influence of the

Sun's gravity. For the Sargenti-Peterson–bound antimatter torpedoes, the overwhelming temptation was to swing up to a higher orbit. As they accelerated relative to their targets, the absorbics were forced to press upward, and the antimatter torpedoes had to press down.

About midway between the two ships they began clashing head-on; and it was here that Tam's act of desperation, if not near panic, turned the tide against the stalker's calm, calculated attack, as a cluster of twenty antimatter torpedoes vanished without incident.

Then another twenty.

And another.

And another.

And one more.

During the last thirty seconds of battle, five hundred absorbic bombs had broken through the antimatter offensive and were lining up dead center on the stalker's prow. There was no option left to the stalker except to make the absorbics detonate as far away as possible. The nearest of Anjin's bombs was still four hundred klicks from impact when the stalker shut down the assault tunnel and let the Sun's chromosphere spill in.

Anjin could just barely see the alien ship, and was struggling hard to get a clear picture when, where the ship had been, the whole tunnel seemed to collapse and a dark spot appeared. It was a darkness of such intensity that he could see nothing except its blackness and its expanding dimensions.

Tam whispered, "You might as well give your

soul to Jesus, stranger. Because your far-from-sorry ass is mine!"

But Anjin did not feel like rejoicing. The intense globe of black, with a surface temperature approaching absolute zero, had spread across ten thousand kilometers; and as it continued to swell over the horizon, Anjin realized with horror that it was also bursting toward him.

"Oops!"

"What do you mean, 'oops'?" Tam asked. "Did we kill them or what?"

"Mostly or what," Anjin answered.

Tam watched the hole in the chromosphere eating up more and more of the pad's field of vision. "What's the range on that thing?" she asked.

"Ground zero is more than eleven thousand kilometers aft. Its edge is moving at four hundred klicks per second. We're keeping just ahead of it at five hundred"—his voice wavered—"but it won't matter."

"Chain reaction?"

Anjin bowed his head. "God help us, Captain. I'm afraid we just blew up the Sun."

19

Gaius

ASTRONOMY WAS FULL OF SUCH INTRIGUING BUT UN-breakable laws. To ground-based observers, an object—or even news of an event—could no more exceed the speed of light than a propeller-driven airplane could break the sound barrier in horizontal flight through sea level air; so a full eight minutes passed before the light of the battle in the chromosphere, traveling at 305,040 kilometers per second, brushed over the Earth. But no creature stared up from the great wasteland that was the world. On all continents and in all seas there was not a single soul to watch the spreading black stain on the face of the Sun.

Four hours away at the speed of light, on the icy plain of Triton, the last Bardo cone was being snapped into position. The ship's dorsal surface was a hastily assembled pile of tanks filled to their brims with liquid hydrogen and oxygen. The gases were derived directly from Tritonian ice. They burned with a dull light and leaked no neutrinos; and after the tanks were empty, they and the engines that emptied them would be thrown overboard by the spidery automatons that crawled over every meter of *Gaius*'s hull. It was thus hoped that its crew of four could lift off stealthily from their icebound research center, and avoid becoming just another gamma burst in Sunspace.

Lenny, Sharon, Vinny, and Robyn were, like the crew of the Cat, members of the Lunarians, a corporation with roots in an eastern American science fiction society. The Lunarians had made their fortune by purchasing a Pacific island no one else wanted and taking advantage of the bargain basement fares offered to anyone willing to risk payloads on the first production model of Powell's gas-powered space cannon. Tons of black, ultrathin Mylar composites were fired into Earth orbit, each package programmed for self-assembly into a slowly spinning disk more than 850 kilometers across. A ring of solar collectors near the disk's center powered an ultralight engine, and when at last the object settled into a geosynchronous orbit fifty thousand kilometers high, both disk and Sun displayed for Earth the same apparent diameter. Each day at noon, the patent-protected disk produced a total eclipse over the isle of Luna, whose tourist and real estate value had, overnight, shot up astronomically.

With equal cleverness, the Triton refugees now hoped to establish the seeds of a new colony, undetected beneath the clouds of Neptune. They waited on what seemed to be an alpine snowfield that was stained an impossible pink under Neptune's ghostly blue light.

Some ninety years earlier, just ahead of the first Voyager flyby, Richard Tuna had predicted an entirely different landscape. He reasoned that Triton's orbit was so far flung from the Sun that liquid nitrogen would not evaporate and blow away on the solar wind, and that lakes, perhaps even oceans, of nitrogen might lie pooled on the surface. As *Voyager II* approached, he had expected to see a world very similar in appearance to his own Earth. "But nothing will be quite as it appears," he had told CNN. "The continents will be ice. The icebergs will be methane. And if—incredibly—carbon and hydrogen have become life, the 'water' that flows within the tree trunk will be nitrogen."

This was nonsense, of course, and Tuna would have been the first to admit that eighty percent of his ideas were nonsense. "Eighty percent of *everyone's* ideas are nonsense," he had said. "The trick is in knowing which eighty percent and in being quick to abandon them."

That, too, was nonsense—but only half nonsense.

What made Tuna different was that he had twenty times more ideas than everyone else; and while this produced twenty times more nonsense, he had learned never to cling stubbornly to a wrong idea—even if it had been a pet one.

"There's *another* complaint I have about God," Tuna joked when the first *Voyager* photos of Triton came through and proved his ocean theory wrong. "If we are to believe God really did have a hand in the creation of the universe, why would he make a mistake like that? All he had to do was place Triton ninety million kilometers closer to the Sun—a matter of just five light-minutes—and we would have seen my beautiful nitrogen seas. So close to a miracle and yet so far."

Like the case of Venus, it was a perfect example of the right world in the wrong place. Because Triton orbited four light-hours from the Sun, its surface temperature was 230 degrees below the freezing point of water. So not even nitrogen could flow liquid. Indeed, one would have expected nitrogen and water to have formed a solid ball of ice almost from the moment of creation.

As it turned out, Tuna had been too quick to abandon a perfectly good theory on the basis of a single "bad" fact—a mistake that was nonsense in its own right. Had he looked more closely, he would have seen that his idea was wrong only quantitatively, not qualitatively.

In two large, natural basins, nitrogen had indeed flowed like water and waves had indeed lapped at Tritonian shores . . . more than 600 million years before Tuna's ancestors crawled out of the sea. To judge from the few craters scattered over the glass-smooth flood plains, Tuna had missed Triton's nitrogen seas by "only" a billion years—a margin small enough to be considered a very close call by the measure of solar system time. Some powerful and still unidentified tidal force—the same force, perhaps, that had caused the partial melting of Miranda and Ariel, thrown the entire Uranian system on its side, flung Triton into its backward orbit around Neptune, and torn Pluto and Charon away from Neptune—had dumped enormous loads of frictional energy into Triton, sending seas of nitrogen bubbling to the surface. The Tritonian and Mirandan meltings were characteristic of a sudden accumulation of heat inside, and an almost equally rapid release of heat at the planetary surface.

Lenny and Sharon had seen in the meltings the signature of a fascinatingly violent event: the passage of a Sunlike star within only one or two light-days of the solar system. Both stars would have torn at their outermost planets and, given the extreme age of the galaxy, and six hundred billion stars with an average separation of only five light-years—each one of them moving on a different course—at least one close brush in Sunspace's past seemed statistically inevitable.

Even at a distance of light-hours, an intruding sun would be too distant to be seen as anything more than a bright star in Earthly or Martian skies, too distant to affect planetary climate and etch recognizable traces in the fossil record. But to the outer planets—those most weakly bound to the Sun—even a light-day was close enough to be felt.

All over Triton there were hints of exploded volcanoes whose lava had been water; and drillings beneath the nitrogen "seas" revealed them to have condensed on top of frozen ice-lava lakes. Vinny suspected that Triton was still reeling from the gravitational tug-of-war. In a region he named Yellowstone Park, liquid nitrogen geysers jetted up from hot spots below the surface. Given that his own Sun was merely a bright star on the horizon, he saw no heat source except the gravitational pulse, and a subsequent fraction of a degree-per-megayear cooling process that was not yet finished, to explain where the energy to drive geysers would come from on a frigid, geologically moribund moon. And if Triton was, to one degree or another, still active after all these years, Vinny could do little more than wonder what greater surprises awaited him on Neptune, whose volume, through which frictional heat would have been distributed, was far greater than Triton's, and whose relative surface area, through which heat could be radiated, was even smaller.

For all he and his companions knew, they were about to become the very last page of human history. But there was nothing left to do except turn the page, as the spiders capped a vent named Old Faithful and jetted streams of hot nitrogen through Lenny's maze of bristle-lined pipes. Each bristle, as it bent and twisted and strained to snap back to its original position, produced a faint electrical current, and the collective whole became a surprisingly efficient charger for *Gaius*'s batteries. Once below the Neptunian cloud tops, those same pipes would derive their power from changing pressures and temperatures.

"Neutrino free," Lenny had said. "Everything has to be neutrino free."

"Surely the power requirements of four people won't outshine the galactic neutrino background," Vinny had protested. "We ought to go nuclear. We'll find all the deuterium and helium-three we'd ever need in Neptune's atmosphere."

But Lenny would not hear of it. He was cautious to the point of paranoia. To him, any neutrino glow at all was an unacceptable risk that might bring with it endless uncertainty as they waited to be proven right or wrong. Why make it a test at all?

So *Gaius* would be launched on a geyser-powered steam catapult, into regions of space where Triton's gravitational pull would slow the ship's outward flight from 2.3 to 0.8 kilometers per second. Under other conditions, without aid of chemical or nuclear propellants, a mere blast of nitrogen steam was just not powerful enough, and *Gaius* would continue to decelerate, until at last its rate of climb leveled off at 0.0 kilometers per second and began clicking backward to −0.1, −0.2, −0.3. . . .

But according to plan, Neptune would be moving into the refugees' path, yanking them away from Triton. Slowly, the ship would begin to pick up speed, to fall up, tail first, toward a planet with seventeen times the Earth's mass. That was when all those tanks of chemical propellant would be needed. And if the braking maneuver over the north pole did not get them killed, and if they managed to target the pole without falling down instead upon the hypersonic winds of the equator, then the plan Lenny had chosen would allow them to draw all the energy they needed by drifting up and down through the Neptunian thermocline—half blimp, half submarine—till the end of time.

The plan Lenny had chosen, and to which they had all agreed, would force them, until they invented procedures for extracting carbon dioxide and silicon atoms from the atmosphere and weaving them into new building materials, to share living quarters barely as large as a one-bedroom apartment. They would be allowed one shower every three days, in water recycled through urine stills. Their food and air would be provided by a four-meter-square box of wet microtubes filled with genetically redesigned algae. In essence, they would be living on artificially flavored slime.

The ship, designed for diving into high-pressure environments, could not even provide the luxury of a window. But this did not matter. Soon there would be very little to see. Neptune was so far removed from the Sun that once *Gaius* penetrated twenty meters below the cloud tops, all natural light would be cut off.

So, as their pads told them that the last Bardo cone was firmly in place and that the steam catapult was charged and ready, they just stood on the nitrogen flood plain, all four of them, looking around for a very long time. There were worms in the sky. On the horizon, directly in front of the rising hemisphere of Neptune, seven geyser-spawned plumes twisted more than ten kilometers into the heavens, ranging from dusty yellow to peach, depending on the slant of the Sun's rays. Here was unearthly beauty, made more unearthly and more beautiful by the fact that they would never see the like of it again.

At Vinny's feet, water and nitrogen—substances he once drank and breathed on Earth—had become the substance of Triton's geology. These were the youngest rocks on the moon's surface, and yet they were astonishingly old. When the cryovolcanoes had spewed the last of them, the remotest reptilian ancestors whose DNA flowed in his veins had not yet appeared on Earthly shores. Vinny lifted the last rock he would ever see and tried to feel the heft of time in the palm of his hand, to understand it in terms comprehensible in the flash of a human lifetime. He tried a thought experiment, knowing that if he started counting forward from the second he was born, he would be thirty-three years old by the time one billion seconds had passed. And as many as a billion *years* had passed since the nitrogen rock he held in his glove had solidified. In all that time, he told himself, Triton had never known the stirrings of life. The sea upon which he stood had never lived . . . until now. Vinny was still running his thought experiment when the horizon, already dark by Earthly eyes, grew even dimmer, as if the distant Sun were passing behind a veil of cloud. But there were no clouds in Triton's sky, and the whole of Neptune had gone into shadow at the same moment. Vinny felt Sharon tugging at his elbow. She was pointing excitedly behind him.

"Look at it! Look at it!" she called through his suitcom. "Something's wrong with the Sun!"

20

Wish Upon a Star

ANJIN GUESSED THAT THEY COULD HAVE SEEN THE sunstorm from as far away as Miranda. He was certain that on Ceres, if people still lived there, they could have seen it without aid of telescopes or binoculars.

The detonation had come within a hair's breadth of setting up a runaway chain reaction. It reached down toward the very core, simultaneously increasing the Sun's mass and freezing a large expanse of its surface. Sargenti-Peterson outran the disappearing chromosphere, just barely, and only temporarily. Behind them, as the refugees watched, an area as wide as the orbit of Earth's moon fell into itself, and the scene aft resembled a crater as vast as Copernicus viewed from its rim. The temperatures and the darkness reached out to the universe, signaling dangers to Sargenti-Peterson that could only be guessed at, but which to the despair of all aboard were bound to be met head-on.

Anjin spent the next two hours rebuilding the ship's sensors and magnetic lenses. Two hours was all he had, for even if the thrusters were not destroyed, Sargenti-Peterson could never hope to make the radical shifts of orbit necessary to avoid so large a storm. For as long as the ship-comet existed, it would circumnavigate the Sun and pass near ground zero approximately every three hours. When he had done all he could, and his pad told him that the edge of the storm lay only two minutes ahead, he dropped his head into his hands and broke into a cold sweat. During those final moments before contact, Tam lifted him from his station and he took her wordlessly in his arms.

Throughout the ship, others had spent the hours building makeshift restraints and harnessing themselves in; but if they entered the kind of shockwave Anjin was expecting, the comet might all but stop short, converting everyone inside instantly into red mist. So Anjin had simply prepared his machines to manage as well as possible, and prepared his mind to receive a shockwave he would probably not live long enough to hear or feel.

He was both puzzled and elated, therefore, when the shockwave never came. The ship simply seemed to bound over what gave the appearance of being a crater wall, beyond which the chromosphere gave way to the open spaces of the corona. Sargenti-Peterson merely adjusted its magnetic trim and bobbed up and down a few times, as if sailing through nothing more extraordinary than a solar flare.

But there was nothing ordinary about the absorbic crater. It was more than ninety-eight thousand kilometers deep—three times deeper than the largest known decrease of the Sun's diameter during its eighty-year cycle of expansions and contractions. And all this damage had required the time it took Anjin to draw and expel a single breath. Walls of bright plasma hovered four hundred thousand kilometers from the center, edging inward as thousands of glowing columns broke through the crater floor, bringing heat from the solar depths. The colors were impossible reds and greens and violets bursting through a crust of black gas; and some were colors Anjin had never seen before.

Across the entire face of the Sun, the chromosphere itself was slowly receding. In three or four orbits, Anjin guessed, Sargenti-Peterson would once again be circling in the lofty heights of the corona without ever changing altitude. He was unable to decide whether or not restoring the thrusters and descending to a lower orbit was a good idea, because he did not know if the Sun would rebound from its present contraction, or perhaps even go nova. The only sure prediction was that he had rendered the Sun's behavior utterly unpredictable.

Harnessed in their quarters, the rest of the crew were joining the engineer and the Captain on their pad screens to stare in astonishment at the changing sunscape. Brilliant outbursts of sapphire pink and champagne orange loomed directly ahead, pulling apart like mist and veiling much of the crater's far wall. The ship-comet streaked through the mist and continued inexorably along its path.

Not even the face of Neptune sweeping up ahead could diminish Lenny's initial amazement. At the highest power of *Gaius*'s scopes, the black spot looked to him like a viral infection spreading across the face of the Sun.

"My God," he exclaimed for the seventh time in

as many minutes. "I just don't believe it!"

"Do you really think they're redesigning the Sun?" said Vinny.

"Engineering it to their own purposes?" asked Robyn. "Does such power exist?"

"It exists," answered Lenny. "Difficult to believe, but there it is. Do you still think I'm hyperparanoid about nukes and neutrinos? Do you still doubt they can find us?"

Lenny's heart was racing. In the beginning, he was just being cautious. He had started out only half believing that whatever had destroyed *Graff*, *Nautile*, and everything else that moved within Sun-space might detect a neutrino glow no matter how small. Born of the weak force, the neutrino's inter-action with matter was also weak, meaning that it could not possibly be shielded from alien detectors, for the vast majority of neutrinos would shine easily through a hull of solid lead and keep on shining through a dozen planets the size of Neptune.

Still, his crew had argued, if the glow could be kept weak enough to match very closely the back-ground neutrino flux of the Galaxy, then small nu-clear reactors might be the safest and most efficient option, making unnecessary the inconveniences and hardships of frugality. But Lenny was taking no chances. When he opted for chemical and mechan-ical means of power production, he had not really believed his enemies were all-powerful and all-knowing. Now, convinced that they could rebuild the Sun, if they so desired, he believed they would find him no matter what precautions he took. They were like monsters in his childhood dreams—im-possible to escape or hide from because they knew everything that he knew, even where he was hiding, because *he* was dreaming them. These destroyers were not only real, but they did not *have* to enter his mind. They could get him without really trying, without really knowing him. . . .

As Vinny saw it, Lenny was spiraling down into deep paranoia, at first not really believing what deeds the Intruders might be capable of performing, then believing in them as one believes in the powers of a god—which was much worse than paranoia. Lenny was far beyond a reality that was bad enough.

At the heart of comet Sargenti-Peterson's largest salt vein, in the cabin that had been Tam's laboratory, some dozen members of the ship's scientific party converged on what was now a dimly lit control room. Some of the men and women wore bandages and casts. Two, including Susan Skurla, were brought in on stretchers; and all of them displayed various scrapes and bruises from the second attack wave.

When they had assembled, and after they had waited ten minutes beyond the agreed time, Tam called the meeting to order.

"All agreed on stepping up production?" she said.

There were grave "ayes."

"Opposed?"

Silence.

She gave a nod to Anjin, and he opened the lines to every pad in the ship.

"This cannot be a command decision," Tam told the attendees. "If we don't all agree on the option,

we're sure to have mutineers, if not outright warfare in the corridors. So I'm putting it to the vote."

Christ no, she thought. All her scientific and political training had not covered a situation like this.
An ironic smile crossed her lips, and she addressed
the pads.

"I shall be brief. As you know, I am diverting most
of the ship's resources to the more-intensive production of absorbic bombs. As you are also aware, we just
came perilously close to creating a stellar chain reaction. My scientific advisers believe that as few as forty
more absorbic detonations could have turned the
trick, converting all the Sun's energy into matter and
causing a stellar collapse that would not have
stopped until it burst forth as a nova. For two or three
days this solar system would have shone more
brightly than a galaxy. The planets and any of our
surviving brethren, and the enemy within our Sunspace, would have ceased to exist.

"Which brings me to the first of three possible
futures.

"We will, very soon, have sufficient numbers of
absorbics to convert this ship into a trigger for the
largest hydrogen bomb ever assembled. Mutual destruction may not be the most elegant way of cleaning the enemy out of our Sunspace, but it's certain
to do the job, and it *is* one option.

"Most of you believe that a few people still survive on Earth or inside Ceres or *somewhere* in this
system. A few realists say not, and I'm with them.
There are, however, a half dozen Valkyries, each
with a husband-and-wife team aboard, scattered as
far away as Epsilon Eridani and sixty-one Cygni. If,
by the slimmest of chances, any of these expeditions

has gone undetected by the enemy, they will probably be safe until, after a decade or two exploring some alien world, they restart their engines and begin the voyage home—at which point their engines' neutrino and gamma glow will make them visible. If they see it in time, a nova might just stop them from getting tangled up in all this.

"Another option is to prepare the trigger, delay pressing the button until and unless we are found, and hope the enemy thinks we're dead and never comes looking for us. We've got Folsome tubes, so we'll always have food and clean water, and there's no question that we've got all the energy we'll ever need. But if what a few of us are predicting, and what the majority of you refuse to believe, turns out to be true—if all that remains of humanity is this ship and a handful of Valkyries—then if we delay too long, the last starships may already be flying home by the time we push the button. Those ships will have only enough fuel for a single deceleration from ninety-two percent of light speed. As they come home and decelerate, they will be picked off as easily as *Graff*, *Nautile*, and *Melville*. In the end, our hesitation, our desire to buy a little more time for ourselves, could guarantee the utter extinction of our species. But that is a *second* option."

"But what if there are survivors on Ceres or Miranda?" a woman's voice called out. "Even if there's only a one-in-twenty chance of that being true, then it's a one-in-twenty chance that we'll be killing more people in this system than we could ever hope to save outside it. Besides, the enemy may already know where all our Valkyries are, in which case we are stewards of nothing."

Tam frowned, then cleared her throat. "I know, but it's all a probability curve, isn't it? We know there must be survivors outside our system, but we've no reason to believe, with any reasonable degree of certainty, that there is anyone left within our system except us and the aliens."

"Which brings us to a third option?" the woman asked.

"Yes. We can't even be certain that all the Valkyries have not already been tracked down and destroyed. The only certainty is that *we* have survived and that our enemies are still out there. If we are all that remains of our species and we trigger the Sun, then we finish the job our enemies began and merely take a few hundred of them with us. Triggering the Sun now, or when we are attacked, accomplishes nothing unless there are humans who are going to survive outside the solar system.

"Since our own existence is all we can count on, the third option calls for building the trigger and using it only if we have been attacked, beaten, and are certain that we are down to our last three seconds. It essentially involves waiting and hoping a little bit longer than the second option allows.

"And if we survive long enough, perhaps our descendants will learn how to move stealthily out of the corona, and perhaps they will even be able to locate the star these bastards came from and, armed as they will be with the ability to trigger novae—"

"My God . . ." Susan interrupted. "This could have happened before. All those exploding stars in the constellation Aquila!"

"Nooo . . ." said Tam.

"Yes! I remember trying to explain Aquila away

as some sort of physical phenomenon, but now the lesson is a bit simpler: if you really want to search the Galaxy for signs of intelligent life, look first for signs of massive stupidity."

Captain Tam smiled and shivered at the same time. She had an appreciation of wit and irony; but this time beads of sweat appeared on her forehead, and in the zero gravity they stayed exactly where they formed. The silence in the cold, cramped room seemed absolute, until Tam shrugged and broke it.

"If I may add to Susan's observation, in a universe where people are blowing up each other's suns, the civilization that hit us with relativistic bombs could be the good news. The really bad news hasn't got out of Aquila yet.

"I don't know where we go from here. All I can offer are these three options, and each breaks down to much the same end. I'll leave you scientists and military types to mull it over, but I'm not sure we have very much time in which to decide."

Two days later, it was voted to complete the absorbic trigger, and then to gamble on some island of human civilization still existing elsewhere in the solar system and on the even longer shot of Sargenti-Peterson's survival: but in the event of a decisive attack, the ship-comet would destroy itself and everything else that lived between the Sun and the Oort Disk.

21

Descent

TO THOSE UNFAMILIAR WITH THE LUNARIAN SENSE OF humor, it would have been difficult to understand why the owners and builders had named this ship *Gaius*. The mad emperor Gaius Caligula had bankrupted the Roman treasury, appointed a horse to the Senate, and devoured his son in public; and while it could truly be said that Hitler was Gaius with good table manners, no one had challenged the Roman emperor's authority until he began to wage war against the god of the sea.

One morning Caligula had ordered the imperial guards to humiliate Neptune by beating the tide back with their swords, and when swords inevitably proved futile against the power of Earth and Moon, he began killing the very men who were assigned to protect him. When even larger groups of soldiers failed to keep the tide from rising, Gaius retaliated with more death sentences and firmed his resolve to defeat Neptune, to his ultimate ruin.

The Lunarians' challenge against Neptune seemed to be going a lot smoother. Even before the last of the tanks were jettisoned, even before *Gaius* reached the ionosphere, Sharon and Robyn had watched the air pressure exerted by atoms of hydrogen and helium climb from the normal interplanetary level of 10^{-20} atmospheres.

"The planet keeps a tight hold on its gases," Robyn observed.

Sharon had a talent for putting her observations into more human perspective. To her, one hundred thousandth of an atmosphere was the pressure of a water strider's foot on the surface of a pond. The pressure was already rising above one atmosphere—the pressure of prerelativistic bombardment air at sea level on Earth—by the time they descended into the outer reaches of the stratosphere. *Gaius* was dropping like a dart. There was nothing to see outside except by the aid of sonoscans; and even then, there was very little to see. At this altitude, in the relatively calm air of the north pole, the tiniest snowflake was far too heavy to remain suspended in the cloud tops and immediately began falling toward the planet's surface. As a result, even the cloud decks, as they scrolled upward past *Gaius*'s nightscopes and sonoscans, lacked detail.

Now that two dozen ropes had been ejected and were streaming behind his ship, producing drag forces that would keep it from attaining too high a terminal velocity; now that everything was proceeding according to plan and his future was becoming ever so slightly more secure, Lenny began to relax, even as deceleration brought with it the return of gravity and his cyberpants activated, slowly squeezing blood from his legs to his torso. Fortunately, such adaptations to hypergravity were only a temporary requirement. If all he knew about the gas giant—about this smallest of all known brown dwarfs—held true, in a day's time there would be almost as much mass above *Gaius* as below, and at most he'd have to stand against only two or three times his normal Earth weight, or as Sharon would have put it, the gee forces every child gets used to on an ordinary swing.

"Ninety atmospheres," Sharon called out. "Denser than water now. We've just crossed the atmospheric pressure on the surface of Venus."

All the larger, hull-based spiders were imploding and becoming useful only as sources of future building materials. The survivors were smaller than mice. They moved by aid of hairlike filaments, and in the greater depths of Neptune they would buoy themselves up, on those hair-thin "legs," with tanks of slush. Their spherical shells were arrays of Bardo cones built on a microscopic scale, and as the air around them intensified from 150 atmospheres ("the pressure inside a late twentieth-century power plant boiler," Sharon announced) to 200 atmospheres ("the pressure inside a charged scuba tank"), Lenny ordered the last of the spiders to turn on their floodlamps and eight million–ASA cameras.

Now he could see clearly for many kilometers, and there were faint hints of swirls within the atmosphere, the first signs of suspended particles—hydrocarbon sleet, mostly. His pad, which was becoming increasingly heavy in his hands, told him that the temperature was rising perceptibly. Like Triton, Neptune was radiating more heat from its interior than it received from the Sun.

At 600 atmospheres, Sharon announced that they had just crossed the threshold of a phonograph needle pressing down on a late twentieth-century vinyl record, which was more than sufficient to collapse a fully charged scuba tank. Two hundred atmospheres deeper, she began comparing the forces trying to get inside *Gaius* with the peak pressure of a fist against a skull during a karate strike, except that Neptune's fists were multiple millions trying to smash through every square millimeter of the ship's Bardo membrane.

At this point, Vinny told her to shut up or he would confine her to her sleeping closet.

"He means it," Robyn added, "and I'll help him. It can be a very lonely ship when three people hate you."

Lenny said nothing.

At 900 atmospheres, *Gaius* crossed through a zone of pressure comparable to the greatest depth of an Earthly ocean, and was now literally falling through an ocean. In one moment they were reclining in their pressure beds, dropping through a cloud of compressed liquid hydrogen and helium laced with methane, acetylene, hydrogen sulfide and ammonia ices; in the next moment they had splashed down upon a world-encircling seascape of ethane and methane. Under a gravitational pull exerted by seventeen Earth masses, the ship did not even bob up and down but sank like a slug of uranium toward some unknown abyssal plain. The splash was barely noticeable on the speedometer, but even in the comfort of a pressure bed, in a high-gravity environment the smallest jolt bore a sting. Sharon likened it in her mind to being in a minor train wreck, but held her tongue.

Ever the explorers, the Lunarians ordered their remaining spiders to search immediately for signs of life in this greatest of all known seas. On their pads they saw the readouts of purines and pyrimidines, amino acids and porphyrin molecules drifting through oceans of gasoline, but no hints that these molecules had ever belonged to DNA or cells—which is just as well for us, Lenny told himself, thinking of the Intruders. It was the universe's ability to sprout life that had gotten him into this mess in the first place. He realized that he was beyond the fear of his enemies now, but he was still determined to escape them. It was a determination, born of a grown child's anger, that his childhood terrors would never find him again, that they would not learn what was in his mind, as they had done in his nightmares. His was an anger beyond all mortal anger, beyond the anger voiced when Pharaoh cursed God and Moses and the death cloud of Thera. It was an anger that could not even be defeated by his death, because it would remain intact until the very end—and then he would no longer be aware to know that he had been defeated.

As his anger swelled and died, and began to swell again, Sharon and Robyn continued to announce the status of the Bardo cones and the pressures trying to get through them. Sensing Lenny's anger, Sharon made no tension-building analogies. None were needed, she told herself. The pads showed that at 1000 atmospheres, the very melting points of the chemicals swirling about *Gaius* were beginning to change.

"Twelve hundred atmospheres . . . thirteen hundred . . . fourteen hundred . . . fifteen hundred . . ."

Now a blast of relatively warm ethane welled up from the bottom; but Lenny's sonoscans showed the sea to be bottomless. Straight down, for tens upon tens of kilometers, laser beams and sonar encountered nothing solid, and passed on without reflecting back to the ship. He ordered the external scoops to start circulating, and tons of noncompressible slush began inflating sacks stowed in the ends of *Gaius*'s system of trailing ropes.

As the ship gained some semblance of buoyancy, it no longer dropped like a stone but drifted down through Neptune. Lenny knew that he could make *Gaius* float like a blimp if he wanted to, but he did not want to. Safety lay in depth, and it occurred to him that if he could find a supply of ice down there, he would have all the excess oxygen he needed to burn the planet's gasoline. He and his crew would be able to generate power wastefully, if they wished, without ever having to worry about leaking a neutrino glow.

"Two thousand . . . two thousand ten . . . two thousand twenty . . . Whoa! I'm picking up reflections north and east!"

At first glance, seen only on the sonoscan, it looked like a turbulent boundary layer. Just another peak in the thermocline. Probing straight down, it was possible to scan right through it. But when Sharon swung the scanners east, she saw a crust of solidifying, cracking, and resolidifying magma stretching to the horizon. To the west, her cameras revealed the rubble-strewn rim of a huge volcanic caldera.

Lenny pumped the intakes, swelled the slush balloons, and slowed *Gaius* to a hover. Switching on every spider-mounted floodlamp and calling attitude-control jets into play, he swept the ship into a graceful banking maneuver, as if it were a helicopter, and aimed the prow at true magnetic north. From an altitude of forty meters, viewed through cameras approximating ordinary human eyesight, the pads would have shown only darkness below. Yet the spider's deep-penetrating cameras revealed a lava lake passing beneath their feet.

The lava, like the hydrocarbon stew that surrounded *Gaius*, was transparent, but its temperature was so much higher that in every direction except straight down it reflected sonar and lamplight and microwave lasers like a silver-plated tray. Unable to contain herself, Sharon immediately christened the volcanic caldera Mirror Lake. From all indications it was spread over thousands of square kilometers.

Eastward, where a thin crust was trying to form, the lake lost its immobility. Giant rafts of ice shuddered and reeled, creaked and boomed through ten thousand vents. There were volcanic fountains on the eastern horizon, but no choking fumes, no steam. At twenty-two hundred atmospheres, it was impossible for bubbles to form without being pressed immediately out of existence.

And strangest of all was the substance of the caldera. The boulders at the volcano's western rim, over which falls of lava half a kilometer high spilled and froze, were composed mostly of water. Here the sheer weight of overlaying nitrogen and gasoline produced new pressure phases, or densities, of ice. The rim of Mirror Lake was Ice Three, which differed from ordinary ice in having more closely packed molecules and a melting point of 34.7 degrees below zero.

More cryovolcanism, Vinny thought. Just like what we saw on Triton. But a water volcano at minus 34.7 degrees centigrade seemed as inexplicable to him as Triton's nitrogen geysers, and for the same reason. Though far below freezing, minus 34.7 degrees was both figuratively and literally hot lava by the standards of the outer solar system. When he tried to visualize how a magma chamber could be kept warm at this distance from the Sun his eyes kept turning toward the sky, toward frictional heating caused by Triton's chaotic orbit overhead. Though Triton whirled around the planet at nearly the same distance that the Moon circled Earth, Neptune's seventeen Earth masses caused Triton to circle five times faster than Earth's moon. It was also circling backward, east to west, in a direction opposite to Neptune's rotation—which explained why, from the icefields beyond Mirror Lake's rim, the ethane-methane ocean conducted to *Gaius* the sounds of the planet's surface quivering and snapping. As near as Vinny could tell, a planetary shell of Ice Three was being continually pulled apart, straining to break into great crustal blocks. He imagined that at the equator the solid, Ice Three surface of Neptune was bobbing up and down, producing an otherworldly tide that could easily put the Bay of Fundy to shame. Quick mental calculations suggested that the current rate of internal heating due to tidal action was enough to sustain chambers of molten ice, or water, inside Neptune, if the interior had, during the past billion years or so, been melted by something else—perhaps, Vinny guessed, by Lenny's vagrant star.

And he recalled with a chill of gooseflesh that Neptune was pulling the satellite nearly seven tenths of a meter closer every year, and in about 660 million years Triton would come crashing down in pieces upon the planet. He tried to divert his thoughts from this inevitable catastrophe to the hope that by the time his distant descendants had to worry about it, they would have found a way out of Neptune. He tried not to think about how he could produce enough descendants. The group was too small, too ill-equipped to give birth to a population that would have a chance of increasing.

Vinny was about to suggest heading for the western rim and looking for a place to drop anchor when Lenny pointed out a patch of clear, uncrusted lava and announced, "Deeper! Deeper! We've got to go deeper."

"But that's crazy," said Vinny. "They'll never find us here."

"Oh, they'll find us, all right. But where we're going they'll have to be crazy to follow us."

"No." Vinny looked around. "Surely you don't agree with this," he implored Sharon and Robyn. But the women uttered no objections, and a horrid sense of fatality passed through Vinny as Lenny circled the clearing, expelled a puff of slush, and allowed *Gaius* to settle belly first on the water-ethane boundary.

For long seconds they floated like a ship in the water-lava lake, while Lenny collected data on relative temperatures, masses, and densities.

Again Vinny looked at Sharon and Robyn. "I don't much relish the idea of looking up through the wrong end of a volcano while our enemies wave good-bye from the right end."

"Vinny, there is no place to go but down," Lenny insisted. "Now bring yourself to order and save yourself!" And then, with a cycling of pumps, the crew compartment slid beneath the surface, trailing long ropes held up by balloons. One of the balloons valved huge billows of warm slush into the sky, and the ropes suddenly picked up momentum in their plunge.

The valving balloon went down with an audible gulp.

Vinny did as he was told: stiffened his spine and diverted his thoughts from the mounting pressure outside. He paid closer attention to chemical analyses from the spiders—and he could not help paying close attention. Life had just turned up in what seemed to him the most unlikely place in the universe. It was very primitive, microscopic life, but life nonetheless. This sea, unlike the one above, was not so much a primordial soup as a very dilute broth; yet the spiders were registering individual cells, occasionally stitched together to form balls or microfilaments.

By their mere existence they generated enough questions to keep the four Lunarians busy for decades. For a start—just for a start—there was the question of what food sources kept the cells alive. Vinny tried to imagine what would happen if the chemistry of this world had been slightly different, so that life could evolve not only under water but up there, on the icy seafloor beyond the crater rim. What would it be like, he wondered, to behold a fish-like creature—if the like could ever evolve here—

erupting onto the ice fields through Mirror Lake? The "fish" would die violently, its blood freezing solid within seconds. If, before it died, it were to embrace an inhabitant of the Neptunian surface, the embrace would feel like the touch of molten lead to the surface dweller. The "fish" would seem an impossible creation—deadly to the touch, living in lava, and turning to stone the instant it was exposed to the ethane-methane "atmosphere."

The ocean through which they were descending 364suggested to Vinny a reference system that had no equal. Concepts of "air" and "rock" and "ocean" became suddenly interchangeable. Water was lava. Ice was rock. And the ethane-methane ocean became simply the lowermost reaches of the Neptunian atmosphere. Once again, the reality of scientific achievement had caught up with and surpassed mythology. For one brief and shining moment, Vinny could reach out and touch and truly feel what the Buddha had meant when he talked about multiple planes of existence; and in the euphoria of that moment, it was possible for him to forget how a black stain on the Sun had affected his pilot and where his pilot was taking him.

At thirty-five hundred atmospheres, the freezing point of water should have been up to minus seventeen degrees centigrade, and still the sea remained fluid, sustained by volcanic upwellings from somewhere far below. There came a sudden, marginally alarming increase in turbulence, and when Vinny checked his pad he saw what he at first took to be a very large field of debris streaming out of the spacecraft—millions of particles everywhere. But closer inspection showed them to be clathrates of methane caged in microscopic needles of ice. He was relieved when he realized that they were not coming from his ship, and that except for further plunging the freezing temperature of water, they were of no consequence.

But Lenny arrived at a different conclusion. His attention was focused on the noise that had accompanied the turbulence. Could that be true? Had it really been the sound of an explosion just a short distance above?

"It's them," Lenny announced. "They're following us." And then, without any further warning or consultation, he barked orders to his pad, and the ship's computer pulled a pin from the largest slush balloon and let it fly up.

"Decoy," Lenny explained.

"Decoy?" Vinny said gravely. "Didn't Mommy ever tell you that when you pull the pin, Mister Hand Grenade is no longer your friend?"

Vinny began calling his own orders to the ship's computer, but he understood that there was not enough space in the remaining balloons to take up a surge of replacement slush, and that the spiders would probably take longer to cannibalize parts of the ship's hull and manufacture a replacement balloon than any margin of error allowed.

The ship already had a sizable negative buoyancy even before Lenny cut loose the balloon. Now the added mass tipped the balance beyond all hope of quick recovery. *Gaius* was falling like a skydiver whose parachute had become hopelessly tangled. At sixty-three hundred atmospheres, the freezing point of water should have been (assuming it was clathrate and salt free) up to 2.0 degrees; but the temperature of the magma chamber itself was climbing higher the deeper they fell.

Luckily, or unluckily, there was no bottom in sight.

At ten thousand atmospheres Vinny became aware of a barely detectible grinding and crinkling sound in the Bardo shield. The spiders were working as fast as they could to halt the descent, but to little avail. There was a sickness in Vinny's stomach, a sickness such as a man feels the instant he turns around and realizes he has just slammed his child's hand in the car door. Sharon looked at him as if to ask, *Are you scared?* He was not scared—only disappointed that all their work and planning had been for nothing.

No one had spoken a word since Vinny's order to the spiders and slush makers. To someone who had never experienced a scramjet plunging out of all rational control toward the Pacific, the quiet resignation of the *Gaius* crew would have come as a surprise; but Vinny was learning that spectacular dangers were sometimes not nearly so frightening when one was in their midst as one expected when only imagining them.

This isn't so bad, Vinny thought. And the thought surprised him, then fascinated him; and fascination brought with it a momentary regret that no one on the outside would ever know how the final plunge had actually felt. No one would have believed him if he had told them it was . . . almost fun.

At twelve thousand atmospheres, the water found a defect at the juncture between two Bardo cones and began to squeeze through, causing them to jam. This set up a ripple effect that resounded through the entire system, causing the shield to respond more slowly to pressures that were already building faster than its ability to adapt. The membrane retained its integrity all the way to thirteen thousand atmospheres, whereupon six additional cone junctions began to fail.

Six hundred atmospheres deeper, a series of loud cracking noises reverberated through the hull. All eyes turned toward the ceiling. No one spoke or even gasped. The Bardo shield quieted before the inevitable cave-in. Vinny took Sharon's hand in his own, and in the stillness he heard Lenny whisper: "It is finished."

In the next instant the sea hammered through *Gaius'* roof with a force of overkill equivalent—as Sharon would have put it—to cracking a walnut by dropping a mountain two and a half times as tall as Everest on it from a height of five meters. The mountain shot through the cabin floor and burst the lower hemisphere of Bardo cones from the inside. The only items not pounded smaller than sand grains were the trailing ropes and balloons. The shockwave merely shredded them to pieces, kicking the slush free of the wreckage and letting it ascend. The remainder of *Gaius* formed a cloud of what had, during its brief life, ranked among the most advanced composite of materials ever invented, and these materials, as they fluttered down, began to separate according to size, shape, and density.

Microdiamonds fell out of the cloud, little industrial grade needles of compressed carbon. They were all that remained of Vinny, Sharon, Lenny, and Robyn. They expanded over a wide area during the long fall through volcanic upwellings and downwellings. Many settled like dust upon an inner, planetary shell of Ice Six. Here the ice melted at a searing seventy-five degrees centigrade, but the seafloor was riddled with volcanic hot spots, and in places the ice was actually warmer than the water above. In those places, frigid downwellings brought a condensing snow of clays, sulfides, and other life-sustaining ingredients—which mingled impartially with the *Gaius* microdiamonds. After a time, some of the diamonds either drifted to or were sucked down vents, where they passed through the Ice Six shell and, as a very rarefied snow, began drifting down toward yet another ocean floor.

At four million atmospheres, Vinny—what was left of him—fell upon a strange world of rock and metal slightly larger than Earth. There were lakes of molten basalt wider than Colorado, and hot sulfide springs of the sort that had sustained chemosynthetic bacteria inside Europa and at the bottoms of Earth's oceans. But the four Lunarians, had they survived, might have been disappointed to see that more than nine thousand kilometers of overlying ice and water precluded biochemistry in this world within the world. Here, where the words "rock" and "sea" took on yet another new meaning, the atmospheric pressure was so great that hydrogen atoms began to conduct electricity as effectively as copper and iron, and carbon, one of the most abundant elements in the sea, could behave only one way: by crystallizing. Where they were free of continental rift zones and pools of incandescent lava, where fine volcanic silts fell like sheets of drifting snow, Neptune's abyssal plains sprouted large, clean crystals.

One of these had grown a brilliant sapphire blue, another ruby red; but like the refugees who had struggled in vain to reach them, they were neither rubies nor sapphires. The red crystal jutted like a mighty obelisk through the floor of a dune field; taller than the Washington Monument; and yet by the standards of Neptune it was little more than a microscopic point of glitter poised on the edge of a diamond cluster wider than the continent of Australia.

22

Face-to-Face

IT WAS TO BE EXPECTED. THE CREATURES IN THE SHIP were—*ugly*. Their faces and their arms were supported by a skeleture so intricate and so refined as to be disturbing to look at. And in the manner of all creatures who had evolved from a hunting existence under sunlight or moonlight, they appeared to be staring right through him.

Fascinating, yes, but not particularly pleasant. And it was an illusion: Thaw Tint need not really worry about being stared through by Hollis and Wayville. It was quite the other way around. Being a member of an eyeless species, he sensed his surroundings as faint electromagnetic pulses and radarlike reflections of his own clicks and squeals. As had been clear from all those painstakingly reconstructed TV broadcasts which had leaked out to space before Earth switched over to cable and VR, human beings, living in a world of light, viewed each other only from the outside, and had therefore developed very different standards of beauty and ugliness.

Now, for the first time, with two of them caged safely below in a bubble of air, he could see what

humans were really like on the inside. There were
lungs and four-chambered hearts and fascinatingly
thick leg bones adapted specifically to life on the
continents. But what fascinated him most was the
depth and intricate perfection of their eyes, like cut
and faceted stones. They seemed as unnatural to
him. And they repulsed him.

Everything about these two brutes repulsed him.
He could not yet force out of his mind the odor that
had stained every object removed through the hatch
of *Alvin*, a damp stench of bad breath and un-
washed flesh mingled with old bilge, old clothes,
and old cooking.

For long days, Thaw Tint observed the creatures
in the darkness of their unfurnished cage. At first
they had huddled on the far side of the room, away
from each other, ingesting whatever foods and
medicines were thrown to them. After a time they
became restless and began exploring, crawling
blindly with outstretched fingers, backing away
from each other whenever they touched. Now they
had marked the room off in paces and could walk
across it without banging their noses. Having lived
with their sun above during the day, and their cities
aglow with artificial light at night, Thaw Tint wondered if there were ever times when the humans
missed the darkness. He suspected that it must
have been difficult to live always in the light. And
yet they seemed so utterly and uniquely helpless in
the dark.

It was time, he decided, to let them see his face.
He swam down from the ceiling and wrapped himself around a small console bound by pipes and rigging. Five of his tentacles completely covered a

touch-tone screen, and as if it were merely an Earthly pad obeying his scrawls and squeals, the screen summoned an array of hastily constructed tubes to life, filling his room with a warm yellow glow.

When *Alvin* was snatched into the sky, Hollis had half expected to see a flying saucer; but the Intruder ship was much stranger than a saucer. She knew at once that it was alien, but there was an eerie familiarity about the craft, reminding her of *Graff*, *Nautile*, or any of the other Valkyries, as if its design had been shamelessly copied by the Intruders. Like a Valkyrie, its core was a ten-kilometer tether. As a giant, retrofitted fishing line reeled *Alvin* in, Hollis estimated that the ship's frame could not have been more than four or five centimeters in diameter. It was a thin, translucent thread of light pointing away from her toward the constellation Taurus. When she saw it for the first time through the porthole of the submarine, with easily recognizable antihydrogen containment vessels and water tanks strung along its nearer end, she thought of a glittering pearl necklace adrift in space, or the beaded tendrils of a Portuguese man-of-war—deadly yet hauntingly beautiful, and beautiful because it was so deadly.

There were subtle differences between the alien ship and a Valkyrie, such as the ominously larger propellant tanks and, of course, the "fishing line," but there were no wild divergences. Hollis guessed that this was not necessarily an act of copying. Just as hydrodynamics dictated that all attack submarines be long and narrow with fins and conning towers in just the right places, and just as all airplanes would have wings, so, too, could all antimatter-driven rockets be expected to look alike. One did not want to intercept a great deal of gamma radiation from the matter-antimatter reaction zones, so the engine was mostly magnetic fields and empty space; and because it was energy expensive to accelerate even a single gram of matter up to and then decelerate it down from relativistic speed, starship design required ultralight construction. Instead of a large metal pusher plate at the bottom of a girder-supported tower and a crew compartment sitting on top of the tower—as would have been the case with a conventional rocket— mass reduction logic put the engine up front, where thick girders were replaced by a long thread that *pulled* the crew compartment and all of its supporting equipment along, like a motorboat pulling a water-skier. Giant pusher plates were replaced by magnetic coils and shadow shields, held in place by a system of thin, translucent rigging that resembled a spider's web. Being as close to nothing as anything could be and still be something, the starship was a glorified kite whose sail was a massless, odorless, invisible sheet of magnetic field lines. It flew on a muon wind of its own creation, dragging everyone and everything along on the end of a string. When all was said and done, the bridge to the stars was nothing more than an elaborate rope trick.

Jonathan had no way of knowing how much time he had spent in the dark. The bastards had removed his watch and every stitch of clothing, before dousing him with disinfectant and throwing him in here. He had heard that spelunkers usually misjudged time; they would stay underground for weeks and believe only a few days had passed. But the big difference was that the spelunkers were having fun. Time passes faster when you're having fun.

How had Einstein described it? When a man sits with a pretty woman for an hour, it seems only a minute. But sit that man on a hot stove for a minute, and it's longer than any hour. Biological clocks ran slower and faster—slower when one traveled faster; faster when one needed to be patient to win the prize of physical affection and the future of one's genes. Theory of relativity? Curse, yes.

After an immeasurable time that might have been days or weeks, the lights came on; but no matter what new horrors the light might reveal, Jonathan Wayville was ready to receive them—and prefer them—to the unbearable torture of sensory deprivation.

He found one wall of his prison to be a window into a dimly illuminated fish tank, slightly larger than a studio apartment. He guessed that it must have been energy expensive to rocket all those tons of water through interstellar space, and that even if the tank provided secondary storage for propellant, the enemy would not have brought it along unless it were absolutely necessary.

A carpet of black, fernlike fronds hung down from the tank's ceiling, looking like a British garden grown disastrously out of control. Two silver, crablike machines hung upside-down among the fronds. At first glance, Jonathan thought they might be the enemy, but he realized immediately that the "crabs" were mere automatons, little different from the "spiders" and "mice" that tended the rigging and engine parts of Earthly Valkyries. Little different, he thought, until one of them uprooted a frond and began hurrying toward the bottom of the tank. He noticed, then, how much shorter and thinner it was than a conventional spider, and how infinitely more graceful.

And there, on the bottom, with its back to him, lay the enemy. The crab rushed over to it with the frond, and without even turning to look, the creature reached out, snatched the black weed, and popped it into its mouth. Seconds later, it belched thick, brown dust out a siphon.

Like Hollis and Wayville, it wore nothing. To judge from its nakedness, Jonathan would have been inclined to interpret the scene before him as meaning that a crab-caged creature like himself had been collected from another world and, like a fish in a tank, was now being fed by its owner. But the console around which the creature's body was wrapped, and the touch-tone screen which, Jonathan guessed correctly, was transmitting actual pictures through its tentacles, made very clear who was master and who was servant in this house.

"Octopuses!" Jonathan cried. "I won't believe it. We've been abducted by octopuses!"

Hollis shook her head, seemingly unaware of her nakedness, looking surprisingly attractive and womanly to Jonathan. He had never even tried to imagine what curves might be hiding under her coveralls, and in a brief moment of admiration for her he felt ashamed of his own gaunt frame. Hollis showed no sign of judging him.

"If it had to be octopi from space," she said, "why couldn't they have been H. G. Wells's Martians in their tripodal war machines? *Those* we could have rounded up in the London zoo before lunchtime!"

On hearing these words, the creature turned around and gestured incomprehensibly. Revulsion and fascination washed over Jonathan in a wave, and his heart was skipping. The thing had no face. It belonged to a species whose flesh was impossibly white yet perfect. It was at once beautiful and obscene, godlike and profane, in that it had escaped its biological cradle to be here, light-years distant, for an evil purpose. Blind because it was eyeless, eyeless because it had never known light, it was a creature that nevertheless exuded a superpresence, as if it were somehow seeing right through him. The historian tried not to stare back, but he could not stop himself.

The enemy made another gesture with six tentacles, and Jonathan's heart skipped another two beats.

"What would be easier for you?" the alien asked through a hidden speaker, impossibly clear and bright and in the king's English. "That I tell you why we brought you here, or that you tell me why you came looking for us?"

"My partner and I did not come looking for anyone!" said Hollis. "We surfaced to find everything destroyed—by you, I presume—and all we did was send up a distress call to our own ships. We weren't looking for you, never knew you were here, didn't want to—"

"I was not referring to you and your partner,"

the alien said. "Forgive me. My English may not be entirely up to crack. I have learned as best I can from old newscasts, old children's programs, and old TV dramas. If my bad English distorted the intended meaning, you must allow me to correct myself. I was not asking why you, as individuals, came looking for me. I am asking why you, as a species, came looking for my people. Why did you begin designing, testing, and flying starship engines? Why did you not stay at home?"

"We built starships because we could," said Jonathan. "And people went out there, my own father among them, because there were no hints of radio, television, or any other kind of broadcasts anywhere except right here. Right in our own sunspace. It was the silence that drew us out. My people wanted to find out whether or not we really were all there was, if we really were all alone."

"Your turn," said Hollis. "Why did you bring us here?" Despite her nakedness, she asked the question with the authority of a church inquisitor.

"Because you are remarkable creatures. Electronic civilizations on the verge of becoming relativistic ones—what could be more fantastic? Or more rare? And you're all gone now, or soon will be. All except you two. We really held out no hope of finding survivors, traveling so conveniently in an unarmed vessel that could be collected and studied."

A picture was projected on the tank wall—translated, Jonathan guessed, into colors from sonic or radar imagery—or whatever means the aliens relied on for "seeing." The greens and reds were in all the wrong places; but there seemed to be far more detail than was necessary to convey the scene to human eyes, the kind of detail a hawk might be able to discern on the head of a mouse from ninety meters above. Silver crabs were swarming over the hull of *Alvin*, inspecting it, climbing in and out of the conning tower and removing pieces from inside.

"Beautiful piece of technology," said the enemy. "Virtually a hand-made machine. A pity that we can't take it with us. Too much mass."

"What will you do with it," Hollis asked.

"What would be easier for you? That we let it burn up in your atmosphere, or that we leave it in orbit? It could still be whirling 'round and 'round your planet, perfectly intact, millions of years from now."

Hollis thought about that for a moment. Throughout *Alvin*'s long existence, the ship had evolved into one of the strangest assemblages of tanks, motors, and computers that ever belonged to humankind. What the robotic doves alone would contain, if they abandoned the submarine in space, might qualify as an anthology of her civilization, Hollis told herself. If a hundred million years hence some other civilization did find *Alvin* whirling around a world that had cooled and become green again, the ship would tell much about its builders' daring and genius, and even their fallibility. *Alvin* would still be here, telling her people's story long after the mounds that had once been the pyramids ceased to be even a memory. But . . . but . . .

"But you killed everyone," she said suddenly. "You killed everything. You came here with that level of hatred in you. Why should you care what is easier for us?"

"Do not attribute to malice what can be explained by logic."

"Or evil."

"No," said the enemy. "Not your idea of evil. All your misfortunes arise from nothing more than a probability curve. Even if you were almost nothing to us, nothing more than an extremely low-probability threat, as long as we had the power to reduce that threat to zero, it was perfectly logical for us to do so."

"Threat?" Hollis said. "We were a threat to no one! Every one of our ships went out there in peace." Her voice was full of bitterness, but it felt good to get it out.

"Probably the strongest reason for your annihilation was the manner in which you hoped to seek out new life," said the enemy. He touched something on his console and the room was filled with music. "April 5, 1985, by your calendar. 'We are the world,' you boasted to the Galaxy—your whole planet, all at once. To this day it remains the loudest burst of coherent radio waves we have ever received. Our equipment locked on the source as soon as the signal swept through our system. That's when we learned about you and began watching."

"I'll take your word for it," Jonathan said.

A new picture appeared on the tank wall, much fuzzier than the view of *Alvin*. It was projected in simple shades of green and white and was more than 90 percent enhanced from what must have been a very weak signal; but one Patrick Stewart and his legendary starship were immediately recognizable.

"Barely more than two years after your proud and daring shout," the enemy explained, "you began to show us this." There came a momentary jumble of green and white static, which resolved itself into Borg and Romulan ships exploding, and a crystal line entity being torn apart, followed by another wave of static and interference, followed by a picture of bright beams shooting down from the *Enterprise* upon a planet . . . and another image of beams striking an alien ship . . . and another . . . and another. . . .

"All fragments of the same story," said the enemy.

Static again, then brilliant flashes from handheld weapons. A living machine burst open . . . an intelligent endoparasite disintegrated . . . a shapechanger glowed red and blue and vanished under weapon fire . . . and then something that reminded Jonathan of an octopus was gunned down and reduced to a scarlet stew. The segments repeated and repeated again, faster and again until they merged into an unbroken green glare.

Jonathan got the message. "Okay. You watch what is now our very old TV and pass judgment?" he said. "Don't tell me you really believed that we were coming after you with the *Enterprise* and phasers."

"Of course not. We knew immediately that no starship could be built to look like that and actually work. We knew immediately that it was pure fantasy, by any physics that we knew or that you could ever know. But it was clearly a fantasy of your hopes for the future. We saw a so-called exploratory ship armed to the teeth with weapons enough to destroy whole solar systems. We saw a species that dreamed of colonizing thousands of stars, of overrunning the Galaxy from end to end like a disease, and wherever you found others, they became subservient to your wishes. And when we looked more deeply, we saw that you really welcomed only humanoids like yourselves into the fold, and even those you welcomed were sometimes treated in the most appalling manner. We saw what you wished for in your deepest selves—"

Glare and static gave way to another excerpt. This time Hollis and Wayville were allowed to see parts of a single story. A world was about to explode, for one dubious reason or another, and behaving as if they were gods holding court on Mount Olympus, the officers of the starship *Enterprise*, adhering rigidly to their Prime Directive of noninterference, decided that rather than transplant a small group of civilized inhabitants and risk changing their culture, the ship's crew should do nothing and allow the entire culture to perish in the coming explosion.

"All those decades," the enemy said. "All those spin-off series, and the basic themes never changed. You became a scary people to us, because you seemed incapable of scaring yourselves. But all this would have been as nothing, except that you then started building real antimatter drives."

"But it was just a TV show," Jonathan protested.

"Our real ships *did* go out with explorers," Hollis

added. "They went out with explorers who sought only knowledge and carried no weapons, only questions."

"The questions your people asked required you to build relativistic rockets, did they not? To really ask is to shape keys. That first antimatter engine shining gamma rays to the stars was your key to the universe. But you never asked yourself if to use that key might be to open the gates to hell. I'm sorry for you, but in your case the answer has destroyed both the question and the questioner."

"Just a TV show!" Jonathan stepped forward, certain that he had heard wrong.

"By a fantasy you revealed your hopes to us," the enemy said coldly and loudly, clearly implying that Jonathan's refutal was absurd. "By a fantasy it started. You would not have needed the *Enterprise* to have become dangerous. Much less would have been enough."

"I still don't understand," said Hollis, still refusing to look naked and stripped of her pride. "Why this massacre? Was it necessary to kill all our people? If our fantasies bothered you, couldn't you have responded with a demonstration! Blown up Venus, perhaps? Simply scared us?"

"People scare best when they're dying."

"Shit!" Jonathan shouted. He punched the tank wall hard, breaking two knuckles. "Where did you get that from? Reruns of an old Bible show?"

"Better. We got it from your own Mister Spock."

Jonathan stood before the tank, shaking his head, cradling his broken fist. "Fuck this," he said to no one in particular. "Don't tell me I clawed my way up from VR addiction just to learn that aliens blew up the Earth because of an old Michael Jackson song and *Star Trek*.

"I won't believe this shit!"

"I won't believe it!"

23

Gaia

A HOT WIND STILL SCREAMED THINLY OVER THE sands of Vatican Hill, where, according to scripture, the Emperor Nero had crucified Saint Peter.

In a chamber beneath Saint Peter's Basilica, the last pope of the Roman Catholic Church had sheltered one of the three lost Arks of the Cross. For nearly a dozen centuries it had lain in Iram's Cave of Blue Light—a half-meter long chest of acacia overlaid with gold—until archeologists of the twenty-first century found it. As with the spectacular but short-lived Peterson discovery, they had been searching for something else. According to legend, Christian armies once carried the golden chest before them, much as the armies of Moses and Joshua were said to have carried the Ark of the Covenant into battle.

When members of the Pontifical Academy of Sciences opened the Ark, they found inside it a fragment of log with a thick iron nail driven through it. The wood surrounding the nail was studded with chips of yellow matter that turned out to be human bone. The Ark, and the Renaissance cathedral above it, had been reduced to fractions of their atoms by the relativistic blast—except for a microscopic sliver of bone that had, in decades preceding, been spirited away by Resurrectionist extremists.

Here, and all across Italy and parts of India, something miraculous was now happening. Fountains of hot water were breaking through the earth. And as the Sun burned through the clouds and the dust whirled and a stream ran forth from Vatican Hill to the dead remnant of the Tyrrhenian Sea, the springwaters filled with bacteria.

24

The Heretics

SIX DAYS AFTER THE STATION LEFT SATURN, WHEN all the obvious dangers of celestial billiards were behind him, Joshua stood before a floor-to-ceiling wallscreen in the mess hall, which made the Belly of the Cat look like a parody of the starship *Enterprise*'s bridge. In filtered white and golden starlight, with every lamp in the hall shut off, he took in the sounds of the sleeping ship, and slipped easily into vivid waking dreams.

He had never wanted followers, not even as a young man on Earth, and especially not during the period of increasing tensions between Karnak and Rome that had threatened to escalate into a holy war. That was when he came to suspect that not just a few of the Resurrectionists were terminally crazy.

Adolescence had been a nightmare unmatched by anything he could remember up till the day Armageddon shifted suddenly, serendipitously, from myth and prophecy to dawning reality. Growing up was difficult enough for most people under the best of circumstances, without adding a cult of fanatics who hung on your every word and expected you, by merely having the genetic makeup of a founding prophet, to be a messiah for that reason.

At the age of fifteen he rejected the throne that the Resurrectionists had tried to thrust beneath him, explaining loudly and at length that he could no more be their anointed one than could the ultimate Elvis impersonator—who painted impressionistic landscapes and expressed no desire to sing despite his indentical genes—live up to his sponsors' expectations. But he failed to convince his viziers that a cloned man merely copied his ancestor's physical structure, that he was growing up in a complex new environment in a completely different time, surrounded by people who did not exist when his gene donor lived. Though the genetic map had survived, preserving the characteristic laugh, the intelligence, and even the emotions of its forebear in identically laid out columns of the neocortex, Joshua alone among the Resurrectionists understood that the soul who dwelt in his neural pathways was someone entirely new.

And yet, when he first read the Gospels, he did indeed notice an odd familiarity in Jesus's words, in the same manner that one identical twin, when reading something written by the other, will sometimes guess what words are coming before he gets to them. In fact, when the words did not come as he expected, he became convinced that these passages were the apocryphal additions made by overzealous writers of later years. Many of these interpolations were quite annoying; a few made him smile. Joshua was convinced that if he and Jesus had grown up in the same century, they would have been able to communicate with each other in the abbreviated manner of speech so unique to twins and so baffling to outside observers. But this did not make them one and the same.

Even so, the more he read of his brother's ancient words, the more he gravitated toward the agnostic order of the Jesuits. The closest he ever allowed himself to approach the Resurrectionist expectation of him was to regard himself as merely the perfectly identical twin of Jesus; but his relentless sponsors persisted in ignoring such pronouncements, insisting that he was the second incarnation of someone who knew the smell of spices and sweet breads wafting from ancient Jerusalem's bakeshops, who knew what the light was like on the day Livia poisoned Augustus, and who could tell whether or not the earth really had trembled with his passing on the cross.

They refused to believe he was anything less than the one and only truth. They refused to believe it even when their one and only truth tried to tell them—when over and over again he tried to tell them—that his time and his surroundings had made another individual of him. He laid out a whole thesis on the separate consciousnesses of identical twins—that no matter how alike they might be, even when one was a clone, there would always be at least one difference between them: differing location in space—which meant that there were *two* of them. The only way they could be one and the same would be to abolish their separate locations, and then, by the law of the identity of indiscernibles, they would be one and the same—which was another way of saying there was only *one*. And still they refused to believe him . . . right up to the day he met Justin.

Justin, too, had tried in vain to convince the Resurrectionists that while they had successfully replicated the mental hardware of the Buddha, his software was that of a man who had not lived before. But his followers, like Joshua's, seemed to lack both the hardware and the software to grasp this insight, and were determined to live by his every utterance except his denials of divinity. Inarticulately, the Resurrectionists wanted to believe that Joshua and Justin did not truly know themselves; but their argument stopped at that point. Playfully, Joshua could see how it might have been made to sound more plausible. Had not Jesus prayed to God the Father in the Garden of Gethsemane, asking if he might be relieved of his mission on Earth? Was not Joshua in fact making the same kind of renunciation? A more intelligent Resurrectionist might have asked him to look more deeply into himself and discover that he was one with his brother, with himself . . . but none of this reasoning, however clever, could refute the biological facts. It could only insist on the truth of an unprovable reincarnation.

Justin and Joshua had struck up an immediate friendship, and it seemed that their sponsors could not have been more pleased when, together, two prophets—one from the time of Tiberius, and another who had lived before Plato began penning his tale of Atlantis—began exploring the nature of the human soul.

But it was the questions that they came up with that finally provoked the Resurrectionists to question what the twins had wished them to question all along, giving new meaning to the old expression, "Be careful what you wish for. You may get it."

First Justin and Joshua asked if it might be true that all religious philosophy was, at bottom, a human hunger for immortality.

An uneasy murmur ran through their communities.

Then they asked if it might be true that human consciousness—what their Resurrectionist sponsors called "spirit" or "soul"—arose from nothing more than a special arrangement of cells in the brain. "Could it be true," Justin asked, "that I am able to ask questions because during the first weeks after conception one small group of cells separated from another small group to become the core of my central nervous system, and that my mind arises from nothing more exotic than specific chemical and electrical signals that are an epiphenomenon not present in the cells themselves? And is it just my good fortune that I am a synergistic sum of all these signals, lucky enough to have arisen from the cells that became the folds of the brain, instead of that *other* small group of embryonic cells that migrated away to become unthinking skin, or liver, or blood?"

The murmur grew louder.

And then the two friends began searching for the meaning of the near-death experience, in which people all over the world, snatched by medical science from the moment between dying and death, recounted stories of leaving their bodies and moving toward light and even, on occasion, being given what looked for all the world like prophetic glimpses of a post-apocalypse Earth. Joshua had tended to regard the experience as an hallucinatory

state brought on by extreme physical stress, because, after all, the patient was still *alive*, and you
can have whatever illusion you like in a living
brain; but what interested him most was that the
Resurrectionists took all near-death visions as gospel. Seizing on this, he asked his followers how, if
they were to accept the visions as really meaning
anything, they would come to terms with the fact
that Christians and Jews, Muslims and Hindus all
met the gods and prophets in whom they had
placed their faiths and not those of other faiths.

"If you believe that God's hand is in this, then
what is He telling us?" Justin added. "If there is
something more to human consciousness than
mere streams of electrons, if the near-death experience is teaching us that man has a soul, then our
souls are telling us that all the world's religions
are equally valid, tailored to the local history and
experience of a people. Even the views of atheists,
who come back claiming to have been in a peaceful place where they met dead friends and relatives, must be valid."

Joshua said, "As for the apparent paradox of beliefs—even those with conflicting views—being simultaneously correct, why shouldn't this be so?
That's how I would have put the universe together,
were I God laying its foundations. In a multiverse
that already manifests every photon of light as a
wave and a particle, with both being contradictory
yet simultaneously correct, wouldn't this be child's
play? If God exists, why shouldn't His will be expressed as pluralism?"

The murmur became a roar.

The Resurrectionists had expected their prophets

to provide answers. But for a world in which every faction prided itself on possessing the one and only true faith, these were the wrong answers. They began calling Joshua an imposter, claiming that he had been resurrected from the wrong DNA, and seeming to notice for the very first time that his hair was "too dark and woolly" and that his skin was "the color of bronze." The pictures that had graced churches for hundreds of years—the stained glass images of an Aryan Jesus—were suddenly judged by his followers to be historically correct. They became afraid of him and began to hate him; and it wasn't just the Resurrectionists who feared him. The Vatican Society of Jesus had always regarded the Resurrectionists and their walking dead as borderline abominations. Seizing upon the sect's internal divisions, the famed Jesuit explorer Ashley Hollis, though she had never met him or spoken with him, closed her mind against Joshua and began calling for his downfall. And thus did Joshua become convinced that religions were inventions for gaining and holding social power, each hewing closely to the impulses, needs, and fashions of its time.

And so, as the Jesuits stirred the glowing coals of discontent, Joshua, being more shrewd and cautious than the sponsors who had summoned him to life, quietly fled Earth before the story of Jesus could repeat itself.

Six days since the Cat left Saturn . . . all the poisons of Earthly persecution were gathering again in Joshua's mind as he stood before the wallscreen and stared into the great pool of darkness ahead. He wondered if all that the Resurrectionists had amounted to was the asking of one question: What if Jesus had come back but there was no one left to save?

The answer hardly mattered, for it was clear to Joshua that even his crèche father must have been on the edge of madness when the end came. He had heard that they actually murdered the clone of Saint Peter . . .

And he wondered, too, about the alien persecution of humanity, about the many decades of travel that would be required to reach the hoped-for safety of the brown dwarf; and as the full weight of these coming decades pressed back on him from futurity, he became aware that someone was standing in the entrance behind him.

He turned to face Justin and said, "I am not Joshua," with defeat in his voice. "I feel closer to Moses, because I expect I won't live to see the Promised Land, much less take part in its conquest."

"Maybe not," Justin replied, maintaining his seemingly unbreakable equanimity. "Unless you live long enough to get to be Joshua, who Moses wanted to be if he had lived."

"Do we have the means to live that long? Do I want to live that long?"

"Of course you do," Justin said. "We're doing phenomenally well, so far. We got away without emitting any signs of our presence. The Luftigs say the only way the enemy could have seen us is if they happened to have a very powerful telescope aimed at nothing except our little patch of the Rings. And they're convinced we owe this happy circumstance to a very timely distraction."

"You mean the solar anomaly saved us?"

"It was rather more than an anomaly."

"What's engineering calling it today?"

Justin took out his pad and called up a telescopic view of the wounded Sun. "Bill calls it a crater. He says a huge area of the Sun simply swallowed itself."

"And he's certain this was no natural eruption?"

"No way. He's talking about a spontaneous conversion of energy to matter. Nature doesn't work that way, or at least it hasn't since the Big Bang. Disaster, my friend. The temperature at the Sun's surface plunged very near to absolute zero."

"Sort of redefines the expression, 'It'll be a cold day in hell when that happens,' doesn't it?"

Justin grinned. "The doomsayers of antiquity believed that when the world ended, beauty would take over. But I don't see anything beautiful coming from all this senseless evil, do you? Our once and sometimes beautiful civilization is reduced to utter nakedness, to the very fear from which it sprang."

"Then we must survive until we can rise up against our enemy. If we are patient and allow ourselves time to grow, we will become strong enough to defeat evil."

Justin put a hand on Joshua's shoulder. "Ever the optimist," he said. "You have just given one of Christianity's oldest arguments for the existence of evil. Without evil we have no understanding of goodness, no basis for comparison. The purpose of evil is that good may fight it and come to know itself."

"Where is the sense in that?" Joshua asked. "I'm

here with you today because followers who judged me evil chased me off the Earth. So much for our understanding of what is 'evil,' or what the word means. It's a very severe gift of DNA, what the Earth gave me. First time around, for my Jewish twin, it was the Jews who became frightened and hateful. This time it was a sect of Christians."

"Allow me to disagree, my old friend, before you carry that story of being persecuted by your own people too far. History does not uphold it."

"How so?"

Justin laughed. "In India we had the story of Saint Issa, who came out of Israel around the time the Roman roads began linking east and west. He was a very bright child. Our scholars found him preaching very remarkable sermons near the River Jordan when he was but twelve years old. They brought him east, where he was educated. And from the description of him, I'd venture to say that it his blood that flows in your veins.

"There are hints of his story even in the Gospels. Remember the three wise men from the east? Where do you think they came from? Where do you think Jesus disappeared to for nearly twenty years of his life?"

Joshua did not answer.

"Have you never wondered why Buddhism and Christianity both urge followers to live a life of service to others rather than one of profit and indulgence, why they both contain the Golden Rule and tell us that 'those who live by the sword shall die by the sword?' Why they both contain stories of an immaculate conception and the promise of a second coming? And why they both advocate a direct approach to salvation rather than the traditional use of rituals?"

"Parallel development? Coincidence?" Joshua ventured.

"You are an agnostic's Jesus, my friend. There are no coincidences."

"But this Saint Issa? He was judged and killed by his own people, wasn't he? Just like Jesus?"

"He was a holy man who associated with the untouchables and railed against the caste system. He drove the Hindus crazy, and it seems they in turn drove him back west. He returned to Israel in his early thirties, during the last year of Emperor Tiberius' reign. And just when he was really beginning to get interesting, Roman soldiers descended upon him and nailed him to a tree."

"Roman soldiers?"

"Yes, Joshua. In India they say it was an ambush by Roman soldiers, with no mention at all of his Jewish followers."

Joshua lowered his eyes and rested his chin on two closed fingers. "So his disciples lied."

"A little, perhaps," Justin said and flashed his easy, ironic grin. "What would you do if you were Saint Peter and you went to Rome hoping to build an army of Roman converts? Would you expect to get very far if you said, 'You filthy Romans, you murdered your own Messiah?' Of course not. Where do you think the old expression, 'When in Rome do as the Romans do' came from? Read this to mean; 'When in Rome, blame it on the Jews.'"

"So that's how you think it all started. The rise and fall of nation states, all those centuries of persecution and Holy War."

Justin nodded. "Ours . . . is a very devious and gutsy species."

Joshua noticed that his friend had almost said, "*was* a very devious and gutsy species."

25

Room Service

THE SHIP WAS UNDER WAY—AND HAD BEEN FOR A very long time—to where, the enemy did not say. A faint vibration was carrying down through the many kilometers of tether into the alien cage that held Hollis and Wayville. The room was now furnished with an ultralight, foamy, yet extraordinarily resilient material which had been fashioned by the silver crabs into an adequate rendering of wood trim and fabric cushions of the Victorian era. Thus furnished, the prison was indistinguishable from a first-class suite at New York's St. Regis Hotel.

The enemy had a name now. He called himself Thaw Tint; and before he cut *Alvin* loose, he demonstrated one commonality between the two civilizations, based on something Jonathan guessed the alien had gleaned from his study of countless "Star Trek" episodes and which he himself understood from personal experience: the love that a captain can have for her ship. And as he took for himself a mechanical dove and the pad on which Jonathan had composed his TITANIC ILLUSTRATED, Thaw Tint—"bless his little black heart," Jonathan later whispered to himself—had told Hollis that his "operating budget" left room for ten kilograms of extra mass to be taken aboard for the voyage, and he asked her if there was any part of her ship she wished to keep as a memento.

There were moments when Hollis blinked away tears before she could touch the robot arm, so hauntingly human in appearance, which stood upright on her writing desk. On one finger she had placed the last object ever collected by *Alvin*, the golden ring that had made a mysterious journey from East Rockaway High School to the *Titanic*. She was sure her great-grandfather would have been most amused to know that more than a hundred years after he began building *Alvin*, one of its robot arms would be carried to the stars as the last relic of human civilization.

As it turned out, the arm had given her cause to think much about *Alvin* and where it had been, and in consequence where in God's universe her enemy might have come from.

Late in the twentieth century, new oceans had begun turning up in the most unlikely places. Saturn's little ice moon Enceladus, when *Voyager II* found her, appeared to be caught in a gravitational tug-of-war. On one side was Saturn. On the other side were Tethys—which sometimes swept past Enceladus at less than one-eighth the distance separating the Earth from the Moon—and Titan, which, though nearly twice as far from Enceladus as the Moon was from Earth, was nearly as massive as Mars. Enceladus' crust was constantly straining and creaking, and as a result Enceladus, unlike comet Sargenti-Peterson and Ceres, had remained warm and wet inside for all the 4.6 billion years of its existence. Despite the fact that it could fit comfortably within the borders of New Mexico, and should have long ago been frozen to the core, it had become one of the most geologically active bodies in the solar system.

Because Enceladus had no atmosphere, water erupting through volcanic fissures in its mantle flashed to vapor, then froze instantly to snow. The first robot probes to park in Saturnian orbit found that Enceladus' surface reflected as much sunlight as freshly fallen snow and saw trillions of twinkling ice crystals occupying the moon's orbit, forming Saturn's outermost ring. Seismic probes revealed a rocky core 155 kilometers wide, telling of a world within a world, a planet so small that a submarine could travel all the way around its 487-kilometer circumference in a single day.

But Enceladus' mantle of ice was more than one hundred kilometers thick. Not even flights across interstellar distances totaling trillions of kilometers could provide an equivalent barrier. And there was nothing of value there, as far as anyone could tell. So the first Valkyries had set off for Jupiter and Alpha Centauri, and Ceres was in the process of being hollowed out when, near the end of man's Earthly existence, funds were finally made available for the launch of Saturn's first permanently crewed research center.

Nearer to home, and more thinly crusted, Jupiter's second largest satellite, Europa, was locked in an even more powerful tug-of-war. Four ice volcanoes were erupting plumes of snow a hundred kilometers into space. Though slightly smaller than Earth's moon, there were no mountains or crater

278 Charles Pellegrino and George Zebrowski

rims on Europa. Its surface was as smooth as a billiard ball, and girded with ice-filled cracks, as if it were warm plastic constantly in motion, with every hill sinking under its own weight.

This ocean, unlike its Enceladan counterpart, was immediately accessible. And so it happened that one of the first Valkyries ever built, flying on a quantity of antihydrogen small enough to be contained in a beer can, was able to carry an entire space station and *Alvin*—and all the other equipment necessary for penetrating Europa's thin crust—on a round-trip voyage lasting only three months. And, oh the sights that had awaited Hollis on the bottom of that hidden sea. She knew of a place where pillars of hardened lava were capped with creatures that looked and behaved like roses. They were colonies of living cells, barely more highly evolved than sponges. Lacking any trace of digestive systems, they lived by inhaling sulfides from basaltic rocks, manufacturing their own food and evolving, without benefit of solar energy, along a strange boundary between plants and animals. And she knew where there grew a mat of fungus-like cells, all descended from the same seed. It thrived so prodigiously on volcanic sulfides that it had formed a carpet wider than Lake Superior, and Hollis guessed that, unless something even stranger turned up, it might actually be the largest single organism in the universe.

But now something stranger had indeed turned up, eyeless and intelligent and warlike. It decorated the floors and walls of its stateroom with chandeliers of ice, and it called itself Thaw Tint.

The enemy had told Hollis that his people were

alarmed when they began to suspect that her people had gone out searching for them; but the very nature of Thaw Tint's existence told her that her people had gotten the story of life in the universe all wrong, and that they might never have found Thaw Tint no matter how much he feared them. Thaw Tint was an ice worlder. There was no doubt about it. Yet all Earth's starships and listening devices had been designed, chauvinistically, to seek civilizations on Earth-like planets—worlds of just the right mass located just the right distance from just the right kind of star. Even a quick look around Sunspace should have made it plain that the right kind of star was not needed, if one was looking for Darwin's warm little ponds. From Europa and Enceladus, Ganymede and Titan, Hollis' people should have guessed immediately that the Atlantic and Pacific were far outnumbered by ice-bound seas, and that all the universe really needed for the production of habitable worlds was the right kind—and not even necessarily *just* the right kind—of gravitational flexing.

The orbit of Jupiter would do just as nicely as Uranus or Proxima Centauri, Hollis realized. We need only look someplace cold, she told herself. Still . . . she could not quite understand how eyeless beings in an underground ocean had broken out to the surface and discovered the stars, or how they had managed to build a civilization in the first place without aid of fire and electricity. The questions raised by Thaw Tint's existence were so new that one could barely furnished criteria for how to go about answering them. But she did understand that her Earth had been a galactic minority all along, if not a downright freak: a rocky world with its oceans outside. There were so many more balls of ice out there, so many more throws of the biochemical dice. It occurred to her, now, too late to be of practical use to anyone, that almost all life in the galaxy must exist inside ice worlds.

Hollis always slept uneasily aboard the ship. It was the vibration of distant engines that kept her awake, and it should not have been so. The cage was quieter than *Alvin* and a hundred times more comfortable. The vibration was felt more than heard. It barely shook the bones and after only an hour, one relegated it to the realm of ordinary background noise. But it was always there, reminding her that the ship was continually accelerating toward an unknown destination.

In fitful dreams she found herself rising to face her God, and from the depths of unexplainable inequity demanding a solution to the timeless mystery of senseless evil.

Hollis got her answer—the same answer given to Job—which at first hearing answered nothing, and at the same time answered all. God spoke to her out of a roaring storm, saying, "Who is this that darkens council by words without knowledge? Gird up now thy loins like a man; for I will demand of thee, and answer thou me!

"Where wast thou when I laid the foundations of the Earth? Declare if thou hast understanding.

"Hast thou entered into the springs of the sea? Or hast thou walked in the recesses of the depth?

Or hast thou seen the doors of deepest darkness? Canst thou bind the chains of the Pleiades or loosen the cords of Orion? Hast thou comprehended the expanse of the Earth?

"Declare if thou knowst all!"

Three thousand years ago, when those questions had entered the oral history of the Hebrew tribes, they were meant to define the wonders of creation and dare man to comprehend them. According to the Book of Job, man was incompetent to cope with the universe. Man, a poor little beast who, measured against the mind of God and the time frames of the Earth, lived for an instant and then died. The roaring storm declared that God's reasons were hidden—beyond Hollis, beyond Wayville, beyond all mankind. The answer, it seemed, was simply this: the universe did not necessarily make sense. The cause of all Hollis's sorrows—the emptiness, her horror at the fate of the Earth—came from a universe now likely to keep more information to itself than she was ever likely to discover from the confines of her stateroom. But that did not discourage her from trying.

When she awoke, with the scraps of the storm still bubbling up from her subconscious, she declared to herself that thou didst indeed have understanding. Had she entered the springs of the sea, or comprehended the expanse of the Earth?

Yes, she told herself pridefully, one could say I've done that.

Walked the recesses of the depth, or seen the doors of deepest darkness?

Yes and yes.

Bound the chains of the Pleiades, or explored the shoulder of Orion?

Yes—if we'd had time, we could certainly have done that, too.

Was it blasphemy to say so? Hollis wondered. In a universe that was not supposed to make sense, did it matter?

After she had showered and awakened Jonathan, the illumination slowly brightened, as it did every "morning." Breakfast was waiting on a "rosewood" table—Earl Grey tea with lemons and honey on the side, English muffins, and a warm dish of something indistinguishable in texture and taste from filet mignon and fried eggs. Hollis could not begin to explain how the silver crabs had managed to replicate Earthly meals without having a chance to taste or analyze them firsthand.

She had barely begun to puzzle over this, as she did every morning, when she noticed that a "porcelain" clock had been added to the room while she slept, and fine "woolen" curtains now framed the place where a cityscape window would have been, but where instead Thaw Tint's tank wall rose to the ceiling.

"Tell me," Hollis said, cutting herself a strip of beef, "what it was like in your iceworld. How did you come to discover space?"

"Why?" Thaw Tint asked.

"Because you understand that it would be easier for me if I knew more about you. That's all. How does one who lives in eternal darkness discover the light-year? On Earth, where the stars are visible at night, men like Galileo were persecuted for saying that the universe was very large and that there existed other worlds. For your own Galileo it must have been a thousand times harder. I can imagine an expedition swimming up to see if and where the sky ended, and finding that it really did end—that you could go up only so far, and you'd bang your head against a ceiling of solid ice. I almost hear your priests on the ground shouting, 'See! What did we tell you? The universe ends at the crystal sphere. We are at its center. And we are all there is.' "

"So you doubt that we should ever have found the outside. Why not? Clearly we did. Are you certain that we had to have a Galileo in our midst? Or a Vatican?"

"No," said Hollis. "It's just that the difficulties must have been multiplied in your case. They *must* have been great. Even if you suspected there was a world above the ice, what could you do about it? Start chipping away at the ceiling? Start tunneling up through it? If your world was anything like Europa or Enceladus, you would have tunneled a lava tube all the way to the surface. Cryovolcanism: the moment they broke through, your explorers would have erupted naked into vacuum—a very poor advertisement for further space exploration. And even when you finally did emerge onto the surface in space suits, what did you think the stars were when you saw them for the first time, after so many millions of years of living without sight of anything like them? How did you even *see* the stars in the first place?"

"What my history could tell you," the enemy said, "if I were to reveal it to you, is that you should not have asked these questions."

"What do you mean?"

"You ask bad questions. And did I not tell you that some answers can destroy both the question and the questioner?"

"How so?"

"You know damned well how," Thaw Tint said with perfectly simulated inflections of bitterness. "If I tell you that my world has an atmosphere, or confirm for you that it does not have an atmosphere, I will begin a process of elimination for you. And you might begin to guess from that where we came from."

"So what?" Hollis asked with genuine bitterness. "You've already told us about Michael Jackson and 'Star Trek.' I'd say that narrows the field down to a couple of dozen light-years. What harm can there be in telling us where you came from or where you're taking us? There's precious little chance that we could manage to escape from this cage with that information, or accomplish very much with it even if we did."

"So why do you want to know?" Thaw Tint sneered. "Why should I give you the answer?"

"Because there is no chance of escape for us. Whom could you tell? Is anyone left?"

"I'll give you that it's an extremely low-probability event—the pair of you ever escaping and breeding a colony where we could never find you; but, no, I cannot discuss my origins, can I? My orders are against it."

Jonathan, who was sitting on the edge of a couch and seemingly lost in thought, looked up suddenly and blurted, "Orders?"

Hollis and Thaw Tint ignored him.

"So which would be easier for you," the enemy

asked, "that I tell you nothing or that I tell you that some of your assumptions are wrong?"

"Orders?" Jonathan asked again. He was standing now. "Who gives *you* orders?"

Thaw Tint made a peculiarly human pointing motion with one tentacle, as if incapable of withholding what was demanded of him. Jonathan looked where the enemy was pointing and saw nothing except a clump of black fronds and two silver crabs.

Now it was Hollis who stood up, but Jonathan came to the realization before she did. "God, no," he said. "Don't tell me this—"

"Surely you don't carry out the orders of your servants," Hollis finished for him. "Are you suggesting that your machines guide this ship, decide what secrets must be kept, and dictate your military strategies?"

"You stupid bastards," Jonathan said, turning his back on the alien. "You let it all get out of hand!"

Thaw Tint inched forward. "What did I tell you? Some of your assumptions are wrong. Now gird yourselves up and know this: it is not the machines who work in our best interests or serve us or belong to us. It is very much the other way around: they keep us here and watch over us only because they find us interesting."

"How did this happen?" Hollis demanded as Jonathan exploded into maniacal laughter. "Were they your machines in the beginning?"

Jonathan's laughter began to drown out her words.

"Jonathan, shut up!" she shouted. "Or the machines swarm upon you from another star?"

Jonathan subsided, but Thaw Tint did not answer.

"Your people started it, then, didn't they?"

Silence.

"What happened?" Hollis demanded. "Did you allow them to evolve minds of their own? How could you have been so stupid?"

Silence.

She glanced at Jonathan, who was chuckling quietly to himself and scratching his genitals.

"You were smart enough to build starships," Hollis pressed on, "and yet you didn't see that it might be dangerous to have slaves who might become smarter than you?" By putting Thaw Tint on the defensive, by confronting him with the disdain of a species he obviously considered inferior, Hollis was hoping to pry more information out of her enemy turned fellow captive. But the tight-lipped alien seemed to catch on to her method and folded up like a hibiscus at midnight, leaving the priest with her questions.

26

The Black Cat

THE CAT WAS SO DISTANT NOW—AND HAD GROWN so small to telescopic eyes—that even with the best 'scopes imaginable, no one aboard had to fear that the Intruders might detect the ship by its passage in front of a star or distinguish the faint blip from identical occultations of stars by the multiple billions of similarly sized rocks. The station's surface was camouflaged with a charcoal-black regolith of carbonaceous silt, and was even pitted to give the appearance of a natural object. As the time came to put the uranium salts on line, to slowly recharge the central core of batteries, the first set of spare, disposable batteries had been drained and were being ground down to dust for rail-gunning aft.

Very carefully, the Cat began laying a faint, slowly expanding cone of dust behind itself. The cone's engineers had realized that even a golf ball–sized relativistic bomb, if hurled against them, could vaporize the entire station in an instant. Anticipating the possibility that their sector of the sky might become the target of a relativistic shotgun blast—with each pellet programmed to

288 CHARLES PELLEGRINO AND GEORGE ZEBROWSKI

seek and destroy any habitat-sized object in its path—the refugees saw that a small target had the advantage of knowing within only fifty meters where a pellet was going to strike. To this advantage, Justin had added the observation that one should stop concentrating on what a relativistic bomb does to its target and consider what the target does to the bomb. It was then possible to see that even a grain of dust looked to a relativistic bomb like a crate of dynamite, and that if one scattered enough grains in its path, a golf ball–sized pellet could be disintegrated thousands of kilometers behind the Cat.

One of the crew had suggested that premature detonation might reveal the Cat's position; but Justin pointed out that it would be impossible for the enemy to distinguish the interception from a collision with naturally occurring interstellar dust, and that even if the explosion was potentially revealing, it was infinitely less dangerous than doing nothing.

The point was moot. Curiously, the dust shield intercepted nothing.

Presently, the Belly of the Cat was full of people. That they had not yet been R-bombed did little to stay their mounting anguish. Joshua knew that before the Promised Land was reached and settled, a healing had to take place inside the people of the Cat. They had to be instructed, made to see a sustaining and nourishing vision, and come to believe in their future survival and growth *as if it were already an accomplished fact*. He had to open a window on the next century and pass the Cat through it.

He reached again into himself, into the clarities

born of atrocity, and saw humanity's militant future. There was no need to hide judgment in the smoke of fear. His people were already fearful and judgmental enough of the aliens. The trick, then, was to exorcise their fear, to whatever degree possible, and hold out to them the promise of a miraculous rebirth.

"What our enemy does not yet know," he announced, "is that it has already saved us."

"What are you talking about?" a tired voice called out.

"We have, in reality, slipped through their natural selection filter. We've been chosen."

A faint, mocking murmur passed through the gathering, but Joshua ignored it and said, "Something very much like this happened sixty-five million years ago, when our ancestors were very small and ratlike. They survived by hiding in the nooks and crannies of the dinosaurs' world. And then one day something destroyed almost all the life—most notably the dinosaurs—yet allowed our termite eating forebears to tread the Earth unimpeded and become us.

"The process is repeating. Now it is we who are very near to being extinct, and we *would* be, if not for one unlikely and still hidden development: the enemy struck too late. Humanity had already begun to metastacize into the Asteroids, into the Saturnian Rings, into the deeps of space. If the aliens had struck a hundred years ago, or even fifty, they would have gotten us all. But instead we live to find the brown dwarf, to settle modestly, for the time being, into the nooks and crannies of our enemy's house."

"For how long?" a young male voice shouted, full of an odd mixture of grief and aggression. "They can catch us at any time."

"If they suspect we exist," Joshua replied, glancing over at Justin. His friend seemed to be smiling with approval—or was it simply the acceptance of the inevitable? Joshua had not been able to escape the feeling that Justin sometimes simply wanted to lie down and die.

"We are the ones who escape," Joshua continued, "at first by pure luck. Then by becoming the strongest, the brightest, the most inventive."

"The most stubborn," Justin said softly next to him.

"We will live," said Joshua, "because even though we know that the enemy is fallible, we shall not count on it."

"But what will we become?" Justin asked, raising his voice, and Joshua felt the stab of betrayal from his friend. But he set it aside, telling himself that no fear, no doubt must remain hidden from public discussion, lest it fester in private.

"And the tactics!" Justin continued. "What will be our tactics? May we hope to defeat the enemy in any of our lifetimes? We can evolve new technologies very fast, but not that fast. We have no tactics. Has anyone a plan beyond the brown dwarf?"

Joshua said, "First we must guarantee ourselves time. First we must live. That's the way of it at a time like this. Amateurs talk tactics. Professionals talk logistics."

"Then I ask you again: what will we become?"

The question was a labyrinth, Joshua realized,

carrying within it a longing for worthwhile effort, for guarantees that could not be given. Joshua nodded, acknowledging his friend's insight into complexities that could not be faced now, then said, "We will become like them in one respect—survivors. All of you here, set your minds on the brown dwarf!" He turned back to Justin. "It's the only place we can go, my friend." The word seemed suddenly strange on his tongue, and he wondered if Justin was in fact still his friend. Could his apparent dissent, or even his questions, pose any danger to the Cat's survival?

A middle-aged man stood up and fixed Joshua with his brown, tired eyes. Joshua recognized him as a nanotech specialist whom everyone called Al. "Let's understand what you're asking of us," the man said. "We're to take up housekeeping somewhere in this dark star system and start breeding. Is that right?"

Joshua nodded, hearing the unbelief in Al's voice, seeing the lack of will in the man's eyes as he stared into them, hoping to instill some of the strength he felt.

But Al had his own strength, and it was different from Joshua's. "You can quit now, false messiah. We all know where this is leading, so don't talk us into sitting through the play to the end. I think some of us would rather signal our position to the enemy and let them destroy us than face the life you envision."

"What's so terrible about the dwarf?" Joshua asked almost casually. "It will become a place of healing for us—*our* place—the portal to the universe for us as a powerful new civilization."

"Or our portal finally to hell!" Al cried out. "Everything we've known, everything we thought we could return to is gone. And you're telling us what Stalin once said to his people as they went into a war, that now there will be fewer but better Russians."

Perfect silence reigned. Joshua could feel the weight of Al's doubts, and how much they were shared by others in the room—and he felt them himself, despite his efforts at self-control. But then, as he thought of how rare the human species had become, the word "logistics" sang loudest to him. The miracle that lay in the new opportunity to restart humanity would not be lost.

"Listen to me!" he shouted. Your doubts are not completely your own. They were placed there by the aliens. We must answer them with a great, inextinguishable resolve!"

"It *is* a wheel," Justin said, his calm voice swelling in the silence.

"If we survive, grow strong, and defeat the enemy, perhaps we'll get off the wheel," Joshua said.

The Buddha smiled. "Long before then our descendants will be looking around with suspicion in their hearts for another species that may pose a threat to us simply by existing. The wheel's circular logic is perfect, convincing and unbreakable, and perhaps even ultimately necessary. Remember, the wheel's logic does not require that there be any actual threat."

"But you do not deplore it."

"I only describe it," Justin said. "To judge the nature of things as they are would be folly."

"Then perhaps we should embrace the wheel."

"Embrace it? What happened to turning the other cheek?"

"Did I say that? *I* didn't say that. Someone else said that."

"Then, once again I must ask: what will we become?"

"A Pentecostal apocalypse, probably."

Loud murmurs of assent burst from many parts of the room. The nanotech specialist glanced down at the floor, looking wounded and forlorn, as if he now saw that he had fallen in with insane people. Then, as the murmurs died away, Justin turned his gaze again on Joshua and said, "Perfect vindictiveness?"

"Perhaps not," Joshua replied. "Strength has options. Perhaps events and relationships can be reshaped in ways that are not yet apparent to us. Maybe a thousand years hence it will be possible to forge a circle of survivor civilizations that can avoid conflict. Maybe such a circle already exists."

Justin smiled. "It may be just such a circle that destroyed *us*."

Louder voices rose in agreement, but it seemed to Joshua that attitudes were becoming prone to shifts without warning and, soon perhaps, without any logical cause. The people were growing exhausted and confused under the pall of constant worry and relentless deliberation. And there was too much to worry about. Even if the enemy never found them, their internal problems might prove overwhelming. At even the simplest biological level there was the question of genetic variability. There was simply not enough variety in a sampling of

humanity this small. New techniques for DNA ma-
nipulation would have to be developed if the species was going to flourish.

"May I suggest a healing," Joshua said, realizing
suddenly that he had to offer something that should
be perceived as both a clear plan of action and an
escape. "May I suggest that we consider biotiming
across to the brown dwarf?"

"And how will that help?" Justin asked, and
Joshua knew that his friend was not objecting this
time; he simply wanted the advantages of such a
course spelled out. You'd better tell them the truth
about themselves, his eyes said to Joshua.

"If we biotime," Joshua said, "there will be no
time for our exhaustion to become internal strife.
Let us save our energy for what must be done at
the dwarf star. Sleep will make the journey short.
And I cannot help feeling that we need the time
away from ourselves, so we can heal our wounds."

And how will you heal yourself? Justin's eyes asked
him silently. "You really think we need the seda-
tion?" he asked aloud.

"A new beginning requires a new awakening,"
Joshua replied. "Sleep has his house, they say, and
we must find rest there. The Cat can take care of
itself, and we'll need all our resources when we arrive."

"But if anything goes wrong en route," said Al,
"I wouldn't want to be in a coma depending on the
judgment of the Cat's robots. Our machines may be
technically sound, but the human brain is still the
most thoughtful computer we can have aboard a
spaceship, and the only one in its league that can
be produced with unskilled labor."

"I agree," said Justin. "Biotiming will make us little different from the VR addict who zones out, or the alcoholic who drinks to escape his problems. The problems are still there when they emerge from their stupors. If we are frightened now and confused in our dealings with each other, sleeping won't solve those problems. They'll still be with us when we wake up. I think we should make the passage the hard way, sober and with our eyes open, so we can learn from it."

"Then I implore you," Joshua said to Justin and the entire gathering, "let's set our doubts aside, stiffen our spines, and plan to survive!" He glanced at Al, and all eyes turned with him to the nanotech engineer.

Al shook his head and shrugged. "I'll ride into hell with you if necessary. Bravely and with my eyes open, I'll ride as far as we can. But let me tell you something, false prophet: You're just as fallible as any of us, and what we are is a cutoff limb of humanity, without much head or purpose, with no place in this universe—until we prove otherwise."

After the meeting was over, and the brother of Jesus sat alone with his friend in the mess hall, the idea came full blown to Joshua. It was almost naive in the simple way that it marked a crossroads.

"It's all in our heads, what happens to us," Joshua said. "That's all that decides it—what we think we can do."

"Of course," Justin replied. "*You* can think of tomorrow and even be right about it, but what about the others? Al doesn't really care whether he lives or dies. It means nothing to him. The only thing that moved him at the meeting was what you and some of the others might think of him, so he put on a brave face, hoping that he might even convince himself. Being cut off from Earth—from its past and future—that's what will continue to sink into them, and you'll see that they're not whole, that they are indeed flailing appendages cut off from a corpse. Maybe you'll even begin to admit that fact to yourself."

"We'll have to put a new will into them," Joshua said, "and into their children, and you'll have to be more helpful. Children will make them want to live again. With children they can start to reach into the future again. That's it, children. And as soon as there is a new generation that will not weep for Earth, we'll be saved. What are we waiting for? Till we get nearer the brown dwarf? Till we put a full light-day between us and the enemy? We have to start right away."

"Maybe you can. They can't. Only you. I think I see that now. You may have to do it because you can't survive without us."

"That's not the only reason," Joshua said.

"What is it, then?"

"I can't help it . . ."

"What?"

"My flock . . ."

"You've spooked yourself with too much history," Justin said.

"No, it's come to find me. You said it yourself: only I can do it."

"You don't have to, you know. Turn away. Let the cup pass and don't drink from it. A moment ago you were just prattling about choices and cross-roads."

"I can't help it. I have no choice. My flock will die without me."

27

The Race of None

IT WAS VERY UNCHARACTERISTIC OF THAW TINT TO break off a conversation and refuse to speak to anyone, even to a machine, for days at a time. For much of his life there had been no company except the silver crabs. Now there were these humans, who filled him with constant fascination but whom he suspected of looking down at him with pity and utter contempt. He knew now that it had been folly bordering on madness to tell them the truth about the crabs.

Jonathan and Hollis were sitting up late one "night," discussing their situation, when Thaw Tint decided to break in on their conversation.

"I've seen enough octopi in my time," Hollis was saying as she adjusted a white terry-cloth robe around her shoulders. "Usually they're quite cowardly."

"That's not quite accurate," Thaw Tint interrupted. "Octopuses, to use the equally acceptable alternative plural, are considered merely shy."

The alien had come back to them with its voice changed—new, but unexpectedly familiar. So, Jonathan thought, he's been watching programs of rather more substance than "Star Trek" and "Sesame Street." The new voice reminded him of Sydney Greenstreet talking to Humphrey Bogart in *Casablanca*. It lacked personal identity, but it was duplicated with such virtuoso skill that Jonathan expected at any moment to be addressed as "My dear Ricky."

"So," Jonathan said, standing up to face the tank, "you've come out of your long sulk at last."

"I hope you've noticed that your accommodations continue to improve."

"Yes," said Jonathan. Judging from one of these improvements, he suspected there would always be gaps in Thaw Tint's understanding of his captives—or fellow captives, as the case might be. A convenience bar had been added, with a lock and key and card that gave instructions for reporting all purchases at checkout time. Thaw Tint or the crabs or both were either too literally familiar with human ways or were making a grim joke. The terrycloth robes weren't bad—one large, one small—but they didn't smell like terrycloth.

"The water isn't warm enough in the shower," Jonathan added with sarcasm. "And my favorite brand of chocolate isn't in the convenience bar."

"I'm sorry the accommodations are not quite perfect," said Thaw Tint, but Jonathan was sure that the alien considered them perfect and was merely simulating politeness. "The water will be warmer."

"I should hope so. You certainly have more than enough heat to exchange."

"Can we get past the chitchat?" said Hollis. "I have to know—are we all there is? Is anyone else left alive?"

"Not on Earth," the alien replied. "That is certain."

"Have you found others? Away from Earth?"

"Yes."

"Are they alive?"

"No."

As Jonathan watched, Hollis got up from her chair and turned her back on the alien, and he realized that Thaw Tint's words had struck her deeply with their implications. He knew what she felt, but pushed it away, telling himself that the time for caring was now past.

"I still don't understand," Hollis said, turning to face the tank. "What did we ever do to deserve such wrath?"

"Wrath?" Thaw Tint asked. "How can you think it was a punishment? Wrath? This was nothing like human beings warring with each other. There was never any anger toward you. Why do you not understand this?"

"But you destroyed the Earth, didn't you?" she asked, as if her question could undo the fact.

"Yes."

"Then the universe makes no sense. . . ."

"For us to wait until you became a threat to us— *that* would have made no sense. We knew your hopes better than you did, better than you know them even now. We know you were testing anti-matter rockets, and as intelligent as you were, we knew that you would soon boost yourselves to even greater abilities."

"You were afraid that we'd become smarter than you?" Jonathan scoffed, and sat down again in his chair. "You should have studied us a little more closely. Doesn't work. Not on vertebrates, at least. Not on Earth. No one was in a hurry to volunteer for human experiments after we tried to give the brain boost to a bunch of apatosaur pups. They taught us how easily you can throw the whole nervous system into chaos and crash yourself. It's sort of like slapping hydrogen and antihydrogen together in your living room: not the sort of mistake you can learn from."

Thaw Tint shifted uneasily in his console. "You would have returned to the problem sooner or later—and give yourselves some credit—eventually you would have solved it. And then, with the intelligence to even further boost your intelligence, to hybridize with your artificial intelligences, and with relativistic rockets at hand, you would have become as a wildfire to us. And there was a very real chance that you would have destroyed us at the first opportunity."

"But why would we want to?" Jonathan asked. "If we became more intelligent, wouldn't we become less destructive for that reason? Wouldn't we seek—peaceful contact?"

Hollis stepped forward. "No," she said, grabbing his arm. "High intelligence doesn't mean you're incapable of evil deeds. The two aren't mutually exclusive. Just look around!"

"My dear octopus," Jonathan sneered, "I may be a bit thick, but I still don't understand why you think we would have destroyed you."

"Because you could not afford not to. What risk of racial death would be acceptable to you? Two percent? One tenth of one percent? *Any* risk at all is too great. Removing that risk would not have involved hatred on your part, only pragmatic fear, as you would say. I'm sure if all your historical records were available to you, they would confirm that one or two farsighted individuals among you had anticipated all that has happened. Only a few such insights would have been enough to set you against us."

Jonathan took a few deep, nervous breaths, and let him see the shock and understanding spread across his face. Even the most irritating of Thaw Tint's revelations—*Star Trek* and Michael Jackson's song—were beginning to make sense. He sat forward in his chair and raked his fingers through his hair, still trying to catch his breath and steady himself.

But the alien went on, saying, "The progression of developments that would have made you a threat are inevitable. We could not have risked even the remotest possibility of your coming out into the Galaxy and washing over us, even if you failed to understand for a short time the folly of *not* destroying us. You see that, don't you?" His voice was very low now, almost croaking like that of a frog, and Jonathan knew that this Sydney Greenstreet would never laugh.

"They make a desert and call it peace," Hollis whispered.

"Tacitus," Thaw Tint said immediately, "a Roman historian who could not step out of history."

"And you do?" Hollis said. "Pragmatism works best in moderate situations. It breaks down in extremes, when real moral issues confront each other. Beware, dear octopus."

"You persist, my dear Hollis, in not understanding this crucial point. It was clearly our survival or yours, sooner or later. Nothing more, nothing less. What is it that we should be wary of?"

"Do you believe in God?" Hollis asked in a sudden, shrill voice, and Jonathan saw that she was about to lose her composure.

"What do you mean?" Thaw Tint asked. "I've seen this reference on your broadcasts, and I've never been exactly clear what you mean by this God."

"A supreme being who watches over the universe, who fucking stands outside of everything the way Tacitus couldn't. Has your culture ever suspected that such a being might exist? Have you ever perceived such a presence?"

"God? But the universe is self-sufficient! Didn't one of your great scientists conclude that in Stephen Hawking's universe there was nothing for a god to do?"

"So, you're godless," Hollis said, as if confronting someone who owed her money.

"Godlessness, as you call it," Thaw Tint replied with what seemed to Jonathan almost like patience, "is the first step toward innocence."

So that's why they destroyed us, Hollis thought, because they're godless, and felt ashamed of her sudden fundamentalism. It was not worthy of a Jesuit. She recalled the words of Saint Anselm: "The fool hath said in his heart that there is no God." But this was no race of fools. No god had ever punished them, and never would. Surely, if there was a God, punishment would have been visited on Thaw Tint and his kind. If this crime was not big enough to bring God's wrath, then nothing would be, or he didn't care, or he wasn't there—but she was trying to resist that final step from agnosticism to atheism, trying to fathom God's mysterious ways, trying to tell herself that it was not for her to judge God, that all of life was a test to make one worthy to see God face-to-face, and that the martyrdom of humanity was just such a test. But did it have to be so extreme—nothing like what was asked of Job or Abraham, nothing at all like the twentieth century's efforts at genocide, unlike anything . . .

"And your people all think this?" she asked in a trembling voice. "You all believe this?"

"What is there to disagree about?" Thaw Tint said.

Jonathan felt the despair coming out of Hollis like a white heat burning deep within her. The priest's entire worldview, built up over a lifetime of thoughtful effort, was being shaken to its foundations, and he knew that her imagination was a self-contained hell of her own creation; and for the first time he felt sorry for her. Facts warred with her emotions and her reason could not deal with either. Here was an intelligent race that did not share human concepts of morality, ethics, or fair play; who in fact saw such notions as self-serving, local illusions.

"You are telling me the truth?" she pressed.

"Why shouldn't I? How can it benefit me to lie about such matters? Why should I protect you? What can I gain from you by lying?"

"Then explain to me how your culture managed to evolve without a sense of mercy. When I view the evolution of my own people, I see man's concept of God evolving as man evolved. Before the time of Babylon's kings, if a member of your tribe killed a member of mine, then it was my duty to kill your entire tribe. Then there emerged the concept of an 'eye for an eye, tooth for a tooth, life for a life.' It was the first attempt to make the punishment fit the crime, and a step toward mercy, preparing the way for the prophets who would tell us, 'love thy enemy.' How did it happen that your culture never evolved beyond the tribal warriors who built Babylon?"

"You make the mistake of equating the story of your evolution with what you call progress. We have no religious beliefs, no cultural moorings, only demonstrable knowledge and a pragmatism that follows what you would call the natural grain of the universe; but this does not make us less advanced than you are. We have no malice toward anyone, of the emotional underscoring kind that is inherited from evolutionary nature. We simply see what is there, and make sure that we see it. Caution is our essential way, born of long contemplation. You might call our conglomerate a culture that is so unparochial that we see it as simply the way to be."

"There you have it," Jonathan said. "The Race of None!"

"An apt description," came the reply. "By comparison, you belong to a race in which mind appears unfortunately linked with a tendency toward imaginative closure—"

"And you have liberated yourselves?" Hollis interrupted.

"Yes. We have no culture as you know it. We follow knowledge where it leads, and where it may lead us on forever, into deepest time, if that is the case, with no closure. We know what we were and what we are, so we don't invent lies about ourselves or the universe."

"You know what you are," Hollis said, "but do you ever consider what you *should* be? Hasn't it occurred to you that you are a race of murderers?"

Jonathan laughed at her question. "Save your breath. To them it's no more than a man spraying bugs in a kitchen. It's an infinite universe—at least a very big one—so come to think of it, why shouldn't there be a killing star here and there? Maybe you get this kind of scared, twisted killing culture in any given galaxy as often as you get individuals who commit murder."

Thaw Tint said, "But even your culture recognizes that killing in self-defense is not murder. We should have no disagreement, since you would have done the same."

"But we weren't there yet," Jonathan said. "And it doesn't follow—logically or anyway you want—that we would have necessarily wanted to destroy you once we learned of your existence."

"Really?" Thaw Tint said, giving a good imitation of disbelief. "Your word alone is scarcely . . . well, not something that my race could take to the bank. I personally believe you, but others of your kind would certainly have had other opinions."

"Oh, yeah?" Jonathan said. "Tell me, how often do you do this—knock off whole intelligent species, I mean."

Thaw Tint did not answer.

And as Jonathan looked surprised at the enemy's silence and thought *gotcha*, Hollis wondered what the Jesuit philosopher John MacQuitty would have made of the present situation. He had seen the human species being called to a great and grand destiny. "And that evolutionary destiny is the discovery of the universe," he wrote, explaining that people would go freely and consciously into a revealing universe, that they would begin to understand loneliness, and that God lay within the loneliness of the cosmos. "Humanity is being called upon to go into a newer, stranger sort of womb than we have ever known before. *That* is what the Earth has really been headed for, during all of its four and a half billion years." And she wondered about what loneliness could possibly mean to a being who had *always* existed, who could never *not* exist, and whose infinity was as much a mystery to itself as her own finitude was to her.

Hollis laughed bitterly to herself and asked, "Have you ever tried to transcend this kind of paranoia? You might succeed by contacting a culture very early, to avoid later violent contact, perhaps by placing observers when the culture is still young, perhaps even by influencing the growth of fundamentalist religions to thwart the advance of space science."

Thaw Tint did not answer, making her feel that her arguments were feeble and naive. Her uncle Gisum had made her feel that way once, when as a little girl she had asked him why all people couldn't be "nice."

And as Jonathan Wayville looked across the room to where Hollis sat in her chair hugging her terry-cloth robe around her, he realized that she was probably the last woman alive, the last female he would ever see, and it startled him to admit how little he knew or felt about her.

Later, when Thaw Tint had retired to some hidden ante chamber, they sat silently for a long time. Finally, she turned her head and gazed at him with crazed, moisture-laden eyes and quivering lips.

"Do you believe that we're the only ones left?" she asked, as if demanding that he lie to her. Jonathan looked back at her, struggling with his primitive, protective feelings that he had never wanted to have pulled out of him, and decided that he would not lie to her, because like Thaw Tint he had no mercy in him. Heaven's gentle rain had simply never blessed him with any, so he could not bless anyone else with it, however much he strained. Besides, what respect he had for Hollis told him that she wanted the truth, and that he would only earn her additional contempt by lying.

He nodded. "Probably. We failed to raise anyone, so either there was no one left or they weren't answering. Somehow I don't believe Thaw Tint lies. Do you agree?"

She nodded, trembling in her chair but making no move toward him.

"What would he gain by lying to us?" Jonathan continued. "He just about said so himself: he'd lie only if there were mercy in him."

"But elsewhere in the solar system . . ." she started to say. "Escape was *not* impossible. Some life will always escape, of whatever you try to kill. Thaw Tint's knowledge can't be perfect!"

"Who knows? We can hope, but we'll never know. I'm afraid we can count on this Race of None being very thorough about it. Maybe they got us all."

"Maybe," she started to say, "maybe Thaw Tint won't ever find out if there are other survivors."

"I'd be very quiet if I were they," Jonathan said, suddenly taken aback by the possibility that Hollis might be thinking of playing Adam and Eve with him. It would not take much, he guessed, for her to put a spin on the Catholic myths that her Jesuit's mind took such great pride in rationalizing ("Human life resembled nothing so much as the Way of the Cross," he had once heard her say). In no time at all he would be cast in the role of the new Adam, and Cain would be killing Abel as the aliens watched from outside the cage—assuming, of course, that their captors permitted such a union to take place. A fruitless union was as far as he would go, given enough time, he told himself. For mercy's sake.

"If their curiosity about us is ever completely satisfied," he continued, "or if they do find other survivors, I doubt that they'll need us anymore," and the words caught in his throat as self-pity overcame him. He clenched his teeth and was silent. Though he had never gotten along particularly well with people, he realized, as he looked at Hollis, that he had needed the mass of humanity around him.

He decided that when Thaw Tint returned, he would ask him for the pad on which he had constructed his TITANIC ILLUSTRATED program. Wasn't every life a *Titanic* disaster writ small? It hits the iceberg and is ripped open when it first understands its own mortality. And faced with this intolerable fact, it seeks to launch lifeboats, in the hope that something of itself will survive; for it knows that it will not survive, even if there are enough lifeboats, because it *is* the ship itself. Art, literature, music, may survive; children will pass the torch before they also pass away. But the sinkings could only be overcome when there was a humankind around the individual to receive his lifeboats, to fish artifacts out of the ocean, to remember. With humanity gone, the old quip, "nobody gets out of life alive" had taken on a deeper, even more horrific meaning. He would sink away completely . . . except, perhaps, in the minds of the aliens. . . .

"Jonathan?" he heard Hollis say from across the room, but it seemed much farther than that. "Jonathan, what's the matter?"

He was certain he had seen his pad lying near Thaw Tint's console, alongside one of *Alvin*'s mechanical doves. And while it was true that the program had been erased, and that he would have to start reconstructing it from square one, surely the alien would not deny him this—well, kindness, if not mercy. Besides, the program now needed more revision than ever . . . and, yes, Jonathan suddenly knew why he needed very badly to be working on it again.

He *had* to return to the *Titanic* because from it he might still be able to launch lifeboats.

III

ORIGIN OF THE FITTEST

Friends may come and go, but enemies accumulate.
                    —*Jim Powell*

28

Spring, A.D. 2096

Deep in the Earth, the hydrothermals were still dreaming, as they had been doing for more than four billion years, evolving new life with which to invade the surface. Gaia, the fecund bitch goddess, was far from exhausted, determined again to display her fertility to the Sun. The recent eradication of life from her surface was merely one of countless interruptions.

The bottom of Manhattan Bay rioted with strange, white colonies of bacteria, some of them clustering into long tendrils that swayed in the currents as if to music. Beneath the place where Radio City had once stood, a new volcanic fissure, venting like a giant undersea snowblower, spewed white clouds of life out over the bay floor, as if preparing the stage for a new show in the music hall.

At Long Beach, great pillows of microbial life called stromatolites were forming a reef. Some of the bacteria could trace their ancestry to Hollis's and Wayville's breath, but mostly they were descended from the geysers that had broken through the foundations of City Hall, sending forth sulfides, and hot water, and heat-loving microbes—which, as they streamed seaward, cut shallow channels through the graves of The Renaissance and The Breakers.

Living off carbon dioxide and mineral-laden hot water, a bacterial mat as wide as the Earth itself had formed a hidden biosphere which for most of man's existence had thrived undetected beneath his feet. It was much like the world Tam had been exploring inside comet Sargenti-Peterson. But this biosphere, like Europa and Neptune, had never frozen to death. It was still quite alive, and even before the coming of the relativistic bombs it had dominated the Earth. Extending kilometers down, and girdling the planet, the sheer weight of the bacterial mat exceeded all the plants and animals on the continents and in the oceans.

Within each bacterium, the DNA was itself a microscopic biosphere, an invisible ecosystem built from competing bits of genetic material utterly indifferent to the needs of the cell in which they lived. The city builders had never understood this, had never appreciated the genetic maps they so vigorously charted as representing something that merely borrowed the body of a human or a bacterium for a while (it did not matter which) and then moved on. In the end, it was DNA that ruled humanity and the Earth. Everything else was vanity.

Where Hollis had beached *Alvin*, the water around the stromatolites was clouding with streamers of brown and red bacteria whose membranes were already evolving precursors of chlorophyll. The rains of Judgment Day had passed, leaving the horizon cloudless and golden hued. The Atlantic was as calm as a quarry pool, and the noon sun shone sapphire pink overhead as the first of what should have been an enduring lineage of sun-loving organisms displayed the rudiments of pseudopodia—which in an epoch or even a millennium, would enable its descendants to move more efficiently and devour their neighbors.

But this was not to be. As if from jealousy of Gaia, the Sun struck back. Directly overhead, a stream of ghostly beads erupted through the corona. The most powerful telescopes ever invented might never have seen them against the backdrop of the blazing pink disk. If the Sun had been eclipsed at that moment by the Moon, and if the objects had been emerging at an improbable angle in which they were not themselves eclipsed, the right equipment might have detected three tiny stars scintillating on the edge of the corona.

There was no hope of anyone knowing what they were or where they were headed. As quickly as they appeared, they disappeared.

And there was no question, if there had been someone to ask it, of their being a natural phenomenon. They burned with great power, yet emitted no neutrino glow.

Nor was there any question of their remaining captives of the Sun's gravity. They were moving at more than two thousand kilometers per second and still accelerating when, where they had been, the solar magnetic fields collapsed. And then, changes that even unaided eyes could see spread over the heavens. In the tidal pools between clusters of stromatolites, shadows weakened inexplicably, yet the sky remained cloudless.

The Sun itself was failing—and failing fast.

On the eastern horizon, the red hull of the Moon was rising; but it faded simultaneously with increasing darkness. Now the tide pools reflected stars. Among them, Saturn and Mars burned brightest. Mars, the nearer of the two was, at this point in its orbit, more than fifteen light-minutes from Earth, and four minutes farther from the Sun. Nearly twenty minutes would be required before Mars could repeat the Moon's vanishing act; but before those twenty minutes could pass, the sky was on fire.

29

The Stars Will Speak

NO ONE COULD SAY WITH CERTAINTY WHEN THE change came over Joshua. All anyone could be certain of was that, as year gave way to year, proving that in the now-timeless world of the Cat there was no particular need to worry or to hurry, proving that Joshua had indeed been right about letting tactics give way to logistics, Joshua began worrying more and more about tactics.

As Justin saw it, the change, although not yet threatening the routines of what was slowly growing to resemble a stable society, had come to Joshua with the arrival of his daughter. The Cat had not yet traveled a light-day when Cherene was born to him. She was celebrating her seventeenth birthday and the ship was still less than halfway to the dwarf when the glare of the nova filled the sky astern.

By this point in the passage, observation screens had been placed throughout the ship, turning the areas around them into mini lounges. When Cherene found her father, less than a minute after the nova was announced, he and Justin were already occupying one of the lounges and were watching the Sun brighten until it drowned out all the stars on the wallscreen.

"Can you get a neutrino reading?" one voice called to another over the intercom.

Justin and Joshua ignored the exchange. They were busy guessing at the technology and the energies involved in what they were witnessing, and Cherene was thankful that her family had voted for moving the Cat a safe distance away from Sunspace. All three understood what was happening but not why.

"Difficult to believe," Cherene observed, "that the first electrons to race through a porphyrin molecule on primeval Earth and to fuel a protocell started a chain of events that have led to this immense destruction."

"Perhaps in such a universe it would be better to return to nothingness," Justin said. "Embrace the oblivion and count oneself lucky."

"It's always better to survive," Joshua said, with his old pride. "You don't experience anything when you're nothing, so you can't tell if it's better. You can only think so when you're alive. Basic logic, Justin. Think, think, think."

Justin smiled. "Perhaps there are safer ways for interstellar cultures to contact each other. It might be done subtly, so that they could get used to each other, first to the very *idea* of there being other civilizations, long before the development of interstellar flight triggers the conclusion that relativistic attack is rational and necessary."

A voice called across the intercom, announcing that the neutrino flux at the core of the nova appeared to be dropping off.

"Do you think it might rebound?" another voice speculated. "Do you think the Sun may re-collect itself and burn steadily again?"

"Doesn't matter now," someone called back. "Nothing can be left alive back there."

Justin shook his head and managed a weak smile. It seemed ludicrous to him that anyone could be concerned with solar physics at a time like this, but he did not laugh. They were still trying to adapt; and, all things considered, they were doing a better job of that than he had expected—better than he felt he could. In spite of the best efforts of immunogenetic technicians to slow the aging process, his hair was graying and thinning under the assault of a deepening depression, and he was gaining weight.

He said, "Maybe someone *had* tried to soften us up for a peaceful contact, but failed. It could have been going on for the last twenty-five hundred years, beginning with the rise of prophets who preached mercy and culminating with literary and media obsessions with alien contact. Sure. Emerging civilizations must be too rare and too important to just bushwhack without first making an attempt to save them—if not for assimilation, then at least for study. Maybe someone was trying to avoid the production of future killers by implanting peace religions in every new human culture. And one by one these religions failed. The Gospels were not very effective in teaching evolution's warriors to love one another, in turning them into holy men."

And slowly, Justin turned his eyes from the wallscreen to the daughter of Jesus' twin—and she was no longer merely his friend's child but a magnificent bronze-skinned woman who was going to be more brilliant than him and her father put together.

Going to be? Justin asked himself. She already was. "No holy men," he emphasized for her. "And let me add that I have never heard your father mention Jesus the Son of God, only Jesus the warrior."

"The Gospels as interstellar insurance?" Cherene asked.

"The Gospels as interstellar damage control," Justin replied.

Joshua lifted his head. "There's not much we can do about it now," he said. "Jesus must be a soldier now, as far as I can see. As for God the Father, I don't really believe in him, and I doubt that I ever will. Prayer, faith—these are ways of making up one's mind. Religiosity is a secular necessity, especially now, but it always was, whatever people told themselves."

With his fingers he sketched letters on his pad and the starscape rotated, allowing the three of them to turn their backs on the dying Sun and gaze forward, where the black maelstrom of the brown dwarf beckoned.

At the center of the storm, the dwarf's heat and resources would hide and nourish a new interstellar devil, if Justin was to be believed. And this new womb, swelling with life's surge, would continue the chain reaction of rational paranoia begun, perhaps, by some long-ago relativistic bombing of some now impossible-to-identify species. Here humanity, as it had once known itself, would linger, increasing in numbers, growing in knowledge, dying to its own disillusionment as it sharpened and transformed its intelligence and bodily aspects into something that would aspire to occupy and control as much of space-time as possible.

Cherene shuddered only slightly as she imagined the future taking Justin's predicted path. She envisioned the community of the brown dwarf changing over time, forgetting the old ways and languages. It would still think of itself as the humanity that had come out of the nearby star, but it would in time become something better suited to fulfill the old dream of spreading out across the Galaxy's bright stellar valleys. Justin and some of the others might disapprove, but what were the choices that she had grown up with? To live, survive, and prevail was simply to follow the way things were, even if one might imagine and even hope that they should have been otherwise. There was a big gulf between what "ought to be" and "is."

"We'll come out from there one day and destroy them," Joshua said. "Disaster," he called out to the starfields, "disaster for you all, for what you are forcing us to become."

"Why not just let vindictiveness go?" Justin said. "Why not just go down into the dwarf forever and concentrate on survival?"

"This *is* survival! Will our mercy save us if they find us again? There is no room for forgiveness. This time I did not come as a lamb led to the slaughter. This time I come with a sword in one hand and a dagger in my teeth." His own words surprised him, because in their now-familiar rancor he had felt a momentary doubt about embracing the way of the warrior, because of the fate it would set upon his daughter and upon her children. The Jesus of the Gospels would have felt abandoned by God the Father after humanity's martyrdom. "Heresy, heresy," his still, small voice whispered; but even the orthodoxies had once been heresies. He told himself that he had to cleave to the realities as paint did to the grain of wood. There was no other way.

His weakness passed, and he put it down to Justin's power of suggestion. His friend knew the truth of things—of what was and should be—but he did not know what to do about it.

Joshua asked, "So you think we've become fanatics?"

"Does it matter?" Cherene replied.

"It's a wheel, my friend," Justin said, "killers beget killers," and Joshua beheld again a widening rift, and suspected that he and Joshua might one day no longer be friends. If Justin's ideas prevailed, the new colony might not last long. Cherene could think for herself, but even with her it could go either way, and being right might not be the side of survival.

An overwhelming sense of new danger came into him, filling him with dismay and self-doubt, but mostly with fear. He did not want Justin or Cherene to see him this way. He needed time to calm down and think. Without a word he turned away from them and walked off toward the bridge, trying to force from his mind all the grief-stained thoughts of the dead Sunspace aft and setting his mind on the maelstrom ahead. It was useless to try, of course, as always. He might just as well have tried beating back the tide with a sword.

He came onto the bridge and found one young man on watch. It was Al's oldest son, Gerd, and while Joshua was coming to view the next generation more and more as an army, it seemed to him that this boy was incapable of harming a fly. Gerd nodded to Joshua as he sat down in the command station.

The nova was displayed front and center. Nothing of dying showed in Sunspace, except for the dimishing output of the star. Not only were we expelled from Paradise, Joshua reminded himself, but it was destroyed behind us as we fled. He wondered if any Intruders had been caught up in the explosion, then switched the view forward, calling up the latest color-enhanced map of the dwarf's ring system, and struggled again to force Sunspace from his mind.

A sudden shift in the constantly updating spectrum revealed that a large iceworld orbiting between two rings might possess a thin, nitrogen atmosphere not unlike Triton's. At once his imagination saw open skies, rolling hills, and blue oceans—and they tormented him with their loss, reminding him that his lifetime and at least several to come would spend themselves with an awesome discipline as the refugees made a life for themselves in the deeps of the black lake ahead. From that cauldron, he told himself, something even more powerful than the Intruders, and perhaps a little more clever—and certainly much angrier—was going to blaze forth. And yes, Justin was right, the black womb would birth a new killing kind . . .

He stood up violently. "Disaster," the brother of Jesus cried out to the impassive stars. "Disaster for you all!"

Afterword: Reality Check

by George Zebrowski

THE SCIENCE HAS TO "CLICK" OR THE PLOT MUST change accordingly. That is the rule we laid down at this book's inception. And we adhered to it—religiously. If we wanted to have a scene in which a Toyota Celica was required to drive backwards at one hundred kilometers per hour and it turned out that a Celica could not sustain one hundred kilometers per hour in reverse, the ground rules required that we find a car that could (a 1967 Dodge Dart slant-six) or rewrite the scene. Be assured, therefore, that when you read about a given planetary position in a given year, or about an object flying at a given speed a given distance from (or inside) the Sun, that the numbers are based upon actual calculations. Some of the rockets described in this novel are true, advanced preliminary designs, and such odd bits of hardware as the rope braking system deployed by the ill-fated *Gaius* team were in fact flight tested on models (specifically for this novel and for Charles Pellegrino's first novel, *Flying to Valhalla*).

How much additional reality is there in this book? Are such wonders and nightmares as relativistic bombs, the cloning of founding prophets, VR addiction, the dominance of hydrothermal life over the Earth, antimatter-propelled starships, and attack from interstellar space, real possibilities? Yes and no, as follows:

1. Relativistic bombs. They violate no known laws, but they require vast amounts of energy for acceleration—which is in fact available. The concept of the R-bomb originated as an unanticipated off-shoot of the Valkyrie brainstorming sessions (an informal "thought experiment" begun by Charles Pellegrino and Brookhaven National Laboratory physicist James Powell in 1984 and continuing into the present). Early Valkyrie designs required the development of the smallest hydrogen bombs (antihydrogen-triggered) ever conceived—smaller, in fact, than an amoeba. By firing sixty of these per second in a magnetic field, it became possible to imagine accelerating a spaceship up to ninety-two percent lightspeed—which is a nice speed to be traveling at, because anyone aboard will be aging at only one-third the rate of stay-at-home observers on Earth. (The bomblet approach is currently being abandoned in favor of a simpler, more efficient engine design: stay tuned.) The realization, by early

1985, that interstellar flight did not present any insurmountable technological barriers and would in fact (assuming civilization could hold itself together) become reality by 2050, raised questions that had never been asked before, perhaps because the whole idea of relativistic spaceflight had always seemed like pure science fiction. One of these questions was: What if we strike a planet with a mass equivalent to a small space station at ninety-two percent lightspeed, or even thirty percent? This led to the concept of relativistic cluster bombs and a re-examination of Fermi's paradox, and to the nick-naming of Powell and Pellegrino as "the Pablo Picasso and Salvador Dali of nukes." (They have yet to figure out which one is supposed to be Picasso.)

2. The Valkyrie brainstorming sessions and their implications for alien contacts as suggested by the relativistic bomb problem—reality. For dramatic reasons we have taken some liberties with the chronology and for obvious reasons some of the names have been changed, but the actual matters arising (as presented in the ill-fated Ed Bishop's file, which allows readers to look over the scientist's shoulders, somewhat like flies on a wall) are so fascinating and chilling in their own right that we have had no real need to exaggerate them in any way.

Ed Bishop is also real. He in fact introduced the authors of this novel to each other at the Rensselaer Polytechnic Institute in 1988.

"George, you've got to meet Charles Pellegrino," Bishop said to Zebrowski over the phone as part of convincing him to come to RPI's science fiction convention, Genericon IV.

"Charles who?" Zebrowski answered.

"You'll like him. He's interested in everything! A real polymath—works in half a dozen sciences at once, and he writes, too!"

Yeah, yeah, yeah, Zebrowski thought to himself. But Ed Bishop was right. Within hours of meeting, Pellegrino and Zebrowski had plotted a short story, "Oh, Miranda!", which became the cover story for The Magazine of Fantasy & Science Fiction *in September, 1991. And the great Bob Eggleton did the cover painting. By the time that story was published, they were already at work on* The Killing Star. *They wrote their outline, Zebrowski came up with the title, then discovered that Pellegrino had once published a science article with the same title! It was a sign.*

We hope Ed Bishop appreciates our extrapolation of his life into the next century.

3. Self-replicating machines—a dawning reality. It is not by our rocket technology that expansion into the universe is limited, but by the current (primitive) state of our computer and robot technology. Between 2005 and 2008, terabit computers—*easily trainable ones*—should become readily available, and from that moment we will be on the verge of creating robots indistinguishable, in their movements and behavior, from colonies of smart insects. The development of self-replicating machines will make possible giant engineering projects previously deemed prohibitively expensive—including solar arrays on the Moon capable of beaming all of the Earth's power needs down on microwave lasers (i.e., clean electricity for all man-

kind*) and arrays of linear accelerators (also on the Moon) dedicated to producing the many tons of antihydrogen propellant necessary to power crewed Valkyrie starships. Pierre Noyes, who brought a breath of fresh air to the Valkyrie brainstorming sessions in 1994 (and who worked with Freeman Dyson on Project Orion), cautions that once machines reach this ant-like level of intelligence, mutation among their replicants—and an evolutionary process far more rapid than anything the Earth has seen in biological organisms—may commence. "We may not be able to prevent it," he says. "Try to imagine a million years of evolution taking place in very smart ants overnight. You need not look to the stars for your Intruders. It is not inconceivable that we will create them right here on Earth."

4. Alien contact, given hundreds of billions of stars in the galaxy, and the ease with which carbon compounds can be nudged to protocell evolution, and assuming a galaxy more than twelve billion years old—a statistical certainty. Fortunately, results from the Hubble Space Telescope suggest a universe that may be only eight to twelve billion years old, and possibly closer to eight. If this is true, then according to the Genesis and Galactic Blight Theory (re: Pellegrino and Crick in *Time Gate*), at the time enough heavy elements had accumulated to allow the formation of life-producing, Earth-

---

*This, of course, presumes a civilization wiser than today's, for if people must worry about those same microwave lasers being turned against nations as weapons, their construction will be prohibited.

mass worlds, Earth (aged 4.6 billion years) was among the very first, if not the first, to form. If this is the case, the reason for the pervasive silence in the galaxy is that most Earth-like planets have not been around long enough to sprout civilizations and (unless old ice worlds are a wild card in the equation) we are alone out to a radius of more than 1,000 light years, and hopefully altogether alone. It would be nice to know that the stars belong to us.

5. The artificial boosting of human intelligence— probably more real, and more near, than you think. According to the latest laboratory experiments, one or two simple brain proteins seem to determine the efficiency with which nerves fire and thoughts are connected. Already there is talk of genetically "tricking" bacteria into manufacturing these human brain proteins, meaning that the first in what will undoubtedly be a series of recombinant, brain-boosting drugs could become available in as few as five years, more than seven decades before they came into use in this novel.

6. The genetic similarities between birds and dinosaurs—more real every day, now that Rocky Mountain Museum paleontologists Mary Schweitzer and John Horner have isolated what appear to be fragments of saurian DNA in a *T. rex* bone. It should be noted that Schweitzer is turning much of what we thought we knew about the process of fossilization upside down. Every new class of paleontology students has learned from textbooks that fossils are mere *images* of once living matter, with none of the living matter remaining intact. (Pellegrino and Wygodzinski proved in 1978 that amberized insects were an astonishing exception to the

rule; but they were only partly correct because amber, while offering the best known protection against the ravages of time, might now be more rule than exception.) As for where this self-perpetuating textbook dogma originated, Pellegrino has been able to trace it back to the discovery of hollow impressions in the volcanic ash of Pompeii during the 19th century. When the hollows were filled with plaster, and the ash was scraped away, images of people could be seen. By analogy, silica and other minerals were said to have replaced bones and shells in the fossil record, and thus did a freak occurrence come to represent the norm.

Now we know better. In addition to Schweitzer's *T. rex*, a second well-preserved bone (an *Allosaurus* femur) came to light when UPS delivered it broken in half to fossil-hunter Mark Newman, who noticed a startlingly intact marrow-like substance spilling out of the interior and remarked, "I know someone who may be interested in this." The bone was promptly passed on to Pellegrino who, with James Powell, identified under an electron microscope what looked for all the world like marrow vesicles and even blood cells whose histology was hauntingly reminiscent of "ostrich." Mary Schweitzer (who appears in Chapter 17) subsequently confirmed that our Jurassic sample looked chillingly like what she was pulling out of the Cretaceous Period. She suspects that as much as forty percent of some fossil bones may consist of original (albeit degraded) organic material. Now that (according to preliminary results) the first minute fragments of *T. rex* DNA may be in hand (with Allosaur DNA next in line) Schweitzer's ongoing analysis suggests that paleontologist Robert Bakker (long thought to be a bit too crazy about birds) was right all along: some dinosaurs were so closely related to birds as to be practically sibling species. After all is said and done, Tyrannosaurs and Allosaurs begin to look like parakeets designed by Stephen King.

7. The mysterious preservation of sheets of paper on the *Titanic*, while sheets of inch-thick steel have deteriorated, is a fact and not a fiction. In fact, in one corner of the *Titanic* debris field, bacterial dissolution had erased boiler casings and iron stairways from existence, leaving only a scrap of newspaper dated April 10, 1912, still taunting us with words of the maiden voyage "of the world's largest luxury liner . . . unsinkable."

8. As with the artificial boosting of human intelligence, several of the fictions presented here threaten to become outdated by the realities of scientific achievement before this book sees a paperback printing. For example, the bags of mail referred to in Chapter 4 have, since the writing of that chapter, been found intact by a deep-penetrating *Titanic* robot named *Robin*. Discussions are now under way to save these documents from advancing streams of iron oxides and bacteria-laden sludge, and to restore them for eventual museum display (we wish George Tulloch and Arnie Geller Godspeed). Meanwhile, a Berkeley pathologist has announced plans to clone an amber-embedded virus of Cretaceous age. Before he risks yanking Leslie Wells's mistakes from the realm of fiction, we beg that he put aside dreams of a *Jurassic Park* until he has taken a second look at Michael Crichton's *first* novel.

9. The dinosaur cloning recipe—which became the basis for *Jurassic Park*—was first proposed by Charles Pellegrino, who agrees with Steven Spielberg that resurrecting the extinct is not science fiction, but science eventuality. In 1988, Pellegrino and Powell proposed—*as a reality*—"Dinosaur World Park, New Zealand." They also, at that time, eliminated two errors from the original recipe: (1) Because insect digestive juices are unfriendly to DNA, and because amber-producing treesap will not likely penetrate quickly to ingested dinosaur blood, mosquitoes ceased to be the insect of choice. Dinosaur flesh preserved on the mouth parts of biting flies will fare better. (2) A "match and patch" approach to reconstructing genetic coding sequences had eliminated any need for borrowing missing bits of code from frogs and other organisms (nevertheless, certain cell organelles, including nuclei and DNA structural elements, will have to be borrowed from present-living cells). Accordingly, the original recipe has been revised and updated for this book.

10. The starship detection method described in Chapter 2—reality.

11. The tunneling effects of a relativistic bomblet through the Earth's atmosphere, as detailed by Powell and Pellegrino—reality.

12. The peculiar chemistry of carbonaceous chondrites—reality. A more detailed account can be found in *Darwin's Universe: Origins and Crises in the History of Life*—which is the book Captain Tam snatched out of the air in Chapter 7.

13. The decline of literacy in favor of computer fastspeak and virtual reality—tragic but perhaps inevitable.

14. VR addiction—go look at what the entertainment industry is downloading into human minds. It's not a long step to *preferring* virtual worlds to reality. In fact, sophisticated philosophical arguments might be made that an artificial reality is superior to the so-called real world which imposes itself on us against our will. VR worlds offer the *experience* of omnipotence if we make a circle of input-output for human minds. You can have anything you like in your mind.

15. The story of the *Yorktown* and Edith Russell's pig—reality.

16. The story of astronaut Fred Haise and the piece of *Aquarius*—reality. Haise's remark about "not dwelling on cracked heat shields" was made to Pellegrino when his candidacy for a space shuttle flight was under discussion in 1983, just prior to the first night launch of the ship Pellegrino hoped would carry him—her prow, titanic; her name, *Challenger*.

17. The 1985 Michael Jackson broadcast of "We Are the World"—reality.

18. The temple of Buddha's Tooth in Sri Lanka—reality.

19. The oral traditions surrounding Saint Issa and the Arks of the Cross—reality. As for the eventual reality of human cloning (although we are set against it)—a dead certainty. And please stand by, for we cannot escape the feeling that Cherene has another story to tell.

20. The deep Earth biosphere of hydrothermal bacteria: the evidence is indeed mounting that the greater living mass of the Earth exists beneath our feet. This is the real Gaia.

21. Project Biotime and its strange connection to life in the ocean depths—reality.

22. Molecular viruses—a purely speculative scenario, but nature does not forbid it.

23. The tale of the talking skull, like the king's horse, is a genuine oral tradition of long standing, brought to our attention by *New York Times* correspondent Paul Helou. Thanks also to Art McAvinue for some helpful insights into Tam's reactions when the absorbic outlet hits the fan.

24. Pancakes (dark rings circling dark stars), also known as "Pellegrino's Pancakes," are turning out to be quite real, and may in fact be more abundant than stars.

25. The battle within the Sun is, of course, pure fiction, constrained only by the hard facts of magnetic field projection, solar physics, and orbital mechanics. The absorbic bomb, through which energy can be converted instantaneously into matter (the inverse of a conventional nuclear explosion) does not yet exist, and may never exist unless, according to Powell and Pellegrino, a sufficient number of magnetic monopoles can be found, or created in atomic accelerators and brought together in just the right geometry to produce . . . Well, perhaps we're all better off not dwelling on how to create this particular nightmare.

26. The ghost universe of neutrinos—reality. Born in reactions involving the so-called "weak force" that governs the decay of atomic nuclei, their interactions with all other matter in the universe are weak—so weak that at night, while you sleep, a constant spray of neutrinos emanating from the Sun's core passes through the Earth before coming

up through your floor. At lightspeed, the spray passes through you and your bed before exiting through the ceiling toward the stars. The trick of generating a neutrino telescope is to capture a few of that very rare minority of neutrinos that happen to stop short in a brick, or in your body, or in a tub of dry cleaning fluid. The trick works only if there are lots of neutrinos, and the fusion reactions at the Sun's core do indeed provide us with *lots* of them. Every second, more than 100 billion neutrinos are passing through the period at the end of this sentence.

27. The story of frozen Tritonian seas, subsurface liquid nitrogen reservoirs, cryo-volcanoes, warm and wet regions inside the asteroid parent bodies, oceans inside ice worlds and the implications of 1 Billion B.C. meltings for the history of the outer solar system were first proposed by Pellegrino and Stoff and (except for their once very hot but very wrong speculation about still-existent liquid nitrogen oceans on Triton) have been rendered real by the *Voyager* space probes.

28. Space colonies—very likely. They'll come in many shapes and sizes, including hollowed-out asteroids, spinning to produce centrifugal gravity-simulation. *Macrolife* (Zebrowski, 1979) was a pioneering science fiction novel about space colonies, and still unequalled for the thoroughness with which it presented and developed the concept, about which Arthur C. Clarke wrote in *Profiles of the Future*: ". . . space habitats, in escalating degrees of megalomania, see my *Rendezvous with Rama*, Larry Niven's *Ringworld*, Bob Shaw's *Orbitsville* and George Zebrowski's *Macrolife* . . .".

29. The sights and sounds experienced during a paranoid descent into Neptune: No one knows for sure how close these are to reality. The temperature and pressure regimes of Neptune, and the attendant geochemical manifestations, are based upon calculations by Pellegrino and Stoff and can at best be considered real possibilities. The various pressure phases of ice are real, having actually been produced in the laboratory using diamond anvils. The pressure analogies provided by Sharon (the force exerted by a water-strider's foot on the surface of a pond . . . a fist against a skull during a karate strike) are real.

30. Relativistic attack—one of this novel's claims to originality is based on the motive that may drive alien species toward violent contact. It is not a motive based on any kind of territorial hostility; it is a motive based on simple, prudent self-defense: nothing outweighs even the distant threat of genocide. Star-crossing invaders will not come, as some older SF depicted, for our resources, to make us slaves, to settle the Earth, even to get our water and our women—or our men! Any culture capable of generating energies needed for interstellar flight would not want anything from us—except possibly to find out what we know and compare notes. Would they want to destroy us for the reasons stated in this novel? The best we can say is that it may never happen, but that hope is not comforting. Perhaps alien cultures are not as scrupulously logical as we assume; but can we take that to the bank? Our radar beacons and leaked television signals may not provoke a response for a thousand years, or we may have a response in less than a century.

What is certain is that we must think about what we are doing, in the light of what is possible and probable. And that is the bottom-line, grim reality that distinguishes "hard" science fiction from every other kind of writing: not that something is merely possible and interesting, or metaphorical, or even aesthetically pleasing, but that it is possible, probable, even likely; that it does not exist only in the imagination, but might confront us in our daily lives—as, for example, an asteroid strike that might destroy most of civilization, moving at a mere thirty kilometers per second (a snail's pace and a mere hiccup compared to a relativistic cluster bomb).

Now is the time to think about relativistic contact, when we are still cradled in innocence, protected (perhaps) by our technological infancy, and no danger to anyone but ourselves.

George Zebrowski
New York, New York
November 22, 1994